FEARLESS
ENOUGH

OTHER BOOKS
BY KELLY ELLIOTT

Love in Montana (Meet Me in Montana Spin Off)
Fearless Enough
Cherished Enough
Brave Enough – August 29, 2023
Daring Enough - November 21, 2023
Loved Enough - February 6, 2024
Forever Enough - April 30, 2024
Enchanted Enough - July 23, 2024
Perfect Enough - October 15, 2024
Devoted Enough - January 7, 2025

Holidaze in Salem
A Bit of Hocus Pocus
A Bit of Holly Jolly
A Bit of Wee Luck - March 2023
A Bit of Razzle Dazzle – June 2023

The Seaside Chronicles
Returning Home
Part of Me
Lost to You
Someone to Love
*Series available on audiobook

Stand Alones
The Journey Home*
Who We Were*
The Playbook*
Made for You*
*Available on audiobook

Boggy Creek Valley Series

The Butterfly Effect*
Playing with Words*
She's the One*
Surrender to Me*
Hearts in Motion*
Looking for You*
Surprise Novella TBD
*Available on audiobook

Meet Me in Montana Series

Never Enough*
Always Enough*
Good Enough*
Strong Enough*
*Available on audiobook

Southern Bride Series

Love at First Sight*
Delicate Promises*
Divided Interests*
Lucky in Love*
Feels Like Home *
Take Me Away*
Fool for You*
Fated Hearts*
*Available on audiobook

Cowboys and Angels Series

Lost Love
Love Profound
Tempting Love
Love Again

Blind Love
This Love
Reckless Love
*Series available on audiobook

Boston Love Series
Searching for Harmony
Fighting for Love
*Series available on audiobook

Austin Singles Series
Seduce Me
Entice Me
Adore Me
*Series available on audiobook

Wanted Series
*Wanted**
*Saved**
*Faithful**
Believe
*Cherished**
*A Forever Love**
The Wanted Short Stories
All They Wanted
*Available on audiobook

Love Wanted in Texas Series
Spin-off series to the WANTED Series
Without You
Saving You
Holding You
Finding You
Chasing You

Loving You
Entire series available on audiobook
*Please note *Loving You* combines the last book of the Broken
and Love Wanted in Texas series.

Broken Series
*Broken**
*Broken Dreams**
*Broken Promises**
Broken Love
*Available on audiobook

The Journey of Love Series
Unconditional Love
Undeniable Love
Unforgettable Love
*Entire series available on audiobook

With Me Series
Stay With Me
Only With Me
*Series available on audiobook

Speed Series
Ignite
Adrenaline
*Series available on audiobook

COLLABORATIONS
Predestined Hearts (co-written with Kristin Mayer)*
Play Me (co-written with Kristin Mayer)*
Dangerous Temptations (co-written with Kristin Mayer*
*Available on audiobook

FEARLESS ENOUGH

KELLY ELLIOTT

Joshua Ty
Hunter
Nathan Christopher
Mason
Rose Marie
Morgan Elizabeth
Lily Hope
Blaze Lucas
Tanner & Timberlynn Shaw
Ty Jr. & Kaylee Shaw
Brock & Lincoln Shaw
Beck Shaw
Bradley Michael
Stella Shaw & Ty Sr Shaw
Avery Grace
Dirk & Merit Littlewood

Shaw Ranch

Shaw Ranch
HAMILTON, MONTANA

DIRK & MERIT

Hunters Cabin

Tanner & Timberlynn

Barn

Ty Sr & Stella

Brock & Lincoln

Ty Jr & Kaylee

Prologue

BLAYZE BROCK SHAW

SENIOR YEAR, COLLEGE - BOZEMAN, MONTANA

We clinked our glasses together before I took a drink of the beer my best friend, Ryan, had just brought to the table.

"Dude, I don't know how you do it," Ryan stated after he tasted his beer and stared at it with a frown.

"You don't know how I do what? And why in the hell are you frowning at your beer?"

He shook his head and looked at me. "This tastes like shit. I can probably make better beer than this."

I shrugged. "Then make it."

A wide grin moved over his face. "I might just do that once we graduate."

"Because you're going to have so much spare time to brew beer." I laughed.

He ignored me. "To answer the other part of your question: I don't know how women just gravitate toward you. Don't say it's your good looks. We already know that brings them over to you, but what makes them actually leave with you?"

I let another laugh slip free. It was true. With my dark brown, almost-black hair and blue eyes, I had definitely inherited my father's good looks. It also helped that I had a fit body—and not one that came from working out in a gym, but from working my ass off on my family's cattle ranch and helping my uncles break in horses and train bulls for the Professional Bull Riders circuit. Plus, I had been following in my father's footsteps as a bull rider, until it became clear to me that my true love was our family ranch in Hamilton, Montana.

"It's called flirting," a voice said from behind us. Ryan rolled his eyes when he looked past me to see Mindy Reynolds standing there. She walked around and slid onto the barstool next to me.

"Come on, Mindy. Don't sit there," he said.

Mindy raised one perfectly arched brow as she glared at Ryan. "And why not?"

He replied, "Because if you sit there, then no women will come over to talk to us."

She let out a fake laugh. "Trust me," she said as she hit the tip of Ryan's cowboy hat, "they won't pay any attention to little ol' me sitting here with the two of you. You both ooze handsome cowboy."

"That's not true, Mindy." I took a sip of my beer and set it back down. "You're a very attractive woman, and either of us would be lucky to be with you."

Ryan gagged while Mindy dropped her head back and let out a true laugh. She looked at me and pointed.

"That is why you have no problem getting woman, Blayze Shaw. Since the first day I met you in kindergarten, you've known how to flirt and make a woman feel wanted. Not the stupid, low, degrading flirting like some do." Mindy shot a look in Ryan's direction. He snarled his lip and gave her the middle finger. "But genuine, make-a-woman-feel-special flirting. My guess would be you've never had a woman tell you no before."

An image of a beautiful young girl with golden brown hair and eyes the color of a spring meadow flashed through my mind.

Georgiana. The one girl I had let myself fall for, and the only woman who'd broken my heart and had made me vow to never give it to anyone again. Okay, I was sixteen, almost seventeen, when I made that vow, but I'd yet to meet a woman who made me want to break it.

Chuckling, I answered Mindy before I got lost in thoughts of Georgie. "Oh, I've had plenty of women tell me no."

"But only after you nearly charmed the panties off of them, am I correct?" Mindy winked.

Lifting my beer up to my mouth, I smiled.

At that very moment, two women walked up to the table. A blonde and a redhead. The redhead looked at me and smiled. "I'm sorry to bug you, but I think you're in one of my classes."

Mindy made some sort of snort-laugh sound next to me. I ignored her and smiled at the redhead. Her eyes locked on the dimple on the right side of my cheek. What was it about a dimple that got a woman turned on?

With a wink in her direction, I replied, "I'm pretty sure I'd remember a stunning woman such as yourself in one of my classes."

Her cheeks flushed and she glanced at her friend, who was staring at Ryan. He wasn't bad on the eyes either. Light brown hair with eyes nearly the same color. He was built like me, though a bit taller and with a smile that had melted his own fair share of panties, from what I'd been told. Including Mindy's, our junior year of high school. That was something they both vowed to never talk about again.

The redhead cleared her throat. "You're not in Professor McNullen's finance class, are you?"

Smiling, I shook my head. "Sadly, I am not. I'm an agricultural business major, though, so maybe we've passed each other once or twice."

She nodded. "Maybe. I was hoping you were; I missed class and need the notes for the quiz, but I'll send a message to our group chat. I'm not doing very well in that class, and if I don't pass my mother will kill me."

I turned on the barstool to face both women. "I got an A in Professor McNullen's class last year. If you need any tutoring, I'd be more than happy to help you," I said with another brilliant smile.

The redhead's eyes lit up. "Oh my gosh, really? That would be so amazing."

I pulled out my cell phone and handed it to her. "Put your number in, and we'll work out a time."

She quickly added her name and number and handed me back my phone.

"Shelby?"

Nodding, she replied, "That's me!"

I sent her a text. "Blayze Shaw. I look forward to helping you out."

Shelby's tongue swept quickly across her lips as she let out a nervous giggle. "Sounds good, Blayze. I'll talk to you soon."

With a nod, I replied, "Talk soon." Little did Shelby know, tutoring was all she was going to get out of me. Oh, I wasn't an innocent, but I didn't make it a habit to sleep around with women. Something my father and uncles had pounded in my head, along with my brother, Hunter, and my cousin, Bradly. Josh and Nathan, my cousins, were still too young to understand.

After Shelby and her friend had turned and walked away, I looked back at Ryan and Mindy.

Laughing, Mindy lifted her beer to me. I clinked it as she said, "And I just proved my point. You could charm the panties off a damn nun."

Ryan shook his head. "The sad part is that you'll probably only teach her about finance."

I laughed because Ryan knew me so well.

I glanced to my left and asked Mindy, "Why are you staring at me like that?"

She narrowed one eye and tilted her head. "Are you still hung up on her?"

I laughed again. "What are you talking about?"

"Come on, Blayze. I've known you far too long. You may be able to charm any woman into going back to your place, but I know you don't sleep with all of them."

"And your point is?"

"My point is, are you still stuck on the one who got away?"

Her question caused Ryan's head to pop up. "You think because he doesn't fuck around he's stuck on some girl?"

Mindy gave him a one-shoulder shrug. "Georgiana wasn't just some girl. And since that summer, she hasn't ever come back to Hamilton."

My heart dropped to my stomach. How in the hell could Mindy read my mind like that?

"Georgiana?" Ryan and I both said at the same time.

With a look that said she wasn't buying my bullshit, Mindy sighed. "Blayze, I'm like a sister to you. I was there, remember?"

I looked down at my beer. Georgiana Crenshaw had been coming to our ranch for as long as I could remember. Every summer. June to early August. She was part of our group. It was always me, Ryan, Mindy, and Georgie. But the older we got, the more I started to see her as something more than my friend. The summer she turned sixteen, she had changed in both her looks and worldliness, and I couldn't stop thinking about her. Dreaming about her. She was the only girl I had ever told that I liked her. Just before she left to head back to Texas, I kissed her behind my father's barn. The kiss turned into something more with me lifting her leg and touching her, and it was then that I asked Georgie if I could make her mine.

I closed my eyes, remembering her big green eyes as she'd stared at me in shock. They'd softened and she'd said yes, and that was the moment I'd given her my whole heart.

I snapped out of the memory and forced myself to chuckle. "I was lucky enough to give Georgie her first proper kiss," I stated with a smirk.

Mindy shook her head. "I think a little more than that happened."

I sighed. "Yeah, that's putting it lightly."

"I liked Georgie. She was funny," Ryan said as he stared at the beer he was holding up to the light.

Mindy smiled and bumped her shoulder against mine. "Don't worry, Blayze. We all remember our first kiss. Some more fondly than others."

Ryan met her glare across the table. "It wasn't pleasant for me either, Mindy."

Mindy and Ryan had somehow ended up hooking up after a pasture party one night. Both of them pretended to regret it, but I knew from talking to them separately that they were glad their first time had been with someone they cared about and trusted. There had been zero feelings beyond friendship.

I hadn't been so lucky. I'd wanted Georgie to be my first, but she'd told me that she had almost made the biggest mistake of her life with me. That I wasn't the type of guy she wanted to give her virginity to. Those words had nearly brought me to my knees. Instead, I'd gone straight to a party where I'd drank too much and ended up sleeping with another girl named Lindsay. Biggest mistake of my life.

Clearing my throat, I raised my beer. "To best friends and being there for each other."

Ryan and Mindy both grinned as they lifted their drinks and repeated, "To best friends."

Chapter One

BLAYZE

FOUR YEARS LATER; PRESENT DAY - SHAW RANCH, HAMILTON, MONTANA

Ryan set two glasses down on the kitchen island and grinned. "Okay, taste it. I made a special brew to celebrate you turning another year older."

I held my glass up and looked at the deep amber-colored beer. After years of listening to him bitch about how bad every beer was, I had finally talked him into brewing his own.

"My birthday was last month."

With a smirk, he replied, "Taste it will you?"

I put the glass to my lips and drank.

My sister Morgan, who had recently turned twenty-one, took the other glass and drank it.

The cold brew hit the back of my throat and glided down smoothly. I could taste a hint of citrus, and I liked it. A lot.

I looked over at Ryan and grinned. "Damn, that's good, Ryan."

"I've had better," Morgan said as she pushed the glass away and folded her arms over her chest. It wasn't lost on me how Ryan let his eyes lower to her breasts before he snapped them back up to look at her. The fact that he was six years older than her and my best friend should have made me want to grab him and punch his lights out for looking at her the way he was, but I felt the opposite. Since Morgan's senior year of high school, I had noticed Ryan looking at her differently. And when Morgan didn't think anyone was paying attention, she would watch Ryan with similar eyes. I wouldn't be the least bit upset if they became a couple. I'd rather my baby sister be with my best friend over some douchebag she met at college. If only she could look past the fact that she couldn't stand him for reasons that were still unknown to me. And to Ryan.

"You've had better?" he asked. "You just turned twenty-one, Morgan. How have you had better?"

She narrowed her eyes at him and leaned forward. "Just because I can now drink legally doesn't mean I haven't ever had alcohol before. I've done my fair share of drinking."

"Let's also not forget how you and Hunter have been sneaking beer out to the barn for how many years now?" I asked as I took another drink.

Morgan huffed. "Don't act all high and mighty, Blayze Shaw. I know you, Mindy, and Ryan were up in that barn loft drinking well before Hunter and I started doing it."

I shrugged. "It's different for you."

Her eyes turned dark, and I knew I was screwed. "And why is that?"

"You're a girl," Ryan said. The moment the words were out of his mouth, he clearly realized his mistake. He took a few steps away from the table.

"Girl? I'm a girl? The last time I looked in the mirror, *Ryan*, I was a woman. I've got the breasts to prove it."

His eyes darted down once again before he snapped them up, his face instantly turning beet red. The poor bastard. I had to bite the inside of my cheek to keep from laughing.

"That's not what I meant, Morgan, and you know it. I'm well aware of the fact that you're a woman."

She leaned forward and gave Ryan a teasing smile. "Are you, now? How are you well aware of it?"

Ryan swallowed hard and looked at me for help. Before I could say anything, my father walked in. I could see the look of relief on my best friend's face. He had been about to go down a path he wouldn't have been able to get off.

"No one invited me to taste the new batch," Dad said as he walked up and looked down at the two glasses of beer.

Without taking her eyes off poor Ryan, Morgan said, "Here, Daddy. Have mine. I don't care for it."

My father, blissfully unaware of the tension between Ryan and my sister, picked up the beer and took a long drink.

He nodded, waited a few moments, and then slapped Ryan on the back. "That's damn good, son. Damn. Good."

Ryan beamed. "Thank you, sir." Then he shot Morgan a look, and I swore to God I thought he was going to stick his damn tongue out at her.

My father's voice pulled me from the show going on between the two of them. "I rang the doorbell, but no one answered. Heard the three of you in here, so I just walked in."

"Yeah, I need to fix that," I said before I finished off the beer.

Dad drank the rest of Morgan's and then handed the glass to Ryan, who promptly refilled it.

"Blayze, I need a favor," Dad said.

"If it's about the north pasture, I've already ordered the fencing to fix that broken wire."

He smiled. "No, that's not it, but thank you for being on top of things."

I nodded. I lived for this ranch and doing a good job for my father and grandfather. There wasn't anything I wouldn't do for either of them. For my entire family, if I was being honest.

"This is something different. A good friend of mine and your Uncle Ty's—you remember him, Jeff Crenshaw, he used to bull ride with me—called me earlier."

My heart felt like it stalled in my chest. "Jeff, yeah, he used to be one of the announcers on NBC, right? He and his family came to the ranch every summer for a few years."

I could feel Morgan and Ryan's eyes on me, but I wasn't about to look at either one of them.

Dad nodded. "Yeah." He looked at me with a knowing look. "His daughter, whom I'm pretty sure you remember, is in Montana to do an interview with the family. It's kind of like one of those *where are they now* things."

My heart felt like it dropped straight to my stomach.

"Is this a piece on just you, Dad, or Uncle Ty, Uncle Tanner, and Uncle Dirk as well?" Morgan asked.

"Mainly me, Ty, Tanner, and Dirk, but she will be trying to interview most of the family. Just not the younger kids very much. Jeff mentioned they'd like to do a special piece on you, Blayze."

That made me jerk upright. My father was clearly trying to act nonchalant when he dropped that little bomb. "Me? Why me?"

Ryan chuckled. "I'm going to guess it's because you didn't follow in your old man's footsteps."

"And that makes for a good interview?" I asked with a hint of anger in my voice. There was a reason I had decided to leave bull riding and that life. And it was no one's business why.

Dad nodded.

"What about Hunter? I'd imagine they'd want to talk to him more than Blayze," Morgan asked. "After all, he's one of the top-ranked team ropers in college. And what about Bradly? He's dang near ready to join the PBR pro circuit."

My father smiled at Morgan and I could see the pride in his eyes—not only for Hunter and Bradly, but for Morgan sticking up for them.

My younger brother Hunter was doing team roping, following in my Uncle Tanner's footsteps. He was damn good and had already won a few events in high school and college. He really excelled at bull riding, but only did it for fun or for charity events—much to my mother's relief. Bradly, my Uncle Dirk's son, was on his way to becoming better than any of us. The kid was damn good on the back of a bull.

"She's planning on interviewing Hunter and Bradly—if they're able to make it home at all this next month," Dad said.

"Wait, she's going to be here in a month?" I asked, trying to keep the horror out of my voice.

Dad took another sip of his beer and nodded. "Yes. She's currently working as a freelance writer for some big magazine. The network Jeff works for just purchased a sports magazine, and his Georgiana has been trying to make a name for herself with it. It's hard for a woman in the sports field. Jeff called in a favor and asked me if we'd do the piece and let her interview the family. I said yes. If interviewing us can help her move her career forward, then it's the least we can do."

"Why? What do we owe her?" I asked, regretting the words the moment they were out of my mouth.

Giving me a hard look, my father said, "Her father is one of my oldest friends. He's never once asked me for anything. Don't let the past cloud your manners, son."

Ryan cleared his throat and pushed a beer in front of me.

I exhaled a frustrated breath. "I was sixteen, Dad. I've let that go."

All he did was raise a single brow before he turned to Morgan. "Georgiana writes for a couple of fashion magazines, *Vogue* being one of them. Jeff said she'd probably be happy to speak with you, Morgan."

That perked my fashion major sister right up. "Of course! I'll help out in any way I can, you know that, Daddy."

My father leaned over and kissed Morgan on the forehead. "I knew you would, sweetheart. You'll like Georgiana. She's twenty-six, and from what her father has told me, she's really into fashion. He's surprised she's still going down the sports-writing path, but at this point he thinks she's simply trying to make a statement."

"I like her already!" Morgan mused.

Dad flashed her a grin. "She just came back from some big event in Paris and the New York Fall Fashion week."

She gasped. "Fall Paris Fashion Week?"

Dad shrugged. "I'm not sure. He didn't say."

"Holy shit, I'd say she grew up—look at this," Ryan said as he turned his phone and showed it to my father.

With a wide smile, Dad replied, "That's Georgiana. She's just as pretty as ever, isn't she, Blayze?"

Ryan turned the phone toward me, though I didn't need to see the picture. I already knew what she looked like, although I hadn't seen a picture of her in about a year or so.

Shrugging, I replied, "Yeah, that looks like her."

My father smirked, and I rolled my eyes. He and Jeff were the ones who found us with my mouth on Georgie and my hand in her panties, on the verge of making her come. Georgie had been horrified, as was I. My father and Jeff were supposed to be off the ranch that day, and still, to this day, I had no idea why they were there or how they even knew where to find us.

Morgan grabbed the phone out of Ryan's hand and stared at the photo. "I always thought she was pretty when I was little, but wow. She's beautiful now."

Ryan nodded. "She sure is. I wonder if she's still shy."

Morgan snapped her head up to look at Ryan and stared at him. I wasn't sure if he could see the hurt in her eyes as clearly as I could. But then that hurt quickly turned to anger.

I took the phone out of Morgan's hands before she snapped it in two. The woman on the screen wasn't a teenager anymore. She was a grown woman who was beyond stunning. I wasn't even sure if beautiful could describe her accurately. Her hair was light brown with streaks of blonde in it. And those eyes. Christ, they were still shockingly green.

Clearing my throat, I handed the phone back to Ryan. "When does she get here?"

Dad put down his mug of beer. "She got in an hour ago, but when she tried to rent a car, they said they were completely out."

"Why didn't she reserve one?" Ryan asked.

"She did, but they're claiming to be out of cars since it's so late in the day. She had delays in Denver." My father looked at me and smiled. "That's where you come in, Blayze."

It felt like someone just dropped lead into my stomach. "Please tell me you're not going to ask me to pick her up, Dad."

"I'm not going to ask you to pick her up, Blayze. I'm going to tell you to pick her up. First thing tomorrow morning. She's staying at the Marriott Hotel in downtown Missoula."

Ryan and Morgan both let out a laugh.

"Why can't Avery go pick her up?" I asked.

"Avery!" Morgan nearly shouted. "She's not even sixteen yet, you dumbass."

"Morgan Shaw," my father said with a warning tone in his voice, although the corner of his mouth lifted some with a hidden laugh.

I pointed to Morgan. "Fine, then Morgan can go and pick her up."

"Oh, I'll go Daddy!" Morgan quickly offered up.

Dad shook his head. "I believe you volunteered to help your mother tomorrow morning with planning the fall festival."

"Crap, that's right," Morgan huffed, crossing her arms over her chest once more. This time Ryan knew better than to check her out with our father standing there.

Morgan went to school in Missoula, so it wasn't out of the ordinary for her to come home on weekends. Especially since her beloved horse, Titan, was here. She lived, ate, and breathed that horse.

Dad focused back on me. "After you pick her up, you should bring her here to the ranch."

"Where's she staying? With you and Mom or Grams and Grandpa?" Morgan asked.

My father shook his head then looked at me. "I'm going to need another favor from you."

I shook my head as well. I knew what was coming. My grandparents were doing a major remodel of damn near their entire house and were staying with my mom and dad. So staying at their house was out of the question. Dad wouldn't want her to feel uncomfortable with Ty, Tanner, or Dirk, so that meant Georgie would be staying with my folks, but something in his eyes said otherwise.

"No," I said. "You've got plenty of room at your house, even with Grams and Grandpa there."

He frowned. "The plumbing in the guest bathroom isn't working because of a root growing into the pipes."

"Grams and Gramps are in my room," Morgan stated. "I'm staying in your old room, and the Henderson's are staying with us because of problems with their new build. Remember?"

I shot my sister a dirty look.

"It's crazy at our house," Dad said, "and I want Georgiana to have some privacy. Your house is perfect for that."

Morgan beamed. "I can't wait to see her again and ask what Paris was like!"

I was still trying to process the fact that I was picking up Georgie and that she was staying at my house. Did he not remember what happened between us when we were younger?

Dad ignored the fact that I was clearly about to have a mental breakdown. "Well, you'll get to see her at Sunday dinner since we've invited her," he said to Morgan. "I expect everyone to be on their best behavior." This time he looked directly at me.

"I highly doubt I'll be sneaking off to steal a kiss, Dad."

"Or play touchy-feely," Ryan mumbled.

Dad and I both shot Ryan a look. He lifted his hands. "Sorry, I couldn't resist."

"Wait, what?" Morgan asked as she looked at me. Then it dawned on her. "Oh my God. Georgiana Crenshaw is the girl Dad caught you almost having sex with? Is that why she never came back to the ranch?"

"Thanks," I said to Ryan.

"Okay, well, this is where I'm going to head on out," Dad said. "Thanks for doing this for me, Blayze. I'll send you her cell phone number, so you can figure out the best time to pick her up."

Dad turned and headed out of the kitchen area toward the front of the house.

I sat there, stunned into silence. I hadn't seen Georgie in more than ten years. And now she was going to be staying with me for a month. A month!

"If I didn't know any better, Blayze, I'd say you were scared to have Georgiana stay with you," Morgan mused.

"Scared? Why in the hell would I be scared?"

Ryan laughed. "Let's see. The last time you two were together, you got caught by your dads about to have sex. Then you acted like a complete ass to her."

"Eww, no! You were so young!" Morgan stated. "What did you do to her?"

"Nothing," I replied.

Morgan frowned. "I'll just ask her myself."

"Your version—I'm positive—will be different from hers," Ryan said with another laugh.

"Just tell me, please." Morgan pulled on my arm. When she got nowhere with me, she turned to Ryan. I knew the moment she batted her eyelashes at him, he'd break.

"What happened?"

And break he did. The bastard opened his mouth and the words just spilled out.

"They were rounding third base when Jeff and Brock caught them. Georgiana was horrified, and when Blayze found her out riding after it happened, he apologized. She told him she was glad they were caught because she would have made the biggest mistake of her life if she gave Blayze her virginity. That she wanted to be with a guy who wasn't a flirt and a player."

Morgan gasped. "She said that?"

Ryan nodded.

I sighed as Ryan went on.

"Then, that night Blayze went to a party and slept with…"

"Ryan," I said in a firm voice.

"He slept with someone else."

"Did Georgiana find out?" Morgan asked as she looked at me.

With a frustrated sigh, I said, "I told her the next day. Then I flirted and kissed as many girls as I could in front of her for the rest of the summer. She asked her dad if they could leave early and that was the last time she came to Hamilton."

"You arranged for her to walk in on you making out with Jasmine," Ryan added. "I think that was when she asked her dad to leave."

"Blayze Shaw! Our father would beat you!"

I scrubbed my hand down my face. "I was sixteen, for fuck's sake. None of it matters. I'm sure she's forgotten all about it."

Morgan laughed. "Trust me, big brother, when a man uses other women to make us jealous, it pisses us off."

Her eyes snapped over to Ryan, who looked taken aback by the comment that had clearly been directed at him.

"Why are you looking at me? I've never done that."

I swore I saw red in my sister's eyes.

She slowly turned her head to me and drew in a slow, deep breath. Ryan and I both took a step away from her.

"The one thing that will turn off a woman is if you're a womanizer. And the two of you have your pictures in the dictionary above the definition."

"What?" we both said in unison.

"Since when does harmless flirting make you a womanizer? I think you need to find a new dictionary, sis," I said.

Putting her hands on her hips, Morgan smiled, but it didn't reach her eyes. "You think by throwing that one word in there, it excuses you, Blayze? *Harmless*. It isn't harmless when a woman is madly over the moon for you, and you use some other woman to push her away. Regardless of her age. It hurts." She looked at Ryan as she finished. "It's far from harmless."

Turning on her heels, she quickly made her way through the house and out the front door. Slamming it as she left.

"I will never understand women. And I have no idea why she is so mad at me," Ryan said.

We stood there for a moment and Ryan slowly shook his head. "A few years back, at one of the charity dances your dad and Dirk put on, I danced with Morgan. I flirted a bit with her and she flirted back."

"And you think that's why she's pissed at you?" I asked.

He shook his head. "No, I think it was the next day.

Turning to glare at him, I growled. "Explain."

He laughed. "No, nothing like that, dude. Emma Myers, you remember her, right?"

"Yeah, you guys were like an on and off kind of thing."

"Well, that same night of the dance, I ran into her leaving. She suggested a mindless hook-up, and I was a bit...wound up."

I raised my brow. "Do I want to know why?"

"Probably not."

"Okay, it's noted that you're attracted to my sister."

Ryan rolled his eyes. "Anyway, Emma stayed the night. I was giving her a goodbye kiss on my front porch and looked up to see Morgan there. The look on her face about gutted me. She looked so hurt, and I didn't know why. She just turned and walked away. After that, she acted like she couldn't stand me."

His eyes lifted to meet mine. "If I thought at any moment that Morgan had feelings for me, I wouldn't have flirted so carelessly with her. Or I guess what I should have done was maybe ask her out. I don't know, she was still in college and your baby sister. I was confused."

I put my hand on his shoulder. "I get it, Ryan."

"That was a few years ago, why is she still pissed about it? If that's what it is about." He pushed his hand through his hair. "Shit, I don't understand women. I have no clue what women think. Want. Need. I'm completely fucking lost."

I scoffed. "Join the damn club."

"What are you going to do about Georgiana? If I remember right, the last words she uttered to you were something like *fuck off, you arrogant asshole.*"

"Yeah, I think it was something along those lines. Listen, if she offered to come here and interview the family, then I'm going to guess she's gotten over it. I have."

He laughed under his breath. "Really? And I hate to break this to you, but I think your dad said you were in that article somewhere too. A piece about why you're not bull riding anymore?"

I pushed my hand through my hair. "Well, she can try all she wants. I'm not giving her an interview."

"And if she brings up what happened between you guys?"

I drew in a deep breath. "I guess I'll cross that bridge when I come to it." I reached over and grabbed my cowboy hat.

Ryan lifted his brows as he gave me a look that silently said good luck.

Chapter Two

GEORGIANA

My phone alarm woke me, and I sat up and fumbled to swipe it off. Dropping the cell phone next to me, I looked around the hotel room and let out a long, slow sigh. The last three days had been nothing but a nightmare. I'd been in New York City for fashion week, then to Paris for another fashion week. Then once I got back, my father informed me about a great opportunity to write an article for *Sports Monthly*. I had a feeling he had something to do with me getting the interview. A part of me hadn't wanted to take it, but I took the assignment anyway, only to find out at the last minute I was going to Montana.

"I can't believe I'm back in Montana," I whispered as I flopped back down on the bed. And the worst part was, I had to see Blayze. I honestly thought I would never see him again.

"Ugh! Why do you hate me, cruel fate?"

I closed my eyes and let out another long breath. Blayze Shaw. The memory of the first time I ever met him popped into my head.

◆ ◆ ◆

My mother took my hand in hers as we walked up the steps to the large stone house. "Georgiana, you're going to love Montana. The Shaws have all kinds of horses to ride and a little boy the same age as you. And Brock rides bulls like your daddy does."

"What's his name?" I asked, looking at the large double doors that waited for us.

"Blayze," my father answered. Then he laughed. "He's a chip off the old block."

"What does that mean?" I asked.

My mother chuckled. "It means he's just like his daddy."

"Oh," I said while Daddy rang the doorbell. A real pretty lady answered and hugged both of my parents, then bent down to look at me.

"Hi, Georgiana! My name is Lincoln. I'm so excited to have you staying with us!"

Smiling, I reached my hand out to her. "It is an, um…it's a…"

"Pleasure," my mother whispered.

"That's it!" I called out as Lincoln covered her mouth. "It's a pleasure to meet you."

Lincoln shook it then stood. "Blayze is going to be over the moon. I apologize now for whatever comes out of that boy's mouth."

My father let out a big laugh. "He's Brock's son. Nothing will surprise me."

"It's great seeing you, Jeff and Callie. How was the trip?" Lincoln asked as she motioned for us to come inside.

"It was great. Georgiana loved Yellowstone. I'm so glad we decided to make it a road trip," my mother stated.

We walked into the house and I looked everywhere, my eyes taking it all in. The house was so pretty, with lots of natural wood. A loud noise came from another room, and a boy about my age appeared.

He skidded to a stop in front of us. Behind him was a man holding a little girl.

"Brock, it's so good seeing you," Daddy said as he shook the other man's hand.

The little boy smiled at me then looked up at my mother. He tipped his cowboy hat. "It's a pleasure to meet you, ma'am."

Smiling, my mother replied, "The pleasure is all mine, young man."

He tilted his head up to look at her. "My name is Blayze. You're real pretty. Would you like to give me your number, so we could maybe have dinner?"

Blayze's dad, Brock, put his hand on his son's neck and gently pulled him back a few steps while my father and mother both laughed.

"I'm so sorry, Callie and Jeff—he's a bit of a flirt." Brock glanced down at Blayze and frowned before looking back at my parents and me.

My father laughed. "Apple doesn't fall far from the tree, Brock."

My mother's smile grew wider as she bent down and looked at Blayze. "As tempting as that is, I'm afraid I'm already married." She pointed back to my father.

With a shrug, Blayze said, "If things don't work out, you know where I am."

Everyone laughed—well, everyone except me. He was a boy! Asking my mother on a date.

Brock pulled him back a bit more and said, "Say hello to Georgiana, Blayze."

Blayze turned and looked at me and smiled. I smiled back. "Hi, Georgiana. Do you like to ride horses?"

I glanced up at my parents and then back at Blayze. "I love horses."

He reached for my hand and gave it a tug. "Come on, I'll take you to the barn. Uncle Ty is out there."

"May I please go?" I asked my mother.

"Yes, but not for long!" she called out as Blayze began pulling me away.

He stopped and turned back to look at my mother, tipping his hat once more. "Ma'am."

Then he started to pull me out of the room. Before we left, I heard my father say,

"You're going to have your hands full with that little cowboy, Brock."

Brock sighed, "Tell me about it."

I threw the covers off me and dragged myself out of bed and into the shower. Brock would be here soon to bring me back to the Shaw ranch, so I needed to get my act together. After a trip to the hotel bar last night and one-too-many drinks, my head was pounding and I felt foggy. I needed to be clearheaded when I saw Blayze. If I even saw him. He'd probably hid the moment he heard I was here, and a part of me couldn't blame him. My stomach lurched as I thought about the terrible lie I had told him.

It wasn't like I was afraid to see him. I simply wasn't thrilled about it. The boy whom I had become fast friends with at ten years old had quickly become the young man I'd had a big crush on. And when Blayze had shown interest in me when I was sixteen and he was almost seventeen, and I'd found myself behind the barn with him, I knew I was in love. Or what my young mind thought was love. And I thought for sure he felt the same way about me. Well, up until I clearly hurt him, and he turned around and hurt me right back.

I stepped into the hot shower and moaned when the heat of the water covered my skin. The moment I shut my eyes, I swore I felt his hands on my body. His warm breath hitting my ear as he whispered, "May I touch you, Georgie?"

I moved my hand up to my lips where I thought I could still feel the tingle of Blayze's lips pressed to mine even to this day. I had been ready for him to make me his. I'd been ready to give Blayze my virginity. I had wanted him to have it, because I'd thought he was the one.

I snapped my eyes open and shook my head. "What are you doing?"

Grabbing the small tube of shampoo, I quickly washed and then conditioned my hair before soaping up and rinsing off. I stepped out of the shower and heard my phone go off.

Once I wrapped my hair and body in towels, I made my way into the room. I picked up my phone and saw a text from a number I didn't have stored in my phone. I swiped it open.

Unknown: Hey, Georgie, I'll be there in about an hour. Meet you in the lobby.

Frowning, I stared at the text message. It wasn't Brock's number—my father had given it to me, and he'd already texted me last night—and there was only one person who called me Georgie.

33

I pressed my hand to my mouth as I sucked in a sharp breath. Was I honestly ready to face him? I talked a big talk, but truth be told, I was scared to death to see Blayze. I knew the moment I saw those blue eyes and that dimple, I'd be a fool for him all over again.

"No! Please, God, no!"

I quickly typed back my reply.

Me: Who is this?

Their answer was almost instant.

Unknown: Blayze.

I dropped the phone onto the floor like it had just burned me and covered my mouth to keep my sudden urge to scream at bay.

Dropping my hands to my side, I started to shake my head. "No, no, no, no! What did I do to deserve this punishment?"

Quickly grabbing my phone, I sent Blayze a text back. It had to be a mistake. Brock was supposed to pick me up.

Me: Thought your father was picking me up?

Unknown: He couldn't make it this morning, so he asked me to pick you up.

"Shit."

I quickly stored his number in my phone. "Okay, okay. Act cool. Normal. Not like the man of your childhood dreams who broke your heart and whom you uttered some really, really mean things to is about to pick you up.

Me: See you soon. If you text when you're here, I'll meet you out front.

He didn't bother to reply; most likely he was driving. I quickly made my way back into the bathroom and stared at myself.

"It's not a big deal. Who cares that Blayze Shaw is picking you up? Who cares that you totally had a massive crush on the asshat when you were sixteen and he ripped your heart out? It's the past, and none of that matters."

If it didn't matter, why in the hell had I taken over twenty minutes to decide what I was going to wear? Then another twenty doing my hair and makeup. I'd barely finished packing up when someone knocked on my hotel door.

"One second!" I called out to housekeeping. Or at least that's who I assumed it was. Instead, when I opened the door, I was struck speechless by the man standing in front of me.

Blayze.

My eyes quickly took him in. His dark hair was cut close to his head with the top just a bit longer, giving it an almost military style. He looked like he hadn't shaved in a few days and had that rough look that made my toes instantly curl. And his eyes. Lord above, I forgot how blue they were.

Then he smiled. The asshole smiled. The dimple appeared in his right cheek, and I was pretty sure my lady bits melted on the spot.

Damn him. Damn him, damn him, damn him!

I went to speak and my voice cracked. Clearing my throat quickly, I folded my arms over my chest. Blayze didn't even bother to hide the fact that he was surveying my body. I mean, hello, I had just been doing the same thing, but he was beyond obvious.

"This isn't the lobby," I said. "And how did you know what room I was in?"

His eyes snapped up and met mine. "I called. Twice. And texted about six times. To answer your question, my dad told me."

I dropped my arms to my sides in surprise. "You did? And…he did?"

Spinning on my heels, I rushed into the room and picked up my phone that was on the bed next to my purse.

"Crap. Sorry about that, I had it on silent for some reason."

"No worries," Blayze said as he walked in. He was wearing a black, long-sleeve T-shirt, jeans that fit him better than they should have, black cowboy boots, and a Montana State baseball cap. Lord, I used to think he was hot in a cowboy hat, but the baseball cap was doing all kinds of things to my body.

Stop it. Stop it right now, Georgiana!

"Are you hungry?"

The change of subject threw me. "I'm sorry?"

"Breakfast. Did you want to grab some?"

My stomach decided to betray me in that very moment. It growled. Loudly.

Blayze laughed. "I'll take that as a yes. Are you ready to head out?"

I nodded and turned away from him to scan the room and give myself a moment to regain my composure. No man had ever put me off balance like this before.

"Let me check the bathroom once more, then I'll be ready to leave."

When I walked back out, Blayze had both of my suitcases and my laptop bag over his shoulder.

"I can grab something."

He winked. "I've got it."

Ignoring the way my stupid heart tripped over itself with that wink, I reached for my purse and followed Blayze out of the hotel room. He stopped right before he got to the door and glanced back at me.

His gaze went to the bed, then back to me. My heart started to pound in my chest as a slow smile spread over his face.

If he said one sexual thing to me, I was going to punch him in the balls.

"Did you leave a tip for housekeeping?"

I blinked a few times as I let his words sink in. "A tip?"

"With all the traveling you do, Georgie, you don't leave tips? I wouldn't have pegged you for that type of person."

My blood instantly boiled, and I dug through my purse and pulled out my wallet. "I'm *not* that type of person, Blayze. You caught me off guard with–"

"My good looks?"

I glanced up and shot him a dirty look. "No, by showing up at my room."

"Kind of the same thing."

With a grunt of frustration, I slapped a ten down on the side table and marched past Blayze and out of the room. An older couple came out of the room across from mine and smiled sweetly when they saw me and Blayze.

"Did you two enjoy your time in Missoula?" the woman asked.

"The fun is just beginning," Blayze said before I could correct her.

"Oh? Honeymoon?" the gentleman asked.

Blayze and I both laughed. Hard.

"No, nothing like that. I'm here to interview him." The words were out before I could stop them.

They both shot a quizzical look over to Blayze. "You must be an actor," the woman said with a blush. "You're so handsome."

"Milly." Her husband chuckled.

"I only speak the truth."

Blayze set one of the suitcases down, tipped his hat at the woman, and crooned, "Why, thank you, ma'am. Coming from yourself, I'm honored."

The husband tossed his head back and laughed. "Good God, son, you've had your practice. I don't think I've seen my wife blush this hard in years."

I couldn't help but smile.

We all headed toward the elevator.

"Tell me, why are you interviewing this young man?" the older gentleman asked.

I cleared my throat as Blayze said, "She's not interviewing me."

Ignoring him, I went on. "It's for a sports magazine, and Mr. Shaw's father was a very successful bull rider."

"Brock Shaw. That's your daddy?" the man asked.

Blayze smiled with pride. "He is, indeed."

Most kids of famous people had a chip on their shoulder, but not Blayze. You could see the pride he had for his father both in his eyes and on his face.

The man smiled back. "So, are you interviewing the father or son?"

"Both," I replied with a friendly smile before Blayze could say another word.

The man stuck his hand out for Blayze to shake. "Larry Morris, and this is my wife, Milly."

Blayze set the other suitcase down as I hit the down button for the elevator. "It's a pleasure to meet you both. I'm Blayze Shaw, and this is Georgiana Crenshaw."

We all exchanged our hellos.

"Do you ride bulls also, Blayze?" Larry asked.

"Not professionally, but I do it for fun or if I'm asked to

for a charity ride. I help my uncle ready them sometimes for the PBR circuit."

The idea of Blayze on a bull made my chest squeeze with anxiety. I placed my hand over my heart and willed the strange feeling away.

Larry chuckled. "I've only been on a bull once, when I was twenty-two, and I broke my arm. Never had the desire to get on one again."

"Oh, that is terrible!" I said while Milly shook her head.

"It was the best thing that could have happened," she said. "I don't know how your mother did it, but there is no way I could have been married to a man who climbed on top of those animals for a living."

We all chuckled. The elevator doors opened, and Blayze motioned for me and Milly to walk in first, followed by Larry.

We reached the lobby and all exited. "You two enjoy your day," Larry said as he gave us both a warm smile. Milly did the same before they headed toward the front desk.

"Do you need to check out?" Blayze asked.

I shook my head. "I did it online."

"Great, let's go get some breakfast. I'm starving."

A few minutes later, we were pulling up to a familiar place.

"Paul's Pancakes! I haven't been here since…well, since the last time I was in Montana."

Blayze smiled as he got out of his truck and jogged around the back of it. I grabbed my purse from the backseat and was about to get out as well when my door opened. I turned to see Blayze standing there waiting for me.

I narrowed my eyes at him. "If you think being sweet is going to make me go easy on you with this interview, you've got another thing coming."

His brows pulled down into a frown. "I can clearly see the type of men you're used to dating."

My mouth fell open. "Excuse me?"

"If you think I have some ulterior motive by opening your door, then you're dating the wrong kind of guys."

I took his offered hand as I slipped out of the truck. "Chivalry isn't dead, but it is rare."

He pulled my hand up to his mouth and kissed the back of it while he winked. My entire body shuddered when he whispered, "That's a damn shame."

Jerking my hand away, I rolled my eyes and prayed he didn't hear my sharp intake of breath.

"Let's keep this professional, please."

He saluted and motioned for me to walk ahead of him. He, of course, walked faster to get around me to open the door and laughed when I exhaled.

A young woman walked up to us and smiled. She spent a few extra moments looking at Blayze before she asked, "Good morning! Just the two of you?"

"Yes," Blayze and I said at the same time.

"Follow me!" she said, grabbing two menus.

As we walked through the restaurant, I smiled. It looked the same as it did ten years ago. The teal booths brought back a rush of memories of me and my parents stopping here to eat.

"It looks the same as it did the last time I was here," I mused as the waitress seated us toward the back of the restaurant.

Blayze slid into the booth. "Why change a good thing?"

The waitress handed us both our menus. "Something to drink?"

"Coffee, black, please," Blayze answered.

"Um, a glass of orange juice and a coffee, black for me, too, please."

She smiled. "Two coffees and an orange juice. I'll let you look at the menu."

"Thanks!" we both said in unison.

I perused the menu. "When I was little, I always got the chocolate chip pancakes. My father would get so frustrated with me because I wouldn't try anything new."

Blayze chuckled. "Man, every time I get the chance to come here I try something different."

Looking up, I asked, "You've never had the same thing twice?"

He was still studying the menu. "Nope. How boring is that."

"Are you saying I'm boring?"

Peeking over the top of the menu, he narrowed one eye. "Did I say that?"

"No, but it feels like you implied it."

He stared at me, then went back to looking at the menu. "I simply said it was boring to eat the same thing over and over. If you took it another way, that's on you."

"That's on me?" I asked.

He put the menu down again. "Yeah, Georgie. I don't know, maybe deep down inside you think you're boring. Or maybe you're afraid to take chances. I don't know. But me saying it's boring to eat the same thing over and over is not saying you're boring as a person."

My mouth dropped open, and I sat there wishing I could come up with a clever reply.

"I do not think I'm boring. Or afraid to take chances. I take them all the time."

Blayze sighed and sat back in the booth. "When was the last time you did something simply on impulse?"

I blinked a few times. "What?"

He smiled and it made my insides heat. "When was the last time you did something on an impulse? You know, something totally unplanned, maybe a little crazy."

I went to speak, but then snapped my mouth shut when I couldn't think of one single thing.

Picking up his menu once again, he softly said, "I thought so."

Before I could say anything, the waitress came back with our coffees and my juice.

"Ready to order?" she asked.

Blayze looked at me and raised a brow.

"Yes." I looked down at the menu and said the first thing I saw. "Three rolled apples, please."

The waitress wrote down my order. "Great pick. And for you?"

Blayze handed her the menu and flashed me a smile that nearly had me blushing. "I'll take the peach Belgium waffle."

"With whipped cream?" she asked.

Blayze turned and looked at her. "The cream is the best part."

I was positive my jaw fell to the table while the waitress let out a breathy laugh.

"Indeed, it is."

When she turned and walked away, I kicked Blayze under the table.

"Ouch! What the hell, Georgie."

"I'm not a little girl anymore, stop calling me that."

His gaze fell to my breasts. "No, you are not a little girl anymore."

I snapped my fingers in front of him. "Up here, Blayze."

Laughing, he pulled his phone out and checked it.

"Do you really think that was appropriate to say to her?" I asked.

He glanced up. "She didn't seem bothered by the fact that I like the cream the best."

I sighed in frustration. "You made it sexual, Blayze."

With a tilt of his head, he studied me. "Or you took it that way."

I folded my arms over my chest as I looked away. "Ugh. You haven't changed at all. You're exactly the same."

"Please enlighten me."

I swung my gaze back to him and tried not to get lost in those sky-blue eyes. "Cocky and a flirt."

Blayze lifted the coffee cup up to his mouth and blew on it. My eyes instantly went to his mouth, and I swore I could feel those lips moving down my neck. When he blew on the liquid, I focused on my own coffee.

"Glad to get that right out on the table," he said. "And your dad thought you were the right person to interview me?"

"I'm sorry?"

He shrugged. "Seems to me that if you hate me that much, it could impact what you write about me—if I was going to allow you to write about me, which I'm not."

My heart dropped. "I don't hate you, Blayze."

The way his eyes pierced mine felt like he could see right into my soul. "You certainly don't like me, and you made that clear the last time I saw you."

It was then I realized how childish I was acting. What happened was so many years ago. Blayze was nearly seventeen at the time, he was handsome and could most likely get any girl he wanted. Yet, it was me he'd chosen to spend that entire summer with. It had been me he'd shown how to rope. Me whom he went riding with every day. And it was me he'd said was unlike any other girl he knew, right before he kissed me. It was also me he'd wanted to lose his virginity to.

I closed my eyes and shook my head. I was an adult woman. A confident, independent, successful woman who was here to do a job. I was letting my sixteen-year-old hurt feelings drive my behavior.

"I'm sorry, Blayze. I shouldn't have said what I said back then, but to be honest I was young, hurt, and angry. And yes, I know it was my words that caused you to…"

I let my words drift off, and he raised a brow in question.

Smiling, I decided to lighten the mood. "And if I'm being truthful, I do like you. Kind of."

The corner of his mouth lifted into the sexiest smile I'd ever seen on a man. When the waitress put our food down, Blayze waited for her to leave. Then he swiped his fingers through the cream and sucked. I couldn't pull my eyes from his mouth.

My breathing grew heavier at the memory of Blayze pushing his finger inside of me, taking it out, and then tasting it. I was so embarrassed at the time, yet I had burned for him to do it over and over again.

"Like I said, the cream is the best part."

Holy crap. I was in so much trouble.

Chapter Three

BLAYZE

"Did you like your breakfast?" I asked as Georgie and I left the restaurant. She had eaten in silence, and I knew it was because of the little stunt I'd pulled with the whipped cream. I couldn't help myself. It had always been fun to tease her. She was so fucking innocent, but even at sixteen I knew there was something about Georgie that told me she'd be crazy in bed. An older football player at school told me about the whole sucking my finger after putting it inside her thing. The way her eyes had widened and heated at the same time…Fuck, I could still feel her heat to this day.

Enough, Shaw, or your dick is going to stand at attention.

She sighed in pleasure. "I'm so full, and it was so good. Good call on stopping here."

"No problem. You don't need anything before we leave, do you?"

Georgie shook her head. "No, I'm good."

"Then let's head on to Hamilton. My mom will be happy to see you."

She smiled as she buckled up. "I can't wait to see your family. I've always had such fond memories of the summers I spent in Montana."

It might have been an asshole move, but I asked, "Then why did you stop coming with your parents?"

From the corner of my eye, I saw her head snap up. "What?"

Quickly glancing over at her, I asked again, "Why did you stop coming to Montana?"

She looked at me with a disbelieving expression, and I turned to focus back on the road.

"I, um…I don't know. I grew up. Got involved with riding and other things. My summers became busier."

I nodded. "I was hoping it wasn't because of what happened between us."

She let out a nervous laugh. "Don't be silly, Blayze. We were young, and it was nothing."

"I don't know if I would say it was *nothing*. I thought what we shared was pretty amazing."

She turned in her seat. "If it was so amazing, then why did you start to flirt with every girl you possibly could after we got caught?"

Giving her a look that silently asked if she was serious, I replied, "Because you said it was a mistake, Georgie. You said you'd regret giving up your virginity to a guy like me."

"Georgiana. My name is not Georgie, it's Georgiana."

"I've always called you that. Why do I have to stop now?"

She let out a long, frustrated sigh. "Because we're not kids anymore, Blayze. We're adults, and I would prefer to be called Georgiana. And I was embarrassed and confused when we got caught by our fathers, let me remind you. You're the one who went out and fucked some other girl, whom you knew didn't like me!"

"What?" I asked in confusion.

"Then you made it very clear how you truly felt about me by making sure I saw how many other girls you flirted and made out with. You were only using me to get into my pants."

I gripped the steering wheel tighter. "First of all, I admit it was a shitty thing for me to do. Lindsay, the flirting, all of it. But if you think I only wanted to fuck you, then you never really knew me. I meant what I said to you."

I could feel her eyes on me. "Why did you?"

"Why did I what?" I snapped out.

"Run off and sleep with another girl that very same day?"

"Male pride, maybe? What you said to me? The fact that you thought I was a mistake? I really wanted you, and not for the reasons you think. I am sorry, though, that I put you in that situation. I really thought our dads had left the ranch that day."

She looked away to stare out the window.

"It was a pretty good kiss, and I didn't regret any of it, Blayze. I'm sorry I hurt you."

We remained in silence for a few minutes. "Did you know you were the first guy to kiss me?" she asked.

Turning to her, I smiled. "You told me I was."

She nodded and let out the cutest fucking giggle. "I forgot. I had no idea what to do, and I was so nervous. But you made it so easy to want to be with you. I didn't come back because I was hurt and a bit embarrassed. I was confused. I guess we both hurt one another."

I reached for her hand and gave it a squeeze. "I didn't regret any of it, Georgie."

She rolled her eyes and sighed. "You're going to keep calling me that, aren't you?"

"It's all I've ever known."

After letting go of her hand, we drove in silence for a bit before I asked, "Are you still riding?"

"Not as much as I'd like to. My job keeps me pretty busy with traveling. I just went to Paris for an article for *Vogue*."

"My dad mentioned that. Congratulations. I always knew you loved sports stuff. It's a strange combo."

She laughed. "I guess I'm still trying to figure out what I want to do with my life. Freelance makes it easy. Dad said that getting this article printed in *Sports Monthly* will open a lot more doors when it comes to interviewing sports legends."

"And that's what you want?" I asked.

She shrugged. "I mean, I've always enjoyed sports, bull riding especially. I thought I wanted to write about, but the more I do in fashion the more I feel like I'm more drawn to it." She smiled soflty. "I think I do the sports thing to make my father happy. I don't know. I work more on the fashion side though. It's my true passion."

"Let me forewarn you now: my sister Morgan is going to college for fashion."

She grinned. "Your dad told me that last night.

"Well, she's going to be on you like a fly on shit."

It was nice we were making polite small talk, but it was time to get to the heart of things.

"So tell me, why is your magazine interested in me? I get wanting to interview my father, but why me?"

She cleared her throat before she began to speak. "Well, it shouldn't be a surprise to you that your family is well known in the PBR world."

I nodded. "And that's reason enough to interview all of us?"

"Yes. I mean, they want the focus of the piece on Brock and your uncles, but you're popular among the PBF family as well."

"Why me, though? Why not Hunter or Bradly?"

When she didn't answer right away, I turned to see her chewing on her lip.

"Spill it, Georgie…er…Georgiana."

She let out a long, dramatic sigh. "Whether you want to believe this or not, people are enthralled by your decision not to follow in your dad's footsteps. They want to know why."

I let out a disbelieving laugh. "Why?"

"Well, from the research I started doing on the plane, you're good at bull riding. Really good. So that makes people wonder why you're not interested in a career in it. You're also popular among both men and women. For different reasons, of course. I'll ask Brock and your uncles questions first, but I'd love to interview your older cousins. Just a little bit."

"What about Avery, Josh, and Nathan?"

"I don't need to talk to them simply because of their age. Um—" She started to look through a notebook she had pulled out of her purse, which actually looked more like a travel bag. "Avery is fifteen, and Joshua and Nathan are both fourteen, right?"

Nodding, I replied, "Yep. Still in high school. You should be warned: Josh and Nate are both really good at team roping and have already won a few events."

"Really? Do either of them bull ride?"

"Both of them do."

"Goodness." She laughed. "Your poor mothers. I can't imagine having to watch my son climb on top of a bull all the time."

"Josh has been on bulls for as long as I can remember. I think Kaylee has a photo of her and Josh riding on one of the bulls when he was like three."

Georgie turned her whole body to face me. "What! Isn't that dangerous?"

This time I laughed. "You'll see that these bulls live a very different life away from the arenas."

"What do you mean?"

I looked at her quickly. "You can ride some of them like a horse. They're gentle giants."

"Ha! I've been around enough of them to know that's not true."

"You've been around them at events, Georgie. Don't you remember when we went over to my Uncle Ty's place and watched him train the bulls?"

She thought for a moment. "I do remember petting them. Wait, we even walked out into a field once and you and Ryan jumped up and sat on one."

"You wouldn't do it, and you cried."

"I did not cry."

"Oh yes, you did! You ran back to the barn crying your eyes out because Ryan said you were afraid."

"As any ten-year-old girl would be! You two were insane."

"Still are."

She huffed. "I believe it."

"I still don't see why you feel like you have to interview me."

Her body slumped. "Blayze, I just found out I was going to be interviewing you not even forty-eight hours ago."

"What?"

Her phone started to ring. "Crap, this is my new editor—he's my go-to for the interview, do you mind?"

"Not at all," I replied.

"Hi, Doug. Yes, I made it fine. Okay."

Georgie started to bounce her leg and I glanced over at her, noticing all the color had drained from her face.

"I, um, I don't think that is going to work for me."

I looked back at her quickly. Her brows were pulled down into a frown.

Focusing back on the road, she said, "I'm going to have to get back to you, Doug. That's not something I'm comfortable with. And…well…hello?"

She pulled her phone away from her ear and stared at it. Did the dick hang up on her?

"Is everything okay?" I asked.

Turning to look at me, she forced a smile. "Everything's fine."

I could tell by the look on her face, everything was far from fine.

I pulled into the gate of our ranch and headed toward the main house. Georgie had hung up with her editor about fifteen minutes ago and had been writing in her little notebook ever since. She bounced her leg up and down, suddenly seeming uneasy. Nervous. She didn't even notice when I turned off the main road that led to my grandparents' house. After a few more minutes of driving, I pulled up to my log house.

"Here we go."

Georgie lifted her head and gasped at the sight before her. "What is this?"

"A house," I replied as I got out and opened the truck door to get her bags.

Georgie got out, too, and shut the door before she made her way closer to the house.

"I've never seen anything so beautiful in my life."

A stunning rock-and-log home stood in front of me. It wasn't overly big, yet it wasn't a small house by any means. Large, round timber logs held up the wraparound porch that overlooked a beautiful meadow dotted with horses and cattle. A stunning view of the mountain ridge at the far side of the ranch made my breath catch in my throat.

I smiled as I followed her gaze.

When I became the foreman for the ranch and started taking over more of the day-to-day operations, my grandfather gifted me with fifty acres of land.

"This house hasn't always been here, has it? I feel like I know this meadow. Do I know this meadow?" she asked, turning to look at me over her shoulder.

A sense of pride bubbled up inside of me. I loved this house and was so proud it was mine. "No. I had it built last year. And yeah, you've been to this part of the ranch when we were younger."

She spun around. "This is...this is...*your* house?"

Looking at my home, I grinned. Rose Marie, one of my younger cousins, Uncle Ty and Aunt Kaylee's oldest, and I had worked on the design of the house for months before my father's good friend, Michael, had drawn up the plans for it.

"Rose Marie and I designed it. You probably remember her, she's one of my cousins."

She blinked at me a few times. "The house? You both designed this house?"

I nodded.

Turning back to look at the house, she slowly shook her head. "It's beautiful. Are those full trees?"

"Yes. I didn't want it to be just a log home, so we incorporated the dry stack rocks. And this pond has always been one of my favorite spots on the ranch. My grandfather gave me the land as a college graduation gift. He said I could either put cattle on it or build a house. I did both."

"Wow, it's stunning. Do you have a lot of cattle on here?"

"My property isn't fenced in, so my cattle roam with the ranch cattle."

"Blayze, this is so beautiful." She looked back out at the small pond. "Wait, is this where we used to ride to go fishing?"

I wasn't sure why my heart skipped a beat that Georgie remembered that little detail. "It sure is. As a matter of fact, the small dock is still there. You can get to it from the house. It's still stocked with fish as well. We can do some fishing while you're here."

"I'd love that."

"Come on in, and I'll show you around and to your room."

Georgie started to walk, then stopped. "I'm sorry, what did you say?"

"I'll show you around the house."

She shook her head. "No, the part about showing me *my room*? Here?" She let out what sounded like a disgusted laugh. "You think I'm going to stay here with you?"

I shrugged. "Beggars can't be choosers, Georgie."

She opened her mouth to say something, then it snapped shut. She turned in a complete circle before she started to laugh.

"What's so funny?"

"You! Did you honestly think I'd be okay staying here with you?"

"No, I figured you'd react exactly this way. Freaked out. But I figured you'd gotten it out of your system when my dad told you the plan."

She put her hands on her hips. "I'm not freaking out, Blayze. If this is some kind of joke, it's not funny. Just take me up to your parents' place. My father said I was going to be staying there."

"Sorry, no can do. They have company."

"They have a huge house! Why can't I stay in one of the guest rooms?"

Sighing, I put her luggage down. "Every room is taken."

"Then I'll stay at your grandparents' place."

I shook my head. "Their place is being remodeled, and they're staying at my dad's."

"Stella and Ty Senior are remodeling their whole house?"

"New kitchen counters and countertops. All the tile and carpets are being pulled up and new flooring is being put in. The bathrooms are getting redone too. So, the entire house is empty. My parents' friends, the Hendersons, are also staying with Mom and Dad since they're having issues with their new build. So, as you can see, it's a full house. Now, you can go stay with one of my uncles if you want, or you can stay here with me where you'll have the most privacy. My father was supposed to let you know there was a change of plans. So what will it be? One of the uncles or here, where I promise to leave you alone because I'm hardly ever here."

She forced a tight smile. "Thank you for allowing me options. I'll stay here. As long as I won't be intruding on your privacy."

"I'm gone most of the day working around the ranch or in town at the office."

"Office?"

"My dad built a community center in town in my biological mother's honor. The Kaci Shaw Community Center. I'm on the board of directors with him."

"Oh, that's right."

I stood there and watched as questions ran through her head. Not many people asked me about my mother, Kaci. She'd died while giving birth to me. My father never talked about her at all until Lincoln came into his life. The only thing I knew about my biological mom was the stories my dad or Grams told me. The community center held mental health offices where a therapist was on staff twenty-four hours a day in case anyone had a mental health crisis. It took my father years before he told me my mother had suffered from depression and anxiety. There was a park next to the community center, the Beck Shaw Community Park, named after my Uncle Beck, who died in the Marines. It had a playground, skatepark, an indoor arena, class-rooms for FFA, and an indoor pool.

"What do you do for the community center?" Georgie asked.

With a wink, I picked up her stuff again. "I'm sure you'll find out while you're snooping into my life. Just think, now you'll have access to your unwilling subject twenty-four-seven."

Georgie's forced smile faltered as she nodded and started up the steps to my front porch. "Looks like I won the lottery then."

I had to bite the inside of my cheek to keep from laughing. "The mega lottery!"

Chapter Four

GEORGIANA

The moment I stepped into Blayze's house, I was captivated. It was a mixture of rock and wood, and I instantly felt a calm come over me. There was a large picture window opposite the front door that overlooked a pond that was fed by one of the creeks that ran through the Shaw ranch. I knew it well because I had played here as a little girl. I'd spent so much time learning how to fish in that pond and swim. I had such fond memories of it, and obviously Blayze did, too, since he built his house near it.

To the right of me was a large living room. A fireplace made from the same dry stacked rock outside went all the way up to the timber beams and the stunning wood ceiling. Large leather furniture filled the living room, adding the right homey touch. A wide pool table sat between the living area and the dining area.

A high-top round table with four red leather chairs housed a small fall bouquet in the center. I turned back to see a quilt draped over the back of the sofa and another fall decoration on the coffee table.

My heart started to hammer in my chest. I had never even thought to ask Blayze if he was dating anyone.

Turning back to the kitchen area, I studied it carefully. The cabinets looked to be knotty alder, stained in a light color to show off the texture of the natural wood. The large island held the countertop stove and an expansive counter with four bar chairs pulled up to it. A hurricane lamp sat on the bar with a bowl of fruit next to it.

There was another large picture window behind the farm-house-style kitchen sink opposite the island. Yet another fall decoration sat to the side of the sink.

Everything was pristine. Spotless. Clearly a woman lived here. The main living area was masculine, yet it had small touches that screamed a woman was present and making it her own space.

"I'd never leave this place if it were mine," I whispered as I slowly turned, taking in the open-concept first floor.

"Thanks. It's my sanctuary, no doubt about it."

I smiled and gave him a slight nod.

"Come on, I'll show you around really quickly, then take your stuff up to your room."

All I could do was follow him as he led me into a large bedroom, which I was guessing was his. Wood planks covered the wall and were stained the same color as the kitchen cabinets.

There was a king-size bed with an old blue-and-white quilt on top and a tan blanket thrown across the bottom of it. One large dresser sat across from the bed, and off to the other side was a nook area that overlooked the water. A large chair with an ottoman sat there just waiting for someone to curl up in it with a warm cup of coffee and a book. Next to it was a small table, and it was then that I noticed the book. I casually made my way over to the window with the excuse of looking at the view.

"What a stunning view. Who wouldn't want to wake up to this every morning?"

Blayze laughed. "It's a struggle to get out of bed sometimes."

Turning to look back at him, I made myself smile. "I bet."

I glanced down and picked up the book, frowning when I saw the title. *The Last Bookshop in London* by Madeline Martin.

He has a girlfriend. Why does that make me feel so…so sad?

Putting the book back down, I hugged myself and faced Blayze.

"Do you like to read?" he asked.

"I love to read. Historical romance is my favorite."

He smiled. "Really? Do you like World War Two-era books?"

"If it has a happy ending," I said with a slight chuckle.

"You should read that one. It's a great book. Morgan left it when she stayed here a few months back. I found it in the spare bedroom. Read it that night until four in the morning. I was fucking exhausted the next day. It has a…what does Morgan call it?…an HEA."

I laughed. "You read a romance book?"

"I like the historical ones. Morgan got me hooked. Not a fan of contemporary romance, but she says I just haven't read the right one yet."

Staring at him like he was insane, I asked again, "Wow, that's kind of crazy."

He tilted his head and regarded me. "Are you saying guys can't read romance?"

"No! I'm not saying that at all. I just assumed it was…"

Lifting a brow, he smirked. "It was what?"

I licked my suddenly dry lips and paused for a moment before I said, "Your girlfriend's."

Blayze's eyes darted down to my lips, and I had the urge to press them together tightly but forced myself not to. Instead, I looked out the window to see a beautiful view of a sprawling pasture with the mountains in the background. A few cattle dotted the rolling landscape, and I thought I spied a paint horse.

"What a beautiful view. Goodness. A view of the pond *and* a view of the mountains. You poor thing, how do you handle living here?"

Blayze chuckled. "The bathroom's in here."

I followed him into a beautiful bathroom that looked like it could be in a mountain spa. His and her cabinets matched the kitchen cabinets. A large oval tub was tucked under another picture window with yet another stunning view. The shower was magnificent and boasted a rock floor with dark tile on the walls. I nearly groaned when I saw the rain-head shower with jets on the side, yearning to stand under it and close my eyes.

"Wow."

It was all I could say. As I turned to walk out, I glanced at the counter and saw only one toothbrush. It also appeared that only one of the sinks was being used. Why I cared was beyond me. I was only here for a month, and I had a job to do. Getting sidetracked by Blayze's personal life was not going to happen. Or, at least, I had to tell myself that.

"There are two guest bedrooms upstairs, each with its own bathroom," Blayze said. "There's also a small theater room with six chairs and a projector and screen. It's fun to watch football games and such up there. Feel free to use it if you want to watch a movie or something. During this time of year we usually have a Halloween marathon."

"We?"

"Me, Morgan, Hunter, and the rest of the Shaw cousins. It's been a tradition for as long as I can remember. We used to do it at Grams and Grandpa's house, but once I moved in, we moved the party over here."

"Sounds like fun," I said.

Smiling, I allowed myself to really look at Blayze. The dimple, his blue eyes that now reminded me of ice blue glaciers that a girl could easily get lost in. There was something different about his eyes. I simply couldn't put my finger on it.

I followed Blayze back through the house and to a set of stairs. Large timber logs held up the second floor and added a rustic feel to the home. The large plank wood floors also contributed to the charm. They looked repurposed, and I wanted to ask Blayze if they were.

"You can take whichever room you want," Blayze said as he picked up my suitcases and headed up the stairs. The railing was black wrought iron. It looked elegant but was a simple pattern that went perfectly with the feel of the house.

The first bedroom had the same wood walls as Blayze's room. There was a queen-size bed with what looked to be an antique bedframe and matching dresser. The other room had a completely opposite feel than the rest of the house. The walls were plank wood, but they were painted in a soft sage green. A chandelier light fixture—that I was positive was antique—hung in the middle of the room. A four-poster bed sat underneath. A beautiful swath of white linen fabric hung around the frame and draped down each leg to pile loosely on the floor, giving the room a feminine feel.

I made my way over to the bathroom and gasped when I stepped inside. It was decorated in black and white. The flooring was an old-fashioned tile. A claw-foot tub was perched under a breathtaking picture window, and a large, walk-in shower that had the same features as the one in Blayze's bathroom was in the far corner. A beautiful antique dresser had been converted into a cabinet and held a stunning black stone sink bowl.

"Jesus, who designed this bedroom and bathroom?"

Blayze smiled as he leaned against the doorjamb. "Rose Marie. I gave her free rein on one room in the house. She stops by every so often to do what she calls a 'refresh.' She can't touch my bedroom, but she usually changes out the quilt and towels in this bedroom and bath and the other one. She also puts out most of the decorations."

Ahh…so that explained the fall décor. "And here I thought you were just in touch with your feminine side."

He threw his head back and laughed. "Hardly. Morgan likes to stay here when she's home from school as well. I think they both just like being away from their folks. This is a beautiful room."

"Rose Marie did an amazing job. She has a talent for design like your mom."

He nodded. "That she does."

"Would you mind if I picked this room? I just love the feel of it. It's comfortable and cozy. I mean, your room is too…"

As my voice trailed off, Blayze rose one brow. I quickly put up my hands. "Not that I was saying I wanted to stay in your room. I was simply saying that it's cozy. Nice. Comfortable. I mean…"

He pushed off the jamb and laughed. "I knew what you meant, Georgie. And you can stay in whatever room you prefer. Even mine, though we'd have to share a bed."

I rolled my eyes and went over to one of my suitcases, grabbed it, and put it on the bed. "I would rather sleep in the barn before sharing a bed with you."

"Ouch," he said softly.

I turned to face him as a sudden thought occurred to me.

Folding my arms over my chest, I asked, "Did you plan this? Me staying at your house? I mean, is this some kind of game you're playing at, Blayze? Because I have to tell you, staying with you wouldn't have been my first pick."

A look of hurt passed over his face, and his eyes looked like a storm was beginning to brew in them. I instantly regretted saying my thoughts out loud. But then I saw the moment the mask fell into place. He gave me the same look he'd given me that day ten years ago when I'd angrily told him that sleeping with him would have been a mistake. A regret I wouldn't have been able to take back. I'd hurt him.

"Trust me, it wasn't planned at all, *Georgiana*." He spat my name out, and I flinched. I hated the anger in his voice.

"I wasn't any happier than you when I found out you had to stay here. Hell, I wasn't happy to hear you were coming at all. And don't even think that I'm going to let you interview me. You're the last person I want to talk to about my private life."

It was my turn to whisper *ouch*, but I kept it inside my head. "Okay," I said as I looked everywhere except at him. "I'll do my best to stay out of your way."

He closed his eyes and was about to say something when I added, "I need to make a phone call. So if we're done, can you leave, please?"

He clenched his jaw as he nodded and headed to the door.

I felt like a complete ass. Blayze was being kind enough to let me say here, and I was acting like a total bitch. I called out,

"Do you think you could drive me around the ranch so I could take a look at it since it's been so long?"

Stopping at the door, he looked back at me. There was something in his eyes that I couldn't quite read, but it caused me to shiver. The easiness between us was gone, and it was clear that a brick wall was firmly in place.

When he spoke, his voice was on the edge of being cold and distant. "In case you forgot, I'm in charge of a large, multi-million-dollar cattle ranch. I don't really have the time to play chauffeur for you."

I let out a bitter laugh. "Seriously? You won't even show me around the ranch?"

He scoffed. "No one consulted with me about this. So let me make it easy for you. Any questions you have or anything you need regarding this interview, you can ask my father."

I opened my mouth to argue, then snapped it shut. Had Blayze truly not agreed to this interview? Before I could ask, he went on.

"The only reason I'm going along with letting you stay here is because my father asked me to for his own reasons. Whatever *secrets* you think you're going to get, Georgiana, let me just inform you now: You're wasting your time."

A rush of anger washed over me, and I took a few steps in his direction. "I was tricked into this, as well, Blayze. I wasn't even told who I had to interview until I was on my way to the damn airport in Dallas. I didn't even have time to go back to my own house after my trip to Paris. My father told me this would put my name on the map as a sports reporter. He knew I would decline if he told me I'd be interviewing your dad and uncles, because he knew I wouldn't want to see you!"

"Then why did you agree to the article if you didn't want to be here?"

63

I balled my hands up into fists. "Because I want to be taken seriously in this business. Everyone thinks I'm just about shoes and fucking hats. I know sports, goddammit. I know how to report on them and write about them, and if that means I have to be an adult and put aside whatever happened between us ten years ago, then I can do that. So whatever this is between us—" I pointed to him, then me. "I can move past it, because it means nothing!"

I practically screamed the last word as it left my mouth.

"There isn't anything between us," he said.

"What happened, Blayze? Not only ten minutes ago, everything seemed fine."

"Are you really going to ask me that?"

I felt my cheeks heat. "I'm sorry I accused you of planning this. I don't know why I said that."

He stared at me for the longest time before he finally said, "I'll start looking to see if I can find you a bed and breakfast in town."

My stomach suddenly roiled. Even though I had talked the talk, I didn't really want to leave. Staying at Blayze's house would give me the privacy I longed for, as well as access to the ranch. If I stayed in town, I'd have to travel back and forth, and I didn't even have a rental car yet.

"What?" I whispered.

"It's pretty damn clear this isn't going to work." He mimicked my action from a few seconds ago, pointing between us. "I'll see if I can find you a place in town."

I stood there, speechless, as I watched him walk out the door. When I heard the soft click of the latch, I stumbled back and sat on the bed.

Why did that hurt so much? Why had I even made that stupid comment? I needed to get my emotions under control when it came to Blayze.

Dropping back onto the bed, I let out a groan. "Shit. That spiraled out of control."

Now it was going to be impossible to get Blayze to talk to me. When Doug—the new editor for the special assignment I was working on for *Sports Monthly*—had called me in the car while Blayze was driving us to the ranch, he had made it clear that they wanted Blayze to be the main focus of the article. That hadn't been what my father had said. Yes, he'd told me they'd wanted an exclusive with Blayze, but the piece was a *where are they now* article. So when Doug told me to focus on Blayze, then dropped the damn bomb on me to find out why Blayze had walked out on his own wedding, I had been thrown for a loop. I could hardly even think straight after I hung up. I decided to talk to my father because clearly Doug was mixed up. I was not writing an article about Blayze, especially when he hadn't wanted to be a part of any article, period.

I slammed my hands on the bed and forced myself not to scream.

My phone rang, and I got up to see it was a call from Brock. I drew in a deep breath and answered.

"Hello?"

"Hey, Georgiana. How was the trip?"

Forcing myself to sound cheerful, I replied, "It was great. Except for the rental car thing, everything else was perfect. They said they'd deliver me a car tomorrow if all goes well with returns today."

"Oh, great. Otherwise, I was going to tell you that we have a few ranch trucks you could drive."

"That's so nice of you, Mr. Shaw."

"Georgiana, I've known you since you were a baby, do not call me Mr. Shaw. You're like family. Call me Brock."

I chewed on my lip as guilt hit me like a sucker punch. *Like family.* Doug had made it clear I needed to dig up as much information on Blayze Shaw as possible. Why wasn't he following in his father's footsteps? What made him pick ranching over bull riding? Oh, and at the same time, I was also supposed to interview the whole family and dig into their personal lives so millions of strangers could get the dirt on the Shaw family.

This was not good. Something was wrong. Something was off. I had never even spoken to this Doug guy before. He'd sent me an email introducing himself earlier this morning. I had even tried to contact Kathleen Marker, who was editor-in-chief of the magazine. My call had gone to voicemail. I needed to call Dad and talk to him about all this.

"Brock, it is," I finally said, trying not to feel like I was suddenly betraying him.

"Blayze texted and said you made it to his place safely. I'm sorry to bunk you up with him, but we didn't have any extra room here at the house, and my folks' place is being remodeled. Blayze mentioned looking for a bed and breakfast for you in town. If you're not comfortable staying with him, we can maybe have you bunk with Ty and Kaylee, or Tanner and Timberlynn."

I cleared my throat. "I wonder if it would be best if I stayed in town? My father just figured with our past and all, I should stay here. Since I'll be interviewing mostly everyone for the article, I think I should maybe try and keep it a bit more professional."

"Nonsense, Georgiana. You'll stay here on the ranch with us. It'll be the perfect way for you to see the ins and outs of it. There's a guest house on the east side of the ranch if you need more privacy. It's a bit tucked into the woods, and Morgan and Rose Marie swear it's haunted. We'll just need to clean it up for you first."

"Um," I said with a nervous laugh. "I think I'll pass on that, but thanks."

Brock laughed. "Well, I don't want you staying in town. We'll come up with something. You're family, Georgiana."

I wanted to head right back to Missoula and tell them to find someone else to do this interview. My gut was telling me to run, and run fast.

"Brock, did Blayze know about this interview? He mentioned that he just found out about it yesterday and that you had agreed to do it as a favor. For whom?"

He sighed. "I told him about it yesterday when I asked if he could pick you up. And yes, your father asked me to do the interview as a favor to him."

My eyes went wide and I had to fight to keep my tears at bay. My father had promised me he wouldn't stick his nose into my career. He had said the magazine had approached him with the idea, not the other way around. He knew how important it was that I made it on my own and not because of who my father was.

"I see. Well, let me thank you then for doing this. I know it's hard to have people poke around in your life. Clearly Blayze doesn't want that, and he told me so."

Brock laughed softly. "Blayze isn't one for sharing his private life, I'll give you that much of a heads up. He's probably going to fight you the entire time."

Little did he know, I'd most likely tell Doug and his bosses that I was doing the original plan for the article—not some gossip column. But first I needed to talk to my father, gosh darn it.

Knowing I needed to say something, I replied, "I always did like a challenge."

"Well, you'll get one with that son of mine. Now, I hope you brought some riding clothes?"

Knowing the Shaws like I did, I'd done a bit of shopping in Missoula last night. Since I had come straight from Paris, I had plenty of business-type clothes, and even a dress or two with me already. What I'd needed were clothes to move around the cattle ranch more comfortably. I knew they wouldn't stop working just because I was there to interview them, which meant I needed to dress appropriately for ranch life—both to keep up with them and to truly get a feel for how things worked on the ranch. My father had told me that the interview was supposed to focus on what life was like for Brock after retiring from the circuit, and how the entire family still played a large role in the world of professional bull riding. That I could do. But the curve that Doug had thrown me about Blayze wasn't sitting right at all, and there was no way in hell I was going in that direction. I wasn't a gossip writer.

"I sure did," I replied.

"Great. Get changed, and I'll be there to pick you up in thirty minutes."

My heart dropped as I quickly looked at my unpacked suitcases. "Um, what will we be doing?"

"I'm going to give you a tour of the ranch. It's been years since you've been here. Thought it would be a good place to start. We'll be on horseback."

Smiling, I started to look for some jeans. "Sounds good. I'll be ready."

Chapter Five

BLAYZE

A light knock on my office door caused me to sigh. "Unless someone's dying, there's a fire, or my mother needs me...go away."

The door opened and Joshua walked in. He was my Uncle Ty and Aunt Kaylee's youngest child.

"Shouldn't you be in school, Josh?"

He smiled that big, bright smile of his. At fourteen, he was the spitting image of his father. His light brown hair, blue eyes, and fit build were already turning girls' heads. Even the older ones.

"We have a school holiday today. Something about teacher in-service day or something."

I nodded, then looked back down at the charts I was working on. "How's high school going?"

He sat down in the one chair that was opposite my desk. I had taken over the office in the main barn when my father had stepped back from the day-to-day running of the ranch. It wasn't anything fancy, but it was all I needed. Just like it had been for my dad.

"It's going. It's weird, though."

Glancing up, I noticed his serious expression. I sat back. "What do you mean?"

He sighed and ran his fingers through his hair. "It's the girls, Blayze. How do you deal with them? They're freaking me out."

I raised a brow. "Why?"

"I had a senior come up to me and ask me if I wanted to go out. I mean, an older girl asked me out."

Fighting to hold back a smile, I cleared my throat. "Tell me you didn't tell your mother."

"God, no!" Joshua said. "I know better. She'd be up at the school threatening her."

That time I did laugh.

"I mean, why would a seventeen-year-old ask a fourteen-year-old out? Then, a group of four sophomore girls sat with me and my friends at lunch, and one put her hand on my thigh and tried to cop a feel!"

"Tried?"

He blushed. "I mean, I thought about letting her, but it didn't feel right so I pushed her hand away. The girl on the other side of me was practically sitting on my lap. My friends teased me the rest of the day because all these girls were throwing themselves at me. Why me?"

I leaned forward. "Bud, you do look in the mirror, right?"

He rolled his eyes.

"You don't look fourteen, for one thing. You're good look-ing, you have a great sense of humor, and honestly, Joshua, you probably have a better physique than some of the senior guys and most of your friends. Well, you and Nathan both do."

Looking confused he asked, "Physique?"

"You're built, Joshua. You've been working on this ranch since you were old enough to clean out the horse stalls. You ride bulls, break horses—you're a built little motherfucker. And Nathan, hell, he's the spitting image of Uncle Dirk."

Josh laughed. "Dad would be pissed if he heard you say that. Also, Uncle Dirk is always telling Nathan he's a mini version of you. A flirt."

I chuckled. "First off, I'm your cousin, not your father, so I can call you a built motherfucker. And secondly, he's spot on. As a matter of fact, I think Nathan is a *bigger* flirt. Do the girls flirt with him?"

Joshua smiled. "Oh yeah. He hooked up with a junior."

"Define hooked up?"

He gave me a confused look. "Really? You don't know what it means?"

I sighed. "Yes, I know what it means. I'm just wondering if what I think it means is the same thing you think it means."

Joshua shook his head as if trying to clear his thoughts. "They messed around in the gym after school. She gave him his first…you know. Then she had him do the same to her, but you know because she's a girl it's not a blow job, it's more of—"

I held my hand up to stop him. "I get what you mean. All he did was oral?"

He laughed. "Yeah, just oral. No way is he having sex. He's too afraid his dad will find out."

I dropped back in my seat, relieved in a sense. But oral sex was a huge thing for these kids to be doing at fourteen and fifteen. Shit. I hadn't gotten my first blow job until my senior year of high school.

"How old were you when you lost your virginity?" Josh asked.

A lump instantly formed in my throat. I cleared it a few times. "What?"

"How old were you when you had sex for the first time?"

I blinked a few times, trying to decide if I should be truthful or not. "I can tell you I wasn't fourteen! Once I got to high school, I started to experiment with things, but I didn't have sex until I was sixteen, and I regretted it."

He jerked back in surprise. "Why?"

I shrugged. "I didn't do it for the right reasons."

"What does that mean?"

I exhaled and looked down at the numbers on my desk, then back up to Joshua. "As great as sex is, it should be done between two people who care about each other. Not just because you want to see how it is or because it feels good. And you shouldn't ever be forced into it by anyone."

"I get that. Did you regret it because you didn't like the girl?"

I smiled. "I really liked this one girl, and I thought I wanted it to be with her. Things didn't work out, though, and one night at a party, another girl was flirting with me. I was angry at the girl I really liked, and to pay her back for hurting me, I slept with the other girl. It didn't mean anything for either of us. She was older than me by a year, she wanted sex, and she really wanted to be my first when I told her I was a virgin. So, when she started making the move on me, I let her. And I instantly regretted it because I knew I'd never get that moment back again."

"And you wish you would have waited for someone who made it more special?"

I forced a small smile. "Yeah. I wish I would have waited for that. Sex is great, Joshua, I'm not going to lie. And what

Nathan experienced is *really great*. Just always respect the girl, no matter what. If she decides you're going too far, you stop."

He nodded. "Dad's already had this talk with me, Blayze."

Laughing, I leaned forward again. "I love women. Always have. I admire them and have the utmost respect for them. I like to flirt and make them smile. Especially girls whom other guys don't necessary flirt with. Every woman is beautiful, Joshua. Some more on the outside, some more on the inside. Just remember, it's not always about how they look on the outside that matters."

He nodded. "I want to find someone like my mom. She's beautiful inside and out, and she doesn't take shit from my dad."

I laughed harder. "No, she does not."

We could hear voices outside in the main barn, and I looked past Joshua's shoulder. "Sounds like my dad."

Joshua stood. "I better get to my chores. Thanks, Blayze. I didn't really want to talk to my dad about this, and Hunter and Bradly would just tease me."

Walking around my desk, I put my hand on his shoulder and gave it a squeeze. "I'm here for you anytime, Josh. If you ever need to talk, or need help with anything…you let me know, okay?"

He smiled. "I will, Blayze. Thanks."

"And hey, once the newness of you wears off, the girls will back down. Some."

Joshua turned to leave, and we both came to a stop when we saw my father standing there with Georgie beside him. I scanned her from top to bottom. She was dressed in jeans, a long-sleeve T-shirt that had a moose on it, and cowboy boots. Her hair was pulled up into a ponytail and parts of it were going everywhere, like she'd just finished riding. My breath stalled in my chest.

"Well, hello," Joshua said as he made his way over to her. Sticking his hand out, he said, "I'm Josh Shaw, and who are you?"

I gaped at him. And he wondered why the girls at school were flocking to him. If the little bastard acted like this, no wonder they were all over him.

Georgie smiled and shook his hand. "Georgiana Crenshaw. It's a pleasure to meet you, Josh."

I put my hands on his shoulders and pulled him back. "And you said Nathan was the flirt?"

He laughed. "I said Uncle Dirk said he was like you. I never said I didn't flirt."

"I am for sure surrounded by Shaw men," Georgie said while my father laughed.

"Go get to your chores, Joshua." My dad jerked his head toward the stables.

"Yes, sir. It was nice meeting you, Ms. Crenshaw."

Georgie smiled and watched as Joshua made his way toward the horse stables. She looked back at me. "Did he learn that from you?"

Ignoring her question, I looked at my dad. "What's up?"

He gave me a slight frown—probably because I just ignored Georgie—but answered, "I'm giving Georgiana a tour of the ranch. Would you like to join us for the rest of the tour?"

My eyes darted over to Georgie, then back to my father. "Sorry, Dad. I'm behind since I had to drive to Missoula this morning. I've got a lot of work to catch up on with the preconditioning and everything coming up."

"What is that, the preconditioning?" Georgie asked.

My father went to answer, but his cell rang. Looking at it, he said, "I need to take this. Blayze, answer Georgiana's question, will you?"

I wanted to stomp my feet and say no, but I knew better.

Dad walked away and Georgie and I both watched him leave. When she looked back at me, she rose a single brow. "Preconditioning?"

Turning, I walked back into my office and kicked the door shut with my foot. She caught it and followed me in.

I sat down, ignoring her.

After sitting in the chair, I saw her glance around my office.

"When your father comes back, I don't think he's going to be very happy to know that you wouldn't answer one simple question."

"Google it," I said.

Georgie sighed. "Blayze, this would be a lot easier, and I would be out of your hair a lot sooner, if you just answered the question."

"Go ask Josh, I'm sure he'd love to tell you about it."

When she didn't move or utter a word, I looked up at her. That was a mistake. She was smiling at me, her head slightly tilted as if she could wait a million years.

Sighing, I sat back in my chair. "It's when the calves are administered vaccinations in one day, prior to or sometimes right at the time they're weaned."

She nodded. "And what is it that you do on the ranch?"

I let a slow smile play over my face. Okay, she wanted to play the game. I'd play. Maybe if I gave her some answers, she'd leave me alone.

"I manage the ranch."

I could see the frustration on her face. "And that entails?"

"I do fiscal management, overall ranch production, financial performance, inventory, and crop rotation, among other things."

She let out a soft laugh. "Do you leave work for anyone else?"

Ignoring her question, I went back to looking at the figures on the print out.

"What did you get your degree in?"

"I'm sure you can Google that, as well, if you haven't already."

From the way she flinched, I knew she was aware of what I'd majored in. "I'm just trying to make conversation, Blayze. And for the record, I really wanted to know."

"Okay, we ready to go?" my father said as he stepped into my office.

Georgie stood. "I'm ready."

"Blayze?"

I shook my head. "I can't, Dad."

All it took was one look from my father, and I knew I wasn't going to get out of this.

Pushing my chair back, I let out a frustrated sigh.

"Who do you want her to ride?" I asked, glancing at Georgie as I walked past her. Her cheeks flushed, and she quickly looked away.

"Your mother's mare, Elly. She's the most gentle one in the barn."

Georgie chuckled. "How do you know I haven't ridden in a while?" she asked my father.

"That's what happens when you live in the city and travel all over for your job."

I headed out of the barn to find Hank. He'd been working on the ranch for as long as I could remember and was the only man my father trusted with his beloved horse Romeo.

"Hank," I said as I walked up to the corral where he was working with a horse.

"How's it going, Blayze? Everything okay?"

I shook my head. "No. There's a pain in the ass woman here, and I have a feeling she's going to make my life a living hell."

Hank let out a bark of laughter. "They always do in some way or another, but they more than make up for it."

I glanced back over my shoulder and watched Georgie and my father step out of the barn. The way the sun hit her golden-brown hair made it shimmer.

"That her?" Hank asked.

"Yeah," I replied, focusing back on him. "That's her. Do you know what pasture Elly and Romeo are in? Dad is taking Ms. Crenshaw on a tour of the ranch via horseback."

Hank took a closer look at Georgie. "Is that Georgiana Crenshaw?"

"Yes, do you remember her?"

He nodded, then looked at me. "Seems to me the last time you two saw each other there was some funny business going on behind this barn."

I rolled my eyes. "Christ, did everyone know? I was stupid and young. The horses?"

He gave me another nod. "Front pasture. Your Duke is up there grazing with them."

Giving Hank a pat on the back, I thanked him, then headed toward the front pasture. It would only take a whistle to get the horses to come to me.

With the help of Decker, another ranch hand, we guided Duke, Elly, and Romeo out to the front of the barn.

"There's my handsome boy," my father said as he walked up and took Romeo from Decker. "Thanks, Deck."

"Sure thing, Mr. Shaw."

"Wow, what beautiful horses." Georgie walked up and ran her hand down Elly's neck. "What breed is your horse, Brock?"

With a proud smile on his face, Dad answered, "He's a Zangersheide. This guy right here has bred some of the world's best show-jumping horses. I paid a small fortune for him, but I fell in love with him the moment I saw him."

"Do you still breed him?" Georgie asked.

Dad smiled and ran his hands over the horse. "Nah. He's retired now and living out his best life with a few gals in the pasture."

Georgie laughed, then turned to Elly. "Beautiful paint."

"My mother adores paints. She's got a good temper, so she should be easy to ride. Do you need help…"

My voice trailed off as Georgie mounted the horse with ease.

I mounted Duke and gave him a pat on the neck.

Georgie was watching both of us. "And the name of your beautiful buckskin?"

"Duke."

"Duke?" she asked with a sly grin. "Any particular reason you named him Duke?"

I smirked. "Because my father said I couldn't name him King."

"Ready to head out?" Dad asked as he walked over to us on Romeo.

Georgie tried to hide her smile and failed. Turning to Dad, she gave Elly a slight kick. "Ready."

Chapter Six

GEORGIANA

I spent the afternoon riding and talking with Brock and Blayze. They showed me around the ranch, introduced me to some different people, and brought me to Tanner and Timberlynn's stunning log cabin that was seated on the edge of a beautiful lake. Tanner was Brock's younger brother and had once been ranked number one in the world for team roping. He currently helped Timberlynn train horses and worked with rescue horses, as well as helping his family run the ranch.

After lunch, we road over to Ty and Kaylee's house. Ty was Brock's older brother and had been forced to give up bull riding after an accident. He and Dirk, Brock's best friend, both raised and trained bulls for the PBR.

Everything had been off the record so far, but I found I really liked Timberlynn and Kaylee. I'd always been fond of them when I was little.

As we handed over the horses to a few ranch hands, I heard a female voice call out from behind me. When I turned, I smiled to see Lincoln Shaw, Brock's wife and Blayze's mother. She was still as beautiful as she was when I was little. Her brown hair was pulled back in a ponytail and her green eyes reminded me of mine. It wasn't often I met another person with true green eyes.

"Georgiana, oh my have you grown up into a beautiful young woman," Lincoln said as she pulled me into her arms and gave me a bear hug. That nagging guilty feeling started at the back of my mind once again, but I pushed it away.

"It's so good to see you again, Mrs. Shaw."

Lincoln laughed. "Call me Lincoln, please. I hope you're hungry. I've made a lasagna and Stella made at least four desserts!"

I smiled. "How are Stella and Ty Senior?"

"You know Brock's parents—still going like they're twenty-five even though they're in their upper seventies."

"If you'll excuse me, I've got some work I need to catch up on," Blayze stated as he stepped up to his mother and kissed her on the cheek.

Lincoln frowned. "You'll do no such thing, Blayze. We have a guest, and it's her first day here. I'm sure work can wait."

Blayze sighed, but he respected his momma enough not to argue with her.

"Now, you take Georgiana here back to your house so you can both get cleaned up. Dinner will be ready at seven sharp." Lincoln looked back at me. "I do have to warn you, Morgan is beside herself with excitement to see you. She heard you were in Paris for a fashion week or something?"

I nodded. "That's right. I do some freelance work for *Vogue*."

Lincoln raised her brows. "Wow, two totally different areas of reporting."

Laughing, I shrugged. "I couldn't decide what I wanted to do so…I'm doing both."

"Good for you!" Lincoln said. "But don't be surprised if she tries to consume all of your time."

"No worries at all."

Brock walked up and leaned down to kiss his wife. "Missed you, babe."

She reached up and kissed him. "Missed you more."

"If you're ready, Georgie?" Blayze said, causing me to pull my gaze away from the happy couple.

"Yes, of course."

As we started down the pathway toward Blayze's truck, Lincoln called my name. Turning, I smiled.

"Tonight is off the record. Whenever you're in my home, you're a family guest. I expect anything shared between the family stays in the walls of my home."

For a moment, I was completely taken aback. Not that I thought Lincoln's request was rude, or that what she was asking was out of the question, but that she could issue a warning with such a sweet smile on her face.

Clearing my throat, I replied, "Of course."

Blayze might have been upset with me, but he walked up to the passenger side of the truck, opened the door, and even took my hand to help me up into his truck. My chest fluttered at the show of chivalry.

When he got in, I was ready for the cold shoulder again. He'd been polite all afternoon, but I was sure it was because we'd been with his father. So when we started down the road toward his house, I wasn't expecting him to speak.

"I want to apologize for the way I treated you earlier."

I turned my head to look at him as he went on.

"I was blindsided by all of this, and to be honest, I'm not really fond of you poking around in my private life. I get wanting to interview my uncles—they were once in the public eye—but I chose not to do that. I don't really understand why your magazine wants you to interview me so much."

I cleared my throat. "First, it's not my magazine. I'm not a staff writer for them."

"But you want to be?" he asked.

Once upon a time that had been a goal of mine, but I was finding that the writing wasn't fulfilling anymore.

"I'm not sure."

He frowned. "I thought that was why we were doing this interview."

I decided to change the subject. "You were in the public eye for a while, though. You rode and competed in high school and some of college. You were set to move up to the Unleash the Beast tour."

"That's not what I wanted, Georgie." His voice was clipped and had an angry tone to it.

Deciding it wasn't worth it to argue with him, I simply said, "I understand. Will you tell me?"

He looked at me for a brief moment. "Tell you what?"

"The real reason you're not bull riding."

"I do bull ride. All the time."

I sighed and shook my head. It was useless. I didn't even want the information for the stupid article. I wanted to know for myself at this point.

"Tell me something," he said. "Why are you—sorry, the *magazine*—so damn interested in me and why I'm not riding?"

I swallowed hard and tried to put a neutral expression on my face. "Honestly, I have no idea why they're interested in you. Maybe it's your looks, and they think your face will sell magazines."

He laughed and shook his head. We spent the rest of the ride back to his place in complete silence.

Once we got back to Blayze's house and I heard him get into the shower, I called my father. It went to his voicemail.

"Daddy, I need you to call me. This assignment is…" I sighed and closed my eyes. "Dad, they changed it on me, and I don't know what to do. This guy Doug Larson called me, and he wants me to focus the article on Blayze and only him. Like in a very personal way. I have no idea who this guy is, and Kathleen isn't returning my calls or texts. Something doesn't feel right, Dad. Please call me."

Hitting End, I groaned and dropped back onto the bed. How in the hell did I end up in this situation? There was no way my father would have told me to do this interview had he known the magazine was looking for a different angle. It wasn't a piece about catching up with the Shaw family, it was to find all their secrets and air them all out. That wasn't even what *Sports Monthly* was about. It wasn't a rag magazine.

Standing, I put my hands on my hips. "I'll write it the way I want to write it. The way I was told to write it in the beginning. Or, maybe I won't write it at all."

Maybe this was exactly what I needed to get me to decide where my career was going to go. I closed my eyes. If only I had that answer myself.

I walked over and opened the garment bag I had hung in the closet earlier and started to look through the outfits I'd brought. I wasn't sure if I should hang them up if I was going to be leaving. In the end, I decided they needed out of the bag, even if just for tonight. After taking the clothes out and hanging them up, I decided on an A-line swing dress. It was long and had a boho look to it, but I loved how it molded to my shape. I'd have to bring a sweater since it was short sleeved, but since we were only going to Brock and Lincoln's house, I figured it would be okay.

After showering, I pulled my hair up into a loose bun on the top of my head, put a bit of mascara on, and then put the dress and my cowboy boots on. I added a few bracelets and a simple, beaded necklace.

A knock on my bedroom door had me drawing in a deep breath before I headed to answer it.

When I opened the door, my eyes nearly bugged out of my head. Blayze had on jeans—something I didn't think I'd ever not seen him in—and a black sweater that showed off his broad chest. His hair was still damp from the shower, and those blue eyes of his traveled up and down my body. I swore they lit a fire to my insides.

"You look beautiful, Georgie."

Feeling my cheeks heat, I looked down and let out a soft chuckle. "Thank you."

When I looked back up, our eyes met. "And you look handsome, as always."

He winked, and I wished more than anything that it wasn't just a reaction to a compliment. It was probably something he did whenever women told him things like that.

Okay, where is that all coming from? Why do I care?

"Are you about ready to go?" he asked. "My mom doesn't like waiting when there's lasagna to be eaten."

I laughed. "Yes, let me grab my phone and a sweater."

With my phone in hand, I followed Blayze through his house and toward the side door that led to his garage.

We spent the ride to his parents' house mostly in silence until Blayze broke it. "I meant to tell you earlier that I'm okay with you staying at the house if you want. It might get to be a pain in the ass driving to and from town each day, and it seems like my dad wants you to really dive into the world of ranching."

I pressed my lips tightly together to suppress a smile. I really didn't want to think about how relieved I was that Blayze had said that. The idea of staying with him wasn't even something I wanted to think about at first, but now it felt weirdly right.

"You don't mind me staying with you?"

He turned and our eyes met for a moment before he focused back on the road. "I don't mind if you don't."

"It will be easier," I said as I glanced out the window to see fields of green pastures slowly turning darker as the sun began to sink behind the mountains. "I'll try and stay out of your way."

"I want you to be comfortable, Georgie. I just need to know one thing."

Turning to him, I asked, "What's that?"

"When you're in my house, everything is off the record."

My heart squeezed. That was twice they'd reminded me of why I was here. I understood, but a small part of me wished I was simply here as a guest. Not a freaking reporter. The knowledge that Brock and his family were doing this to help me with my career made it all seem a bit worse. I felt like an intruder.

"Of course, Blayze. I would never write about something that I felt was told to me in private."

He nodded. "Good, I'm glad we both understand that."

I instantly started to twist my hands together, and I had to force myself to keep them still in my lap. Turning over my phone, I frowned. I hadn't heard from my father yet, and I really needed to talk to him. I did, however, have a voicemail from Doug that I had no desire to listen to at the moment.

"Okay, I hope you're hungry. My mother loves to feed people," Blayze said as he pulled to a stop behind a few other vehicles.

Smiling, I opened the truck door and started to get out.

"I've got it," Blayze said as he jumped out of the truck, dashed around the front, and held open the door for me.

We walked up the steps, and the front door flew open as a stunning young woman with brown hair and eyes the same color as Blayze's came running out.

"Georgiana!"

My eyes nearly popped out of my head. "Morgan?" I gasped, taking in the woman before me who had been a child the last time I saw her. "You've grown up!"

Laughing, Morgan pulled me into her arms. "Love the dress!"

I chuckled in return as I looked at the dress she was wearing. It was almost the same as mine, but in a light blue and with quarter-length sleeves.

"And I love yours."

Morgan linked her arm with mine and started dragging me into the house. "Everyone's dying to see you again. The littles don't remember you. Hell, I don't even know if they were born yet when you were last here."

"Language, Morgan, dear," Lincoln said as she gave me a friendly smile and a kiss on the cheek. "Good to see you again, darling."

"Thank you for having me. And to answer your question, I think Joshua and Nathan might have been like four, and Avery Grace was five?"

"That sounds right!" Lincoln said.

"Come on, Georgiana, let me introduce you to everyone!" Morgan pulled me through the foyer and into the large living room. My mouth nearly fell open as I looked around at all the people there. I instantly recognized Stella and Ty Senior, the Shaw family monarchs. Ty Senior stood, followed by Stella.

"It's so nice to see you both again," I said, reaching my hand out to shake theirs.

Stella pulled me in for a hug. "My, you've grown into a beautiful woman. Hasn't she, Blayze?"

Blayze cleared his throat. "She has."

"Lord, I remember how you flirted with this girl from the first moment she arrived on the ranch," Stella said.

"Who hasn't he flirted with?" a male voice said from somewhere in the room.

"That's my brother Hunter," Morgan said, guiding me over to another stunningly attractive young man. Did all these kids have the same blue eyes?

"It's good seeing you again, Hunter."

Hunter was still in college, but was also doing professional team roping. He'd won a college championship the year prior.

Taking my hand, he shook it. "It's nice seeing you again, Ms. Crenshaw."

"Please, call me Georgiana."

A brilliant smile erupted across his face. "Will do."

Morgan pulled me over to a stunning blonde with blue eyes. I was pretty sure Blayze had said earlier she was twenty. The blue eyes in this family, my goodness. "This is Rose Marie."

"Just call me Rose."

"Rose, you've grown up and so beautiful."

She flashed me a brilliant smile. "And so have you. I've read your articles in *Vogue*; you've got an amazing eye for fashion. I have to ask, why use your talent for a sports magazine?"

"Rose Marie!" Kaylee said with a look of surprise on her face.

"What? I'm only asking a question, and I'm speaking the truth. She has an eye for fashion."

With a soft laugh, I looked at Rose. "I love both. I grew up with a father who lived and breathed everything rodeo. And my mother was a fashion model. I guess I wanted a piece of each."

Rose nodded. "I can see that."

Morgan moved me onto the next person. "And this is Lily."

I stared at her. "You were so little the last time I saw you."

The young woman in front of me had dark brown hair and eyes the color of honey. She laughed. "I'm nineteen now."

"Wow, are you still obsessed with horses like your mother and father?"

"Yes!" she answered, smiling brightly. "I'm going to school for Equine Business Management."

"That's amazing. Keeping the business in the family I see."

Lilly nodded. "Sure am!"

"And here we have our next world champion bull rider, Bradly," Morgan said as we walked up to a young man with almost-black hair and eyes the color of onyx.

"I've been hearing some amazing things about you," I said with a smile.

Bradly took his hat off and gave me a nod. He was the spitting image of his father, Dirk Littlewood. Dirk was Brock's best friend, and had won a number of PBR championships himself.

I could tell from the get go that Bradly was shy. Not a flirt like the other boys.

"Thank you, ma'am."

My brows shot up. "Please, Bradly, call me Georgiana."

He smiled, and two deep dimples appeared on his cheeks. Lord above, he was going to be a heartbreaker, if he wasn't already.

"Then please call me Brad."

Nodding, I replied, "Will do, Brad."

"Now we move on to the high school brats!" Morgan said with a laugh. "This is Avery Grace."

She rolled her eyes. "Ha ha, Morgan. It's nice to meet you, Georgiana."

Avery Grace was adorable. Unlike her brother, Brad, she had light brown hair, and her eyes were…her eyes were amazing. They were a deep sapphire.

"Your eyes are breathtaking," I said as I stared into the depths of them.

Avery Grace giggled. "Thanks. My mother has violet eyes, so she teases me that my eyes weren't sure if they wanted to go green like my daddy or violet like hers."

"Well, they're mesmerizing."

She blushed. "Uncle Brock said you're an amazing rider. I'd love to go riding with you and talk about fashion!"

I couldn't help the smile that spread over my face. I looked around the room. "It's clear the girls like the fashion side of me, and the boys like the sports side."

Everyone laughed, and I caught Blayze's gaze. He winked at me again, and I tried to ignore the dip in my stomach.

"We've met," Joshua said as he stepped up, took the back of my hand again, and kissed it.

"Excuse me," the boy beside him said, "but we haven't met yet. I'm Nathan Shaw. If you need a real man to show you around the ranch, I'm your guy."

Groans filled the room, along with a bit of laughter.

"Are you sure he isn't your son, Brock?" Tanner said with a smirk.

I grinned. "I feel like we've met before."

A wide smile appeared on Nathan's face. Another good-looking kid with Shaw brown hair and eyes so silver they almost looked fake. "A mini Blayze in the making," I said as I glanced back at Blayze.

Nathan frowned. "There's nothing mini about..."

"You even think about finishing that sentence, Nathan Christopher Shaw, and you won't see the light of day for a month," Timberlynn said with her arms crossed over her chest. Tanner was attempting to look stern, but it was clear that he was fighting to keep his laughter in. As were Ty, Dirk, Brock, and Blayze.

"Now that you've met the brood, let's eat!" Lincoln stated as she clapped her hands together, and everyone hurried out of the large living room. I remembered where the dining room was, and was about to head that way when someone took my hand to hold me back. An instant rush of warmth shot up my arm and through my body. I looked over to see that it was Blayze.

"I'm sure you already know this, but we need to keep the three underage kids out of the article."

I tilted my head and studied him. Did he really think I would write about high school kids?

"Nathan and Josh are into bull riding," he said. "Not as serious about it as Brad, but they do enjoy it."

"I already said I wouldn't put kids in the article, do you not believe that I'll stay true to my word?"

He shrugged. "To be honest, I'm not really sure what this article is about. My father said it was a *where are they now* piece, so I'm not really sure why you even want me in it."

I folded my arms. "We already went over this. You rode in the lower circuit and were damn good. The readers want to know why you picked ranching over bull riding."

The corner of his mouth rose, but with more of a smirk than a smile. "Let's keep them guessing. My reasons for not going pro aren't anyone else's business."

Sighing, I shook my head and looked away for a moment before I focused back on him. "I'm not here right now to talk about interviews or articles, Blayze. I'm here to enjoy dinner with your family."

He narrowed his eyes at me, trying to assess if I was telling the truth or not. God, why did that hurt so much. Did Blayze really think of me as another random person who was writing about his family? It hurt more than I wanted to admit.

He studied me, then drawled, "Right."

As he walked away and headed to the dining room, I pulled out my phone again to see I had another missed call from Doug and nothing from my father. I quickly typed out a text.

Me: Dad, I need you to call me ASAP.

Chapter Seven

BLAYZE

It was clear that the entire family adored Georgie. The girls hung on every word she said, and the boys, well, those little bastards were only thinking one thing.

After dinner, Lily grabbed Georgie's hand. "We're going out tonight to a western bar in town. Will you join us?"

"Who's we?" Georgie asked.

"Me, Morgan, Blayze, Hunter, Brad, and Rose."

Georgie raised a brow. "I didn't think all of you were twenty-one yet."

Rose added, "The bar is for eighteen and up. You get a stamp on your hand if you're over twenty-one."

"Please come," Morgan begged. "It will be so much fun."

Georgie smiled then glanced over at me, almost as if seeking my approval. "If you're tired, I can drop you off at the house," I said.

"She isn't tired!" Morgan said. "Are you, Georgiana?"

With a slight chuckle, Georgie shook her head. "I'm not, but I haven't been out in a long time. Well, I've been to parties, but they're always work related."

"Well, you better be ready, because the moment you step into The Blue Moose, the guys are going to take notice," Hunter said with a wide grin. He wasn't wrong. They would.

"Okay then, I'd love to go."

Morgan did a happy dance along with Rose and Lily. Hunter and Brad rolled their eyes.

Mom walked into the dining room and smiled. "What's with all the excitement?"

Morgan spun around. "Georgiana agreed to go to The Blue Moose with us!"

Smiling, my mother walked up to Georgie. "Honey, if you're tired after traveling and the busy day you've had, it's okay to say no."

She waved her hand in a dismissive way. "Honestly, a night out sounds kind of fun. I don't even know when I last went to a bar."

Mom grinned at her. "Well, then you should go and enjoy yourself."

Rose walked up to Georgie. "You can ride with us. We'll meet you guys there!"

Before I could even say anything, the girls whisked Georgie out of the room.

My father clapped me on the back as he came to stand next to me. "Seems like the kids all like Georgiana."

I nodded. "Seems like it."

"Are you still upset about the interview?" he asked, turning to face me.

"I've made it pretty clear to Georgie I'm not interested in participating."

Dad nodded and rubbed at the back of his neck. "Folks are curious, Blayze. You were on a clear path toward a successful bull-riding career and then…"

His voice trailed off.

"You know that wasn't what I wanted. And if she starts asking questions, the whole shit show will come up again. You and I both know that if she tries to write about me, then she'll start asking questions around town, and she'll find out what happened. I want it to stay buried. Not that I think it will hurt the family, I just…I want to forget about it."

Dad sighed. "I know, son. You do not have to participate. But maybe you should tell Georgiana why?"

I let out a harsh laugh. "Hard pass, Dad."

He shook his head, a look of disappointment on his face. "I don't want you to take your anger toward Lindsay out on Georgiana."

I gave my father a hard look. Ignoring that comment, I asked, "You really think she's here to do a *where are they now* piece?"

"That's what her father said, and we're friends. I trust him."

"Fine. If that's what she really wants, I'll help her navigate around the ranch, talk to who she needs to talk to. But I don't want anyone knowing my business, Dad. I wasn't in the spotlight like you, Ty, Dirk, and Tanner. I didn't ask for any of this."

He nodded and glanced down at his beer before focusing back on me. "I don't know if she knows about it or not, Blayze. Her father knows, but I don't think he's ever told her."

"She doesn't know. How in the hell could she?"

"Lindsay could very well talk."

"And if she does, I'll sue her for breach of contract. She signed the NDA."

He nodded but didn't seem convinced.

"There's no way she'll talk. The last thing she would ever want to admit is that she was left at the altar."

He let out a humorless laugh. "She is a little vain."

"A little?" I asked with a mock surprised look on my face.

"Go on, have some fun, Blayze. And think about telling Georgiana about Lindsay."

I stared down at my beer. Georgie already knew Lindsay was the girl I'd slept with to get back at her. What in the hell would she think if she knew I almost married her—and why.

I finished off my beer and nodded. "Maybe."

The sound of country music filled the air as I walked into The Blue Moose. A Rascal Flatts song was playing and the dance floor was crowded with people. After a quick glance around, I headed to the side of the bar where I knew everyone would be. I'd called Ryan and Mindy and they had already planned on being here tonight. Saturday was when the younger crowd was at the bar; the rest of the week was for the older bunch.

It wasn't long before I saw the group of them sitting at a table. Sitting at an adjacent table were Ryan, Mindy, and a few other folks from high school.

Morgan, Rose, and Georgiana were missing, but Lily, Hunter, and Brad were all sitting down. Hunter and Brad were both talking to women I didn't recognize. Most likely tourists. Lily was talking to one of her friends.

I stopped at Ryan's table and gave him a slap on the back. He turned and flashed me a wide smile. "Dude, it's about time you showed up."

Leaning down, I kissed Mindy on the cheek. "How's it going?"

"Good!" she shouted over the music. "I got a glimpse of Georgiana. Still as pretty as ever."

I rolled my eyes, and Ryan laughed. "It wasn't two minutes before someone asked her to dance."

Trying to ignore a pang of jealousy, I pulled a chair out and swung it around, straddling it as I looked out over the dance floor. "Good for her."

I could see Ryan and Mindy exchange a look.

"No sparks between the two of you?" Mindy asked.

Glancing at her, I laughed. "We were in high school, Mindy. There's nothing there anymore."

I wondered if my two best friends could tell I was lying through my teeth. From the moment Georgie had opened her hotel door this morning, I'd been thinking about her non-stop, and it was pissing me off.

Mindy nodded. "That's good, because she's already danced with like four different guys. The girl can't come and sit down before someone else asks her to dance. She just might be getting lucky later."

Lifting my hand, I motioned to the waitress for a beer while I ignored Mindy. I knew she was saying those things on purpose to get a rise out of me, and I refused to let it work.

"Like I said, good for her."

I tried not to make it obvious that I was scanning the dance floor looking for Georgiana. My searching came to an abrupt stop when I saw her dancing with Tim Jones. The way Georgie was looking up at him while laughing made me want to put my fist through his face.

The song ended and she quickly stepped away and seemed to thank him before making her way off the dance floor. Another song started—"Sounds Like Something I'd Do" by Drake Milligan. Glancing at Mindy, I raised a brow.

"Want to kick it up?"

"Hell yes!"

We both stood, and I took her hand. I'd been dancing with Mindy for as long as I could remember, and I always liked it. We could cut a rug on the dance floor, no doubt about it.

I drew Mindy into my arms, and we started to two-step, throwing in a bit of swing dancing as well.

"Tell me you're not using me right now, Blayze Shaw."

Giving her a shit-eating grin, I replied, "I have no idea what you're talking about."

"We haven't danced in forever, and the one night a girl from your past is here, you want to spin me all around the floor."

"You're thinking too much."

"Am I? Then go ask her to dance. Next slow song."

Laughing, I looked down at Mindy. "Why? What in the hell would that prove?"

Her eyes turned soft, and I saw something I really hated seeing. Pity.

"That you're not scared to let someone in, Blayze."

Looking away, I bit the inside of my cheek and counted to ten in order to get my emotions back in check.

"I'm not scared of falling in love, Mindy. And I am not even remotely interested in Georgie that way."

She took a step away. "Really? Because when you saw her dancing with Tim Jones, you looked like you were ready to come unglued. You've got to learn to trust again."

"I'm not interested, Mindy. Will you drop it?"

Mindy exhaled and looked down at the floor, then back up at me. "I'm sorry I pushed you. If you're not interested, you're not interested."

Turning on her heels, she headed off the dance floor.

"Fuck," I mumbled as I pushed my hand through my hair and looked around. It seemed like no one had paid attention to that exchange.

I made my way back to the table where Mindy and Ryan were sitting. Glancing over, I saw Georgie in conversation with Rose.

I sat down and looked at Mindy. "I didn't mean to jump at you."

She gave me a sweet smile. "It's okay. I was being pushy, as usual."

I laughed.

Turning to look at Georgie, I sighed. If only to prove to Mindy I wasn't afraid, I stood and made my way over to her.

"Would you like to dance, Georgie?" I asked with my mouth right at her ear. She shivered, and I kind of hoped it was because of me.

Rose's face lit up, as did Lily's. I had no idea where my sister Morgan was—most likely dancing.

The song changed as Georgie stood and took my hand. She had the most beautiful smile on her face, and I had to fight the urge to pull her out of the damn bar and take her back to my house.

Once we got on the dance floor, I drew her closer to me.

"I love Blake Shelton," Georgie said as Blake belted out the words to "Sure Be Cool If You Did."

"It's a good song," I replied, looking at the top of her head. I was afraid that if I looked at her face I wouldn't be able to control the urge to kiss her. Hell, I'd had the urge to kiss the woman in my arms from the moment I first realized what kissing was.

Georgie looked down and stared at my chest as we slowly danced across the floor. I shouldn't have been surprised she could two-step so well. She did grow up in Texas, after all.

Neither one of us spoke while we finished out the dance. When it changed to a pop song, my sister showed up and grabbed Georgie and pulled her into a circle with Lily and Rose. That was my cue to leave.

It seemed like the entire bar was dancing to the song. I took one look over my shoulder, caught sight of Georgie, and nearly tripped.

"Be careful there, Blayze," a voice said from in front of me. "If you're not careful, people will start to think someone has finally caught your eye."

My heart felt like it turned to stone. "What are you doing here, Lindsay?"

She smirked. "Probably for the same reasons you are."

"I highly doubt that," I said as I tried to walk around her. "Who is she?"

Drawing in a breath to show she was trying my patience, I asked, "Who is who?"

"The girl you were dancing with. Your sister and cousins seem to know her well. She looks familiar."

"Old family friend," I said, pushing past Lindsay. No matter many how times I ran into her, the anger was still there.

"You're still mad?" she called out from behind me. I barely heard her over the music and the talking.

Spinning around to face her again, I moved closer. "Leave me alone."

"Oh, for fuck's sake, Blayze. You weren't in love with me, and it all turned out fine in the end."

"Go away," I growled.

She smiled. "It appears I still know how to bring out emotions in you."

Lindsay ran her finger down the side of my face, and I jerked back. "Should we explore those again, Blayze?"

"Fuck off."

Turning, I headed toward the men's bathroom, thinking Lindsay wouldn't be stupid enough to follow me. I should have known I'd be wrong. I never could predict what in the hell she would do next.

"Blayze," she called out.

I ignored her and kept walking.

"I'll follow you into the bathroom, and you know I will. Won't that get all the tongues wagging in town."

Coming to a stop, I slowly turned in the deserted hallway that led to the restrooms and stalked over to her. She didn't even budge when I came to a towering stop in front of her.

"We don't have anything to say to each other, Lindsay."

"Oh, now is that any way to talk to your ex-fiancée?"

I pushed her hand away when she started to move it toward me. "What do you want? Does Lane know you're here?"

She dug her teeth into her bottom lip before running her tongue over the dents she'd left there. "He's riding in Kansas City tonight. Probably fucking some little buckle bunny as we speak. Seems to me he shouldn't be the only one getting to have all the fun. What do you say, for old times' sake?"

"Blayze."

The sound of my brother's voice was a relief.

"We're done here, Lindsay," I said as I gave her a cold stare.

"Little brother, maybe?" she whispered. "I seem to have a way with the Shaw men."

I leaned in closer. "You stay the fuck away from my family, do you hear me? No one wants you near us, Lindsay. Get that through your head."

She pouted, then sighed. "Looks like I won't be able to compare notes—for tonight, at least."

I took a step closer to her and she stepped back, clearly realizing she'd pushed me too far.

"If you don't get out of here, I'm going to drag you out."

"Blayze," Hunter warned.

Lindsay let out a nervous laugh. "I think I would be into it rough like that. I am, after all, married to Lane. We've played with that version of sex. Even had one of the buckle bunnies join us."

I snarled my lip up at her. If she thought that would pique my interest in her, she was seriously deranged.

"Everything okay here, Blayze?" Betty Jane, the owner of The Blue Moose, asked. For as long as I could remember, she was in charge of the bar. Even told us a few stories about my father and uncles.

"I believe Lindsay here was just leaving," Hunter said as he stepped between the two of us.

I hated the way Lindsay let her gaze move over my brother. She tsked, then turned on her cowboy boots and held up her hands. "I was just leaving, Betty Jane. Don't get your panties in a twist. Doesn't look like either Shaw brother will be warming my bed tonight."

I wanted to launch at her and Hunter sensed it. He put his hand on my chest. "Let her go, Blayze. You know she isn't worth it."

We all watched Lindsay walk out of the bar. Betty Jane turned back to me. "I'm sorry, Blayze. I had no idea she was back in town, and Hank is new at the door. I'll be sure to let them all know she isn't welcome in here."

I pressed my hand to the back of my neck to rub at the instant tension there. "No worries, Betty Jane. Thanks for stepping in."

She smiled and tossed a hand towel over her shoulder before heading back to the bar.

A memory flashed through my mind, and I closed my eyes to force it away.

"What about Lane?" I asked Lindsay as she pulled her shirt over her head and tossed it onto the floor.

"Lane and I are done, Blayze. He left me a few weeks ago. It's you I want. It's you I need."

"This is just about fucking, right?" I asked, my voice slightly slurred from too much alcohol.

"I'm not looking for anything else. I want you, and I know you want me too," Lindsay said as she walked over and straddled me. "Just like last time. It doesn't mean anything. I want you to ride me like you ride those bulls, Blayze. Will you do that for me?"

Smiling, I reached up and unclasped her bra. "Only if you ride me like you ride those horses."

With a laugh, she leaned down and brushed her lips over mine. "Deal."

Hunter put his hand on my shoulder and gave it a squeeze, pulling me from the memory. "If it helps, I think Morgan kept Georgiana pretty entertained. I doubt she saw anything."

My eyes darted across the bar as I scanned the dance floor. "Good. The last thing we need is her putting her goddamn nose in my business."

Hunter frowned. "Blayze, what is it that you have against Georgiana? I honestly can't tell if you like her or not."

I swallowed hard. "I'm hitting the bathroom, then I'm heading home. Make sure Georgie gets back to my place, okay?"

He nodded. "Will do, big bro."

With a smile, I hit him on the side of the arm. "Thanks, I owe you one."

"That's what brothers are for, right? To save you from crazy exes."

"She isn't an ex."

His smile faded. "Right."

Chapter Eight

GEORGIANA

Morgan and Rose had done a great job of trying to keep my eyes away from the area where Blayze was talking to a drop-dead gorgeous woman. She had long, curly blonde hair and was dressed in a skin-tight dress that left nothing to the imagination. When he started for what I was guessing were the bathrooms and she followed, my heart sank like a piece of lead. She looked familiar, but for the life of me, I couldn't place it.

They stopped at the entrance of the hall. When a nearby young guy got Rose and Morgan's attention, I turned so I could watch. Another guy walked up to me so it was easy to pretend I was dancing with him while I watched the scene play out.

Whoever she was, it wasn't a friendly encounter. Hunter walked over, followed by an older woman—the bartender I'd seen earlier. The blonde woman turned on her heels and marched out of the bar, a smug smile on her face. Who was she? I'd met her before, I just knew it.

I danced two more songs before I tapped out and let the younger girls keep dancing. As I made my way off the dance floor, a man and woman who had been sitting at the same table as Blayze, smiled and waved me over. I ordered a bottled water from the waitress and walked over to them.

"You probably don't remember us," the young woman said.

I shook my head. "I'm sorry, I don't."

She laughed. "I'm Mindy, one of Blayze's best friends. This is Ryan."

I turned to see the handsome guy sitting where Blayze had been. He shot me a big smile, and I instantly remembered him. He had the most amazing smile.

"Ryan!"

He laughed and hugged me. "That's me." When he stepped back, he gave me a quick once over. "You've grown up, Georgiana."

"So have you." Laughing, I pointed at the empty chair next to them.

"Please, sit," Mindy stated.

"Wow, I can't believe it," I said as I sat. "I haven't see y'all in…years!"

"I think we were sixteen." Mindy smiled.

"Something like that." I returned her smile. When the waitress handed me a bottle of water, I gave her money and a tip. Then practically downed the water.

"Hard to keep up with the younger ones," Mindy said with a wink.

"Yes, it sure is. I mean, Morgan is only six years younger than me, but after tonight I feel old."

I took another drink and glanced around. "Blayze dancing?"

The corner of Ryan's mouth twitched with a hidden smile. It was no secret that once upon a time Blayze and I liked each other. But we were sixteen, and that was ten years ago.

"He left," Mindy called out.

Forcing myself not to show my shock, I repeated her words. "He left?"

She nodded. "Was he supposed to give you a ride? He made it seem like you came with Morgan and the girls."

After blinking several times, I smiled. "I did. I guess I assumed I'd leave with him since I'm staying at his house."

Mindy damn near spit out her beer while Ryan's hidden smile became a full-on grin.

"You're staying with Blayze? At this house?" he asked.

I nodded. "Yes. I was going to stay with his parents, but his grandparents are staying there while their house is getting remodeled, and they have some other guests as well. So, it was either stay in town or bunk at Blayze's house."

"Interesting," Mindy stated.

"Not really. I'm here for work, and Blayze and I are old friends. That's it."

They both nodded but exchanged a quick glance.

I decided to take a chance and ask them about the person Blayze had been talking to.

"Who was that woman Blayze was speaking with? They didn't seem to be getting along."

"No one," Ryan answered.

"Lindsay," Mindy said, then snapped her mouth shut. When Ryan shot her a disbelieving look, I quickly figured out I wasn't supposed to know who the woman was. That explained why Hunter tried to block my view of her.

"No one," Mindy quickly added, and I nodded and gave them a small smile. Surely they both knew I would remember who Lindsay was. She was only the girl Blayze had slept with after our heated exchange that day we were caught by our fathers.

After a few minutes of small talk, Ryan got up to get a few more drinks, and a good-looking cowboy came to ask Mindy to dance. I was left sitting alone, except for a girl who looked to be around my age. I hadn't noticed her earlier, so I wasn't sure when she'd sat down.

"Hi, I'm Georgiana Crenshaw."

She held out her hand for mine. "Wendy Reynolds. I'm Mindy's sister."

My eyes went wide. "Wendy! I remember you! How have you been?"

With a sweet smile, she replied, "Tired. I'm almost finished with vet school."

"Oh, wow, congratulations."

"Thank you. My sister dragged me out tonight, even though she knows I hate it."

I nodded.

"Listen, I sat down at the tail end of you asking about the woman Blayze was arguing with."

With a curious look in her direction, I said, "Yes?"

"I don't know why no one ever talks about it—well, actually, I do. Blayze was starting to ride in the professional PBR circuit, though he only did a few rides before he quit, I think. Anyway, they were engaged."

A million questions popped into my head that I wanted to hurl out at Wendy.

Had Lindsay been the reason Blayze left the PBR? Even when I'd been tracking his career, I'd never understood why he'd walked away. I was glad about it, deep down, since I would have never wanted to see him hurt. But did I really believe he simply left to be a rancher?

"Engaged? What happened?"

"He left her at the altar."

Oookay. So *that* rumor was true. "He left her at the altar? Like, he didn't show up for his own wedding?"

"Oh no, he did," she said as casually as if she was talking about the weather. "When she walked down the aisle and turned to face him, he said something to her that no one else could hear and then walked away. Just left her there. To be honest, she deserved it."

I blinked a few times as I processed everything Wendy had said. "He left her? Why did she deserve it?"

Wendy glanced over at Ryan, who was still at the bar. "You didn't hear this from me, but she lied to him to get him to marry her. I'm guessing he found out the truth, and then left her at the altar as a revenge kind of thing."

"What did she say?"

Wendy shook her head. "That's his story to tell. I just didn't want you to think there was something going on between them since I overheard Ryan and Mindy talking about what happened between you and Blayze."

My mouth fell open. Jesus, this girl was a gossip encyclopedia.

"I saw the way Blayze looked at you when you were dancing with him," she said. "I've never seen him look at another woman like that. As big of a flirt as he is, he's never really had a serious girlfriend. I don't think he's ever been out with anyone more than a couple of times."

I wanted to ask her more, but Ryan returned. Her words played havoc with my mind.

"I got you both a beer if you want it," Ryan said as he set four beers down on the table.

Wendy smiled. "No, thanks. I've got a test tomorrow."

I grabbed mine and downed it.

My mind swirled the rest of the evening and well into the night after Morgan had dropped me off at Blayze's house. I laid in bed and tried to wrap my head around the fact that Blayze had been engaged. He had been about to be married, but it sounded more like a trap. Was Lindsay blackmailing him with something? What had changed that made him leave the woman at the altar to be embarrassed like that? It wasn't something I could picture him doing. Not the Blayze I knew—not even this Blayze. We may have had a rocky start this morning, but he wasn't cruel.

When morning finally arrived, I had maybe gotten four hours of sleep, if that. After washing my face, brushing my teeth, and pulling my hair up, I slipped into jeans, boots, and a long-sleeve T-shirt. It was Sunday, and I wasn't sure if Blayze or Brock would be working. If they were, I was planning on following Brock around. It would be my first official day as the reporter here to write a story about the Shaw family and where they are now. As for Blayze, I wasn't the least bit interested in learning anything for the article—but for myself, I was beyond curious. And if I was honest with myself, jealous as hell that Lindsay had been about to marry him.

After trying to call my father again, I started to get worried and sent my mother a text. The smell of coffee lured me into the kitchen where I found Blayze drinking a cup and reading the newspaper.

Smiling at the sight before me, I walked in and took the mug he had set by the coffee machine and filled it with liquid gold.

"I haven't seen anyone read an actual newspaper in awhile."

He glanced up with a look of surprise at seeing me in his kitchen. I knew he hadn't forgotten I was there since he'd left out an extra coffee cup.

"I like holding it and reading it. Probably has something to do with watching my grandfather read one all those years. He still does."

Nodding, I took a sip of the coffee. "You left early last night. Did you even stay an hour?"

"Bars aren't really my scene anymore."

I tilted my head. "What is your scene?"

He looked up again. "I like to be outside doing things that make me happy."

"Such as?" I asked.

"Riding, roping, bringing in the cattle. Hiking, water rafting, yoga."

I nearly spit out my coffee. "I'm sorry, did you say yoga?"

He smiled softly. "Don't seem so surprised, Georgie. It's a great form of exercise, not only for your body but your mind as well."

"What were you doing this morning? I looked out my window and saw you sitting outside."

With a half shrug, he replied, "Meditating."

"Meditating?"

"Why does that surprise you?"

"I don't know. The Blayze I knew was always so on-the-go. I can't imagine you just…being."

He frowned slightly. "Well, sixteen-year-old Blayze is a lot different from twenty-seven-year-old Blayze."

I'll say.

"Are there good hiking trails around here?" I asked. "I'd love to get some hiking in. Morgan said she'd go hiking with me when she was able to. She mentioned heading back to school this morning, though."

"There's a lot of good hiking, but I recommend you go with someone else. Always."

I slid onto the barstool. "Maybe you could take me?"

He didn't bother to look up at all. "Maybe."

I exhaled and stared out the window. It was a beautiful fall day. The dark gray mountains looked like a painting against the soft blue sky. I'd never been to the ranch during fall or winter, and I was dying to know what it looked like.

Turning back to Blayze, I was about to ask him if he had any photos of the ranch when my phone rang. Relieved to see it was my father, I jumped up. "I need to take this. Excuse me."

Blayze gave me a single nod and went back to reading.

I slipped out the back door and made my way out onto the porch. The last thing I wanted was for Blayze to overhear this conversation. It was chilly outside, and I instantly wished I'd grabbed a light jacket or a sweatshirt.

"Dad, are you okay?"

He chuckled. "Honey, did you forget we were going on that overnight cruise in the Gulf to gamble?"

I closed my eyes and cursed. "I forgot about that. How did you do?"

"Terrible. Now, what's going on?"

Glancing over my shoulder once more, I made sure the coast was clear before I began to speak.

"Dad, you told me this interview was a *where are they are now* piece. That I would be focusing on Brock and his brothers and maybe a bit about Blayze."

"Yes, that's right."

Sighing in frustration, I said, "Well, that's not what Doug Larson is telling me. He wants dirt on Blayze and wants most of the focus to be on him."

"Who in the hell is Doug Larson?"

"I guess a new editor for the magazine. He's treating this like a tabloid rag, Dad. He actually told me he wanted dirt on not just Blayze, but the entire family."

"Dirt?" Dad asked, sounding confused. "What kind of dirt?"

"Apparently Blayze was engaged and left the girl at the altar. Doug wants to know why and thinks there's more to why Blayze stopped his bull-riding career right as it was heating up. I don't think they care about the real reasons he never became a bull rider. I'm also supposed to find out if Hunter is a playboy out on the circuit. Dad, I don't write gossip columns. I write sports articles. If this is what they think they're going to get me to write for them, I'm not doing it. What's going on over there?"

"That doesn't seem right, Georgiana. Are you sure you heard him correctly?"

"Yes!" I stated, rather offended he would think I was wrong. "He called me on the way in from Missoula. That was when I found out about Blayze being engaged. Then he told me to dig deeper. That every family has their secrets. Dad, this isn't the magazine you worked for. Something has shifted."

I could practically hear my father thinking over my words.

"Okay, I want you to stick to the original story: *where are they now*. Nothing else. Not even anything on Blayze. Do I make myself clear?"

"Yes, very. I was already going to drop the whole Blayze thing. He never gave me permission to interview him, and clearly doesn't want anyone in his business."

"I don't blame him. He's not in the spotlight like his brother or cousin. I'll talk to Kathleen Marker and see what's going on. She may have a rogue editor and not even realize it. I highly doubt *Sports Monthly* is going to become some gossip magazine. Of course, there is a new owner, so that might be why things are changing."

I chewed on my lip. "I'm not writing anything other than an article about where Brock, Ty, Tanner, and Dirk are now. I'll write about the ranch and that's it. I don't even want to bring Hunter or Bradly into this piece."

"That's good, sweetheart. I'll get it taken care of."

Relief flooded through me. "Thank you so much, Dad."

"No problem, sweetheart. Just keep what this Doug guy was asking you to dig up to yourself."

I chewed on my lip. I didn't feel comfortable keeping this from Blayze or Brock. It felt like they needed to know the intentions of the magazine, if it was truly their intentions.

"Dad, I'm not sure I even want to do the interview anymore. If the magazine is looking to print something like this, it only tells me that if I don't do it, someone else will. I think I should tell Brock at the very least."

"Not quite yet. Let me talk to Kathleen first."

A feeling of dread washed over me, but I'd do as my father said. He'd worked for the magazine after he left his PBR broadcasting career, but only did an occasional article now and then. So it would make sense why he hadn't been in the know of things changing with the new owner.

"Fine. But, Dad, make it quick, okay? I don't like keeping this from them."

"Will do, sweetheart."

I ended the call and drew in a long, deep breath before I made my way back into the kitchen. Blayze was now at the sink washing out his coffee mug.

He glanced back at me. "Work call?"

With a shake of my head, I replied, "It was my dad. I hadn't been able to get a hold of him or my mom. I forgot they went out on this gambling cruise off the coast of Texas."

Blayze smiled as he dried his hands off on the dish towel. "Did you want to drive up to the barn with me? Unless you don't plan on working on a Sunday. But you could at least shadow me or one of the ranch hands."

"Yes! If you don't mind. I have a rental car that's supposed to be delivered today, so hopefully I won't need you to chauffeur me around much longer."

With a weak smile, he said, "It's not a problem."

"Let me go grab my work stuff and a jacket. Feels like it's a bit cooler out today."

"I'll meet you out front. Just lock the door on your way out."

I nodded, then rushed to the room I was staying in. After grabbing all my stuff, I put it in a bag with my phone charger. I had no idea how long I would be gone today, and I needed a working phone.

As Blayze drove us up to the main barn, I pulled out a notebook and got busy taking some notes. I wasn't sure why because I was almost positive I wasn't going to write the article. But I found myself curious about what Blayze did on the ranch. I wanted to know more about him for my own personal use. "Do you mind if I ask you only ranch-related questions?"

He shook his head. "Go for it."

"Okay, yesterday you mentioned the conditioning of the calves. What happens this time of year with all the cattle? I never see a whole lot when we drive around on the ranch, and I only saw the ones in that front pasture on our horseback ride."

"Well, for starters, you're only seeing a small part of the ranch. They're out there, just a bit higher up. We'll start bringing them down to the lower pastures here in the next week. The ranch has different divisions."

"Meaning?" I asked.

"One part of the ranch is used for growing things like alfalfa and silage for hay. One pasture is barley and millet, or winter wheat. Tanner and Timberlynn run another division of the ranch. They not only train horses, but they breed them. Specifically roping horses. And Ty and Dirk run the bull breeding and the training for the PBR bulls. Our ranch produced last year's number one bull in the PBR."

"Titan," I said as I wrote down some notes.

"That's right. He was a fun bull to ride."

"You rode him?"

He nodded. "In the beginning, when Ty was training him."

"Do you think I'd be able to see him work a bull like that? Training-wise? I would love to see that!"

Blayze shrugged. "I don't see why not. I'd think it would be good for your article."

"Oh yeah, it totally would be great for the article. Plus, I really want to see it!" I said with a smile. "What do you feed the cattle? I know they don't simply graze on grass."

"No, ma'am," he said with a chuckle. "They eat a balanced diet. Native pasture, good quality hay that we grow, and supplements if it's too dry for the hay due to a drought, or if we get snowed in."

"Speaking of winter, what in the world do they eat when there's snow on the ground?"

"Well, the first thing we need to do is make sure they're all healthy during the late summer and fall. A lot of work goes into making sure they're fed and happy in the winter. Our cattle are horn-trained, which means when we honk that horn, they come running from everywhere."

I smiled at the picture that brought to my mind. "So I take it you grow the hay for winter consumption?"

"Yes, and we also sell it. But yeah, we grow most of our hay for the cattle and the horses. The healthier the cows are, the better they are at breeding and calving. We have a pretty strict winter-feeding program."

"Do you only put out the big bales?"

"Sometimes. If the cattle are fenced off, we'll do what's called 'laying down the feed.' We spread it out for them."

"How many tractors do you have?"

Blayze laughed. "A lot."

He pulled up and parked next to a few other trucks. "Looks like my dad is here."

"Yep. Do you guys ever take a day off?"

He winked. "Cowboys don't know what that means. Will you need a place to work in the barn?"

I attempted to hide the surprise in my voice as I responded to his kind gesture. "I saw some tables outside the barn. I can always sit there if I need to."

Blayze stared at me for a moment before his smile grew. "Not when it's cold outside. I'll make an area for you. That way you don't have to go back to my house or up to my folks' house to work."

"Um, thank you."

Blayze tipped his cowboy hat and got out of the truck. I knew by now to wait. He was going to come open my door whether I wanted him to or not. He walked to my side, opened the door, and waited for me to gather up all my stuff. Once I was out of the truck, he smiled and said, "Have a good day, Georgie." And then he was gone.

I spent the rest of the day shadowing Brock, as well as Clay and Decker. Every now and then I'd see Hank, but he seemed to be more of the foreman-type guy on the ranch.

As I watched Blayze fill his father in on a few things that were happening on the ranch, it was clear to me that Brock had handed over a lot of the day-to-day operations to his son and was focused on charity work. Though he clearly wanted to be kept up to date with what was going on with the ranch. He met with Blayze once in the morning and once in the afternoon, if time permitted. Every. Single. Day. When Blayze said cowboys didn't know what a day off meant, he wasn't kidding. But after talking to Clay and Decker, I did learn that they rotated week-ends off. I was glad to hear it. I also found out that most of the ranch hands had worked here for years. Some started when they were sixteen years old and had been here ever since. The pay was good, they were treated well, and they all felt like they were part of the family.

As the day wound down, I found a quiet corner in the barn to work, tucked away in one of the stables where a mare had been stalled to let her hoof heal. I heard voices coming and knew I should stand and make it known I was there, but when I heard Blayze and a female voice I didn't recognize, I froze before slowly sitting back down. I shot the mare a pleading look when she looked at me, and then silently asked myself why I was trying to reason with a horse. In the end, she went on eating her feed and ignored me.

"Thank you for the horseback ride, Blayze."

"It wasn't hard being in the presence of such a beautiful young woman today."

I rolled my eyes as the woman let out a giggle. "Your reputation precedes you."

"Oh? And what is that?"

"A flirt. My father warned me about you. Told me to make sure you didn't try anything."

"Me?" Blayze said in a mocking way. I slowly crawled across the stall and peeked out through the small opening. Blayze had his hand over his heart as if he'd been wounded.

"I only call it like I see it," he said.

She smiled. "You're too sweet. What are you doing for dinner tonight?"

The young woman talking to Blayze had on tight black riding pants and a matching riding jacket. When Blayze stepped to the side a bit, I was able to get a good look at the woman. It wasn't Lindsay. She was just as pretty, but a bit younger. Maybe early twenties. Her dark brown hair was braided and hung over her shoulder, and she was giving Blayze a look that said she was more interested in dessert than dinner.

"I'm sorry, Sara, I've got plans tonight."

"You can't break them? I promise I'll make it worth your while."

I pretend gagged and looked up at the mare who was now standing next to me, wondering what in the hell I was doing.

"As tempting as that is, I can't."

The woman stepped closer and wrapped her arms around Blayze's neck. I felt my entire body go rigid with...anger?

"Blayze, I'm offering you my body for the entire evening. Tell me you don't want your hands on this."

The mare leaned down, and I swore she was trying to watch it all play out as well.

Reaching his hands up to unclasp hers, he gently put them down at her sides. The mare snorted next to me, and I had to press my hand to my mouth to keep from laughing. I liked this horse.

"You probably need to go meet up with your father, Sara. I'm sure he's finished his meeting by now."

Before I could even blink, she'd pressed her mouth against his.

My eyes widened in horror, and the mare next to me started to hit the ground with her hoof.

Blayze stepped away. "I need to get back to work. You can show yourself back to the house, or I can have one of the ranch hands accompany you."

Sara looked like she might have been pouting when she backed away and let out a dramatic sigh. "I guess your reputation isn't all it's cracked up to be. Your loss."

Blayze didn't say anything until Sara was out of the barn and around the corner. He sighed and pushed his hands through his hair.

"Why do all women say that?" Hunter asked as he appeared out of thin air.

"Who the fuck knows?" Blayze said. "Do me a favor, Hunter—don't randomly hook up with girls just because you can."

Hunter laughed. "I saw what happened to you, big brother. That is the last thing I want to go through."

Wait? What happened? The broken wedding? I wanted to jump up and demand answers, but instead I slowly made my way away from the door. I pulled out my phone and typed in the search bar:

Blayze Shaw. Hamilton, Montana, wedding.

Nothing.

I waited until I heard their voices grow distant before I got back to work. I wasn't the least bit interested in finding out about Blayze's history for the magazine article. No. I wanted to know because the thought of him giving himself to another woman that way made something in my chest ache. And I had to know what happened between Blayze and Lindsay. I just had to know.

Chapter Nine

BLAYZE

I shut the door to my office and sagged against it. It wasn't like I wasn't used to women throwing themselves at me. Hell, it had been happening since I could remember. I loved women, loved flirting with them, but when a woman threw herself at me as aggressively as Sara just had, it was nothing but a turn off. Not that I would even think of doing anything with Sara. For starters, she was going to be working with me, and secondly, there was only one woman who could currently make my blood boil—and she was currently somewhere around the barn.

Georgie.

The first girl I ever truly wanted to kiss. The first girl I wanted to go further with. The first girl who made me feel like I was going crazy when she rejected me. The only difference was, I wasn't sixteen anymore. I could have easily slept with Sara. Taken her in my office and fucked her brains out. But she wasn't who I wanted. I wanted the one woman I couldn't have. The one who was sleeping in my house. The one I had hurt and now couldn't seem to get out my head.

There was a light knock on my office door, and I glanced up. My breath caught in my throat at the sight of Georgie standing in the doorway, her bag over her shoulder and her hair a mess with hay stuck in it.

"Who have you been rolling around with in the hay?" I asked.

She giggled, and it was music to my ears. "A very beautiful chestnut mare who allowed me to work in her stall with her earlier. It was the only place that was quiet."

I smiled but couldn't help wonder if she'd been in the barn when I had. "I'm sorry I didn't get a chance to clear you some office space, but I made you a make-shift desk right there if you want to use it. I'm not typically on the phone, and half the time I'm out on the ranch somewhere."

"Thank you, I'll remember that next time. It was peaceful in the stables, I have to say."

"The horses tend to make me feel at peace. When Hunter was little, my mother used to find him out here asleep in his favorite horse's stall. Even though the horse wasn't there, Hunter said he liked the smell of it. She said I used to do the same thing. If I thought I could, I'd probably still sleep in one."

Georgie crinkled her nose. "Well, I do like the smell of the hay, so if you kick me out of your house…"

Her voice trailed off as we both laughed.

"Did you get a lot of information today?" I asked.

She nodded. "I got to see a wonderful side of your father, and everything he does for charity, as well as for the town of Hamilton."

I leaned back in my chair. "My father is pretty passionate about giving back. Has been for as long as I can remember."

She gave me another nod. "He mentioned a charity rodeo coming up that will be held in the indoor arena at the community center he started. He said it's to raise money for the mental health foundation he helped start in your mother's name."

"Dad does it every year. It's a fun time, you should go."

"I will, for sure. Avery Grace was telling me about the street dance afterwards. Apparently there's a boy she likes, and she asked me to help her pick out a dress. We're going shopping in a few days."

"That's nice of you, Georgie."

She half shrugged. "I love shopping, so it's no hardship for me."

We stood there for a few moments before she cleared her throat. "My rental car came today."

"Good. Is everything okay with it?"

"Oh, yeah, it's fine. I was going to head into town and grab something to eat for an early dinner. Do you have any recommendations?"

"You in the mood for pizza?"

"I'm always in the mood for pizza," Georgie said with a chuckle. "Do you want to join me? I mean, only if you're free."

A small part of me wanted to say no. A very small part of me. And for reasons I couldn't name. But before I could listen to my head, my mouth went off.

"I'd love to. Are you ready to go now? I can drive."

A brilliant smile spread across her face, and I had the strangest feeling I'd done the right thing by saying I'd join her for dinner.

"Since you know your way around, you can drive."

I grabbed my cowboy hat and put it on. With a wink, I motioned for her to head on out. "After you, ma'am."

Georgie dug her teeth into her lower lip and blushed. I had no idea what had made her flush, but I loved seeing the color on her cheeks. She stood there for a few moments, and when her eyes dropped to my mouth, I nearly bent down to kiss her. Before I could do anything, though, she turned and headed out of the barn and to my truck.

She put her computer bag in the back seat and climbed up into the passenger side. I shut the door and headed around the front. When I got in, she was looking something up on her phone.

"Where are we going?" she asked.

"A place called Figaro's Pizza."

She typed something in, and I started to drive. We remained silent for a bit while she appeared to study the menu. "Yum, everything sounds so good. And it's rated the best pizza in Hamilton."

"Do you really think I'd take you anywhere less? I don't mess around when it comes to pizza."

"I guess not. I do appreciate you coming with me. I hate eating alone."

"I'm not a fan of it myself," I said. "But if it means getting some decent food and I have no other choice, I'll do it. I imagine with your job you eat alone a lot."

"I do," she replied with a nod. "I'm starting to get tired of it."

"You don't like traveling?"

She turned her body some to face me. "I love to travel. But traveling for fun and traveling for work are two very different things."

"That's very true. Where are some of your favorite places you've been?"

She sighed and seemed to daydream a bit while she thought about her answer.

"Anywhere with mountains. Estes Park is one of my favorite places. Italy. Anywhere in Italy or France, actually."

I laughed. "Never been to any of those places."

From my side of the truck, I saw her tilt her head. "Do you want to travel?"

"Yeah, I wouldn't mind it. Just haven't found the time or the person I want to travel with."

"Mmm," she said as she faced forward in her seat again. "What kind of pizza is your favorite?"

That was a clear change of subject. "I like the twelve-topping classic."

Georgie started to read on her phone again, then snapped her head to look at me. "You like pineapple on your pizza?"

"Yeah," I said, laughing in disbelief that she would even question it. "You don't?"

"I've never had it, but it sounds gross."

I turned my head to look at her. "Wait. You've *never* had pineapple on your pizza?"

Her nose crinkled up again, and damn if it didn't make my cock rock hard.

"No. Who puts fruit on a pizza?"

I let out a defeated sigh. "Georgie, we have got to fix this today. Like, this is life or death kind of shit."

She let out a bark of laughter. "Life or death, huh?"

"Yes! Why haven't you ever tried it?"

"I don't know," she replied. "It doesn't sound good. I'm not one for taking risks."

"Risks?" I repeated with a disbelieving laugh. "Risks? It's pizza, for fuck's sake. It's not like I'm asking you to get on a bull."

Laughing, she shook her head. "And I wouldn't do that either. Nor would I go whitewater rafting, zip-lining, or anything else that I deemed dangerous."

"Did you just say you think eating pineapple on a pizza is dangerous?"

She nodded. "Yes! Some people get very offended when you put it on pizza."

I was positive I was gaping at her.

"What? We can't all be fearless, Blayze."

I pulled into the parking lot, parked, and then faced her. With narrowed eyes, I asked, "You think I'm fearless?"

"Of course you are!"

"How do you figure I'm fearless, Georgie?"

"Well, for one thing, you ride bulls."

"And that makes it so?"

She shrugged. "Do you like to whitewater raft?"

"Yes."

"Zip line?"

"Never done it, but I bet I would."

"Do you snowmobile up in the mountains in the winter?"

I laughed. "You're joking, right?"

She shook her head and opened her door. "You clearly don't remember that I've never even climbed a tree."

After getting out, she got her computer bag and put it over her shoulder before walking toward the front of the truck.

"Holy shit, I totally forgot you've never climbed a tree."

"See, you're fearless, and I'm not."

I held open the door of the restaurant for her and winked. "I can be fearless enough for both of us."

Georgie stopped walking and stared up at me. I had no fucking idea why I said that, and clearly neither did she. She blinked a few times and then headed into the pizza parlor. But there had been something in those green eyes that said she'd be on board.

◆ ◆ ◆

I waited and watched as Georgie took a bite of the pizza. She chewed. Stopped. Chewed some more then stopped. When she lifted her gaze to mine, I couldn't help but smile. I could see it all over her beautiful face.

She liked it.

"Well?" I asked before I took a bite of my piece.

After finishing up chewing, she set the pizza down, wiped at the corners of her mouth and looked down at her plate.

"I like it."

"What was that?" I said as I leaned forward. "I don't think I heard you. Speak up."

Her eyes lifted to meet mine. "I like it. There. You happy now?"

Laughing, I nodded. "I am very happy. I told you that you'd like it."

"Everything okay here?" the waitress asked, grinning down at both of us.

"It's delicious, thank you," Georgie said as she picked up her pizza again.

The waitress nodded. "Another round of beer?"

"I'll take one. Georgie?"

She gave the waitress a thumbs up.

After eating the entire pizza between the two of us, I looked over at Georgie. "What are you doing tomorrow?"

"Tomorrow?"

I nodded.

She pulled out her phone. "I don't have any interviews planned tomorrow. Your mom mentioned something about making some pies in the afternoon for a fall festival at the church."

"Yeah, they do a fall festival every year with all kinds of booths for kids. They have a chili cook-off as well as sell a bunch of other food. All the proceeds go toward the youth program at the church."

Georgie leaned back in her chair. "That sounds like fun."

"It is kind of fun. Was more fun when I was younger, though."

She flashed me a smirk. "Do you still go now that you're older and it's less fun?"

"Every year—and don't look so surprised. I'm not that much of a bad boy, Georgie. Only when I'm requested to be one."

Her eyes turned dark and she chewed on her lip before she glanced around the restaurant. I would have paid top dollar to know what was going through her mind at that moment.

"If you're free in the morning, I can take you to do one of my favorite activities," I said.

She narrowed her eyes. "Is there a chance I could die?"

I laughed. "No matter what you do in life, there's always a chance."

She crossed her arms over her chest. "Tell me what it is."

"No. I want you to take a chance on something for once, Georgie."

She huffed. "I take chances all the time, Blayze."

"Do you?"

"Yes," she stated. "Sometimes."

I rolled my eyes. "I want you to live life without knowing exactly what's around the corner for once. Put your perfectly planned-out day to rest just for tomorrow. After that, you can go back to your organized, safe life."

"What about the pies?"

"I'll have you back in plenty of time for pie."

"Why did that sound sexual?"

"Maybe because you wanted it to."

She huffed and moved around nervously in her seat before she looked at me. "Fine. We can go do whatever your favorite activity is."

"I said one of my favorites. It's not the favorite."

She stared at me for the longest time before she simply nodded. I nearly laughed. She knew she wanted to ask me what my favorite was but stopped herself. Had she asked, I would have said sex just to see her blush.

"You ready to head on back?" I asked.

Georgie swallowed hard. "Yes, I have some work to do."

"Don't stay up late." I stood and waited for her to do the same. "We'll be heading out early tomorrow."

"Pffft. I'm an early riser, Blayze."

As we headed out of the pizza parlor, I put my hand on her lower back. "If you say so, sweetheart."

Chapter Ten

GEORGIANA

I flipped over onto my left side, hit my pillow, and sighed. I needed sleep, but I couldn't stop thinking about Blayze. Those damn blue eyes of his when he'd said he could be fearless enough for the both of us. Or his stupid flirting during dinner. Then…the topper was his hand on my lower back, that low seductive voice, and the word *sweetheart* tumbling out of his mouth.

"Ugh!" I said, rolling onto my back. "Stop thinking about him, Georgie. Stop!"

I forced myself to close my eyes and concentrate on my breathing. "In. Out. In. Out."

Focusing on my breathing had worked in the past. The only problem was, the repeated in and out of my breath only made me think of sex. And that made me think of Blayze and then that got me horny as hell.

"Fuck it!" I whispered, throwing the covers off and getting out of the bed. I tiptoed over to the dresser and opened one of the drawers. I reached in and rooted around until I found my vibrator. When I pulled it out, I smiled.

After a quick glance at the clock, I saw that it was four thirty. Blayze would hopefully be fast asleep and wouldn't hear me anyway since his room was downstairs.

I raced back over to the bed and jumped in. It was freezing in the room. Slipping my hand into my panties, I closed my eyes and touched myself. When I wasn't getting turned on enough to get wet yet, I thought of blue eyes and dimples.

"If you say so, sweetheart."

"Touch me," I whispered, picturing Blayze in his office, me on his desk.

"If you say so, sweetheart."

"Put your mouth on me," I said in a raspy voice as I played with my clit. No man had ever given me oral sex. Ever since Blayze had made the comment about the whipped cream after he'd picked me up, I had been having dreams about his face buried between my legs.

Squeezing my eyes shut, I pictured Blayze's soft, plump lips sucking and tasting me. I turned the vibrator on and slowly worked it inside of me.

"Go deep," I whispered as I pushed the vibrator in.

"If you say so, sweetheart."

"Oh God, yes. Faster, God yes!" I whisper-shouted, my other hand coming up to play with one of my nipples as I imagined it was his mouth on me. I moaned in pleasure. "Oh, God."

My breathing was hard and fast, and I had to remember to stay quiet. The image of Blayze over me, his long, built body moving in and out of mine was nearly my undoing.

I could feel my toes curl up as my orgasm built. My mouth fell open, and my whimpers grew louder.

Knock. Knock. Knock.

My eyes flew up. I pulled the vibrator out and threw it across the room.

Thunk!

Oh my God, it hit the tub.

Then a vibrating sound started on the tile floor.

"Shit!" I whispered as I tried to get out of bed but got tangled in the covers instead.

"Georgie? Is everything okay?" Blayze asked, knocking again.

"Fine! It's fine!" I called out, tripping over the stupid rug and nearly diving head first into the bathroom. I grabbed the vibrator and fumbled with it, causing it to turn on more and make the most obnoxious sound.

"Fuck!" I whisper-shouted again.

"Georgie, open the door. What's going on in there?"

Thank God I had locked the damn bedroom door.

"Hold on!" I cried out, finally getting the damn thing to turn off. I dropped it onto the floor and rushed into the bedroom, nearly running into the wall. I cracked the door open and fought to breath normally.

Blayze looked at me with a worried expression on his face.

"Are you okay?"

I nodded.

"What was that loud noise?"

"Um...a book."

Both of his brows rose. "A book?"

"Yep," I said, nodding my head much faster than I needed to. "A book. I was reading and you scared me, so I threw the book. It hit the tub."

"You couldn't sleep?"

"Why do you say that? I mean, what makes you think I couldn't sleep? I wasn't thinking of anything or doing anything...what I mean was that I was reading. That's doing something."

He blinked at me a few times before he gave himself a little shake. "I only thought maybe you were having a hard time sleeping since it's so late at night and you were...reading."

"I was. Reading. And having a hard time sleeping, but it had nothing to do with you."

Oh God. All the stars above, what in the hell was wrong with me? I closed my eyes and prayed for the floor to open up and take me.

"I guess I'm glad to hear that."

I tried to look casual. "What are you doing up? Why are you at my door?"

"I was getting up to make us some coffee."

"Before five in the morning?" I said with a slight laugh.

He nodded. "Yeah, we need to leave the house by five for-ty-five."

My mouth fell open. "Why?"

"We need time to drive to the trailhead. Dawn is five min-utes after seven, and that gives us less than thirty-five minutes for the sunrise to reach the spot I'm taking you to."

I was positive I was staring at him like he'd lost his mind.

"Dress in warm layers and wear hiking boots. You did bring some, didn't you?"

"Um, I have hiking sneakers, does that count?" I asked as I crinkled my face up in confusion. I wasn't sure if it was lack of sleep, being robbed of my orgasm, or...both, that had me confused.

He nodded. "That'll work."

Blayze turned to leave and I called after him, "Wait, are we going hiking? Is that what we're doing this morning?"

With a quick glance over his shoulder, he replied, "It is, indeed. How did you guess? The clues I just left you?"

I rolled my eyes. "Ha ha. So, we're getting up now?"

He turned and faced me. "Are you too tired to go? Did you want to get back to your…book?"

Why did he pause before saying book? Oh dear Lord above. What if he'd heard me?

"How did…how did you know I was up?" I asked.

A slow smile played across his face. "You must have said something while reading your book. I heard you."

"I did. I always talk out loud when I'm reading. No! I read out loud. So, sometimes I read the book. I read what's in the book."

He nodded. "Hence reading out loud."

"Yes!" I said as I pointed at him.

"Okay, well, I'll let you get ready, and I'll meet you in the kitchen. Remember, layers."

"Layers! Got it!"

"Bring your book along, too, if you want. We might find a spot or two to relax and you can read out loud to me," he said as he started moving away from me.

"Okay!" I shut the door and leaned against it. I put my hand on my chest and let out a long breath. Then I giggled. What would Blayze Shaw do if I pulled out a vibrator instead of a book? I chewed on my lip, then snorted.

"Jesus, Georgie, get ahold of yourself."

Thank goodness I took Blayze's advice and dressed in layers. I had already stripped off my jacket and tied it around my waist, then put it back on as we hiked farther up the trail into the mountains.

"Are there bears?" I called out ahead of me.

"Most likely."

I stopped and looked around.

"What about cats?"

It was his turn to stop. "Like meow cats?"

I couldn't help but giggle. "I mean like the kind that will eat me."

"Yep, those too."

Hustling faster, I quickly caught up to him.

"Okay, if anyone asked, I'd tell them I'm in shape," I said. "I work out nearly every day, but this hiking is kicking my ass!"

Blayze glanced back at me. "Not much farther. Pick it up a bit so we can get there on time."

I rolled my eyes as I followed him, the light from the head-lamp he gave me at the beginning of the trailhead lighting my way. Dawn had appeared just like he'd said it would once we'd started to hike, but it was still dark out. And I wasn't even going to think about all the things I kept hearing running off and what they could be.

"I'm going to have blisters," I mumbled as I stumbled up and over a rock. The trail had been pretty easy at first, but this last half mile was giving me hell. I was positive we were going straight uphill.

When I looked up from the trail, I saw Blayze coming up on another couple. I wonder if the guy had dragged her ass out of bed as well. When I looked at her face, I had my answer. She was leaning over, gasping for air.

"You said you hiked!" the guy said.

The young woman shot him a dirty look. "Like around a flat lake, not up the side of a freaking mountain!"

He sighed. "I promise, baby, it'll be worth it. You're almost there. We have to keep going if we want to make it in time for the sunrise."

She stood up, and I was almost positive I saw her look at the edge of the trail where there was a nice little drop off. Probably contemplating if she was going to push him.

"Here, you lean on me, I'll lean on you," I said to her. "I think I see the end of the trail. Maybe we can drag each other up the rest of the way."

The girl looked relieved. "Oh, thank God. Another person just ran by us. They ran! Like this wasn't the slow climb to death."

I couldn't help but giggle.

"Can you push me up?" she asked.

"The trail is wide enough that I think we can pull each other up."

She nodded, and we started up the trail. When I looked directly at Blayze, he held up his hand to block the light.

"Oh, sorry," I said, clicking the headlamp off. It was getting lighter outside, and I didn't need it anymore.

"You didn't hike up here without a light, did you?" I softly asked my new climbing partner.

"No, he gave me a flashlight. At least your guy gave you a hands-free version."

I shook my head. "Oh, he's not my guy. We're friends. He thought this would be…I guess he thought it would be fun."

She groaned. "What the hell is wrong with men? By the way, my name's Candace."

"Hey, Candace, I'm Georgie."

"Nice to meet you, Georgie."

As we came to the end of the trail, Candace's boyfriend

reached for her hand while I took a moment to catch my breath. I heard Candace gasp.

"Oh my God, Lance!"

It was, no doubt, a stunning view of the valley. I just wasn't sure I really gave two shits by that point. My lungs burned, my legs felt as if they were going to cramp up on me, and I had finished off my water ten minutes ago.

I was clearly not in good shape.

"Come on." Blayze wrapped his arm around my waist, and we walked the last few feet. When I got to the top, my breath caught.

"Blayze," I whispered, looking at the bright pink sky with hints of orange. The snow-topped mountains went from pink to white in a matter of seconds as the sun began her climb.

"We made it in time." Blayze took my hand in his. Butterflies went off in my stomach and I tried not to think about how good his touch felt.

The bright tip of the sun peeked up over the mountains as a burst of light appeared over the mountaintops. Sounds of birds waking, leaves and bushes rustling echoed around me as I heard everything wake up around me and come to life. A flock of geese flew above us. It was beautiful.

Blayze tugged my hand and jerked his head for me to look. When I turned, I saw Lance down on one knee and Candace crying.

I pressed my hand to my mouth and fought to hold back my tears as I watched him asking her to spend the rest of his life with him.

Spinning around to Blayze, I whispered, "I bet she feels terrible for wanting to push him off the trail now!"

His eyes went wide. "Did she say that?"

I shook my head and looked back at the happy couple hugging, both of them in tears. "No, but I saw it written all over her face."

Blayze chuckled. "Well, it looks like it was worth the climb for her. How about you?"

Glancing back at the beautiful view before me, I nodded. "It was so worth it. Thank you for bringing me up here."

"You're welcome. It's one of my favorite places to hike, especially for that sunrise."

As I looked all around me, I exhaled. "I see why. It's stunning."

A few other people soon joined us on the mountaintop to take in the view. Eventually the clicks of cameras replaced the sounds of nature, and I found I missed the peace of it all. Whispers turned louder, and that romantic moment disappeared.

Romantic moment? Was that what it had been? It certainly had been for Lance and Candace. And Blayze had held my hand as the sun came up. A gesture I hadn't thought much about at the time, but now seemed to consume my every thought. Well, that and how I wanted to slap my hand over a lady's mouth who kept saying over and over how high she was and how sick she felt.

"Ready to head back down?" Blayze asked. "There are a few stops we can make if you want to soak up the fresh air. Did you bring your book?"

My cheeks instantly heated. "No, I wanted to be in the moment."

He smiled a brilliant smile, and I felt my knees wobble a bit.

"Then how about we make our way back down and grab some breakfast before we set off on another adventure?"

"Another one?" I asked with a weary laugh.

"This one will be easier, I promise."

Returning his smile with one of my own, I replied, "Then let's go grab some breakfast."

We ate breakfast in a darling little café in the heart of Hamilton. Afterwards, we strolled down Main Street, and I took in the charm of the town. I had been so young when I visited before that I never really understood how beautiful Hamilton was. Fresh flowers hung from baskets on lamp posts every few feet, and some stores had benches out front that were flanked by more flowers. Most stores had fall decorations out, and I found myself breathing in a deep breath as we walked.

"What do they do when it turns too cold for plants?" I asked as I pointed to the hanging pots.

"They're replaced with decorations."

I turned around in a circle. "What a charming little town. I don't really remember it, even though I was old enough to."

Blayze glanced around the street as well. "It is charming. I don't think I'd want to live anywhere else."

"Really? You've never had the urge to be in a bigger city?"

He laughed. "College was enough city living for me. I've always been happiest on the ranch. Always will be."

I nodded. "You'll stay on the ranch even when you marry and have kids?"

"Hell yeah. Hopefully I find a bride who's down for being a rancher's wife."

"Your mother seems to enjoy it."

Blayze smiled as if fondly thinking of his mother. "She does. She works as an interior designer, which I'm sure you already know. She only takes on a few clients now and doesn't work as much as she did before. I used to love sitting in her office and watching her with all the swatches, and seeing how she put colors and patterns together. She has a real talent for it."

"If her home is any indication of her work, she'd be highly sought after in Dallas." I chuckled.

"I bet she would."

"May I ask you a question, not off the record?"

He shrugged.

"How does your mom feel about your brother riding bulls?"

"I'm not sure. You'd have to ask her."

I nodded. It was going to be like pulling teeth to get Blayze to talk to me. But then he surprised me and went on.

"I'm sure she worries. I would think any mother would. But my mother would never let her fear dictate what her children did with their lives."

"No," I said with a soft smile. "She doesn't strike me as being that way."

Blayze stopped and motioned toward a store. I glanced up. Chapter One Bookstore.

"A bookstore!" I said.

"I figured since you were up late last night reading, you must be a book lover."

My face instantly heated as I nodded. "I love to read."

"So do I."

I gave him a wink of my own. "I remember that conversation we had in your room about the romance novel."

"That's right. I can do more than ride a horse and be handsome."

Rolling my eyes, I laughed as he opened the door to the bookstore for me. We walked around for a while in silence as we both picked up and flipped through different books. When I glanced over at Blayze after a bit, he had a few books in his hand.

I was about to walk up and ask him what books he'd chosen when a woman around our age came into the store and saw Blayze. She smiled and made a bee-line straight for him.

"Hey, Blayze!"

He smiled politely when he saw her. "How's it going, Liz?"

I didn't miss the way she let her eyes wander over him. My gosh, did all women openly eye-fuck the guy? I wondered if Blayze ever got tired of it. If he did, he didn't show it.

She smiled "It's going. Are you going to the street dance next weekend?"

"Most likely."

"Great! Will you save me a dance?"

Blayze tipped his cowboy hat and flashed her a panty-melting smile. I tried not to let it bother me, but damn it all to hell, it did.

"Sure, I will. How are your folks?"

Looking as if he'd asked her to give him the sun and the moon, she beamed up at him. "They're doing real good. Daddy is thinking of retiring."

"Really?" Blayze asked. "Your brother taking over the cattle?"

"Bobby? You couldn't drag him back to Hamilton if you offered him a million dollars. We'll most likely sell them off."

Blayze nodded, seemingly lost in thought. "If he needs any help, you tell him to let me know, okay?"

She grinned. "I will. Listen, you should come on over for dinner tonight if you're not busy."

I could tell that Blayze was about to look my way, so I engrossed myself with a set of books and acted as if I wasn't even aware he was having a conversation.

"Maybe. I need to see how my day goes."

Pfft. More like needed to see how fast he could ditch me. Liz was another beauty. Dark blonde hair that was cut to her chin. She had on workout clothes, and her insanely fit body was on full display for everyone. She was probably the type of woman Blayze went for.

They said their goodbyes, and I watched Liz head to the back room of the bookstore. Great, she worked here. I quickly grabbed a book and opened it when I saw Blayze making his way over to me.

"What are you reading?" he asked.

"Something interesting," I said as I shut the book and stared down at the title. *The Cure for Stupidity.*

I groaned on the inside.

Blayze leaned in closer. "Using Brain Science to Explain Irrational Behavior at Work?" Turning his head, he frowned. "Is this for you or someone else?"

Ignoring his question, I slipped the book back in place before heading to the romance section. Running my finger along the spines, I stopped when I found one of my favorite authors. Julia Quinn. I drew the book out and smiled at the title. *Just Like Heaven.* Historical romance was my favorite genre.

I tucked the book safely against my chest and kept looking. Next I found Evie Dunmore. I had that book on e-book but decided I needed the paperback as well.

"*Bringing Down the Duke?*"

Spinning on my heels, I nearly ran into Blayze. "It's one of my favorite books."

He simply nodded. "You like historical?"

"Romance. I like historical romance."

A crooked smile tugged at his mouth. "I gathered. What's a good book for me to read?"

"In historical romance?" I asked in a bewildered tone.

"Yes."

I remembered him mentioning he liked it, though not contemporary romance.

The idea of Blayze reading a romance novel made my insides warm. Handing him Evie Dunmore's book, I said, "This one."

Blayze took it, turned it over, and read the blurb. With a single nod, he placed it with the others in his hand and then proceeded to walk over to the checkout area. "We should get going if we want to make it to our next adventure."

I swallowed the sudden lump in my throat. My feelings were all over the damn place. I didn't want to have romantic thoughts about Blayze. I didn't want to visualize what it would be like having him read a book to me. I didn't want to hit the woman from earlier who'd asked him to dinner. But I did, in fact, want all of that.

And that wasn't good. It wasn't good at all.

Chapter Eleven

GEORGIANA

When Blayze drove us back to the Shaw ranch, I didn't think much about it. When he turned to the left almost immediately, I simply wondered where we were going. But the farther we drove, the more I realized we were going somewhere I hadn't been on the ranch before. He pulled up to a gate and punched in a code. The brand on the gate was the same as the one on the main ranch gate.

"Where are we going?" I asked.

"Ty's arena."

"His arena?" I asked cautiously.

"Yep."

"W-why?"

Blayze turned to look at me. With a shit-eating grin, he answered, "To get you up on a bull."

"Oh, hell no, Blayze Shaw! No way!"

His head fell back, and he let out a laugh that made my toes curl in delight.

"I refuse to get on a bull, Blayze."

Reaching over, he took my hand in his and gave it a squeeze. "Do you trust me, Georgie?"

I blinked a few times and wanted to shout that hell no, I didn't trust him. But those words wouldn't come out because they weren't true. I did trust Blayze. I had always trusted him. From the first time he'd talked me into swinging off that cliff on a rope swing into the lake with him when we were teenagers, I knew he would never do anything to physically hurt me or to cause me hurt.

My chest ached as I let my mind wander. What would have happened if we never got caught? If I had given myself to him that day? Would we still be together?

"Yes, but that doesn't mean I'm getting on a bull."

He glanced back at me one more time and winked. "Trust me."

I huffed and folded my arms over my chest. "Something tells me I'm going to regret this."

"Hope not," he said as he pulled down another road, this one not as driven on. Pastures lined both sides of the road, and a few bulls were sprinkled throughout the grass. Most ignored us as we drove by, but some lifted their heads to see who'd interrupted their peaceful lunch.

A large barn came into view, and to the side of it was an even larger arena. There were chutes, three large gates, and what looked to be fake people made out of cardboard placed around the fence.

"Are those…"

"Pretend audience members. Believe it or not, some folks get really nervous riding in front of other people. It's good practice for them to ride in front of fake people."

"I never knew that was a thing."

145

Blayze pulled up behind a black truck and parked. "Sure is."

He got out of the truck and jogged around to my side, opening the door and holding his hand out for me to exit the truck.

Shaking my head back and forth, I said, "No. No. I'm not doing it, Blayze."

With a wicked gleam in his eyes, he reached into the truck and scooped me out.

"Blayze!" I cried out as he kicked the door shut and headed toward the barn with me in his arms.

I heard a deep male laugh near the entrance to the barn, and turned to see Blayze's uncle, Ty, standing there with Ryan.

"I'm pretty sure women don't like to be manhandled, Blayze. No matter how good looking you are."

Blayze set me down, and I had to take a moment to balance myself. Not because he did it too fast or because I was on uneven ground. No, it was because my body was up against his, my mind was spinning, and my knees were weak. Lord, what was it about him?

"Georgie here would like to ride a bull," Blayze announced with a smile.

"Um, no, Georgie would not," I said.

Ty raised a brow. "Are you sure about that?"

Nodding, I answered, "I'm so sure it's not even funny how sure I am."

"How about you watch one being ridden then," Ryan said.

Okay, if Ryan was going to ride a bull, I would be totally fine with that.

Pointing to him, I blurted out, "Yes! I would love to watch you ride a bull."

Ryan laughed. "Oh, hell no. I'm not stupid. I was talking about him."

When I saw he was pointing at Blayze, my heart did a weird little jump.

Ty tossed gloves toward Blayze. "Let's do it."

Turning to face him, I grabbed his arm before he followed Ty and Ryan into the barn. "Wait, you're not riding one, are you?"

He smirked. "Why, Georgie, if I didn't know any better, I'd say you were worried for my safety."

Dropping my hand, I scoffed. "Don't be ridiculous. It's just...I thought it was Ryan who was going to be riding."

Blayze laughed. "Come on. You'll get a front-row view for your article."

The mention of the article made my stomach twist. I had gone back and forth all morning, debating if I wanted to tell Blayze the truth about what was going on. Instead, I decided to trust that my father would get it all figured out and fixed. I wasn't even sure who Doug Larson was.

I followed Blayze through the barn and around back to where I'd seen the large arena. There were a few bulls in the chute, and I caught sight of Bradly and Hunter. I knew Hunter mostly did team roping, but he also rode bulls, and I was curious to see if he would be riding one of these.

As we walked toward the arena, I caught up with Ty. Even though I had been to plenty of bull-riding events, I had no idea how any of the training worked. "So, how do you do this? Do you put a rider on once the bull is mature enough?"

"No, we flank and place a dummy first," Ty said.

"What?" I asked.

"We'll show you."

I nodded and realized that Blayze had disappeared. Not wanting to make it seem like I was searching for him, I followed Ty.

"This is called a practice arena," he said as he reached down and grabbed a rope. "This is the flank. It's a soft cotton rope and has an eye on the end right here and a tail on the opposite side. I'm going to drop this down on one side of the bull, then use this hook to grab it and bring it up and around the bottom of the bull."

I nodded. "What's on the hook?"

"It's a piece of copper coated with rubber so neither of us gets hurt."

Not realizing I was holding my breath, I finally let it out.

"I'm going to pull it through the eye just enough to where it won't come off," Ty continued. "It's not tight or hurting him in any way."

"Okay," I said.

"Next, I'm going to put this dummy on him. It's a seven pounder and has a latch that this pin will go in once we get it around his body."

I looked at the silver box in Ty's hand that was the dummy. "How does it come off?"

Ty held up a remote. "By hitting a button. Now I'll put this on just like I did the rope."

I watched Ty ease the dummy onto the bull's back. He pulled on the rope and got it tight enough to where it wouldn't fall off when the bull bucked.

"This is the quick release pin that goes in the flank and attaches by making a handle with the rope."

He pulled the rope and made a couple of loops.

"How long do you let him buck?" I asked.

"We ease him into longer times. With this guy I'm going to let him go for six seconds."

I could feel my heart starting to race with excitement.

I watched Ty let the bull out. I saw the bull buck like crazy....and couldn't help but smile.

"And you increase the weight over time?" I asked Ty.

He kept watching the bull as he kicked and turned. "Sure do. Then they move on to riders."

"What was it like the first time you got on a bull?"

Ty smiled. "I was scared to death and excited at the same time. No matter how many times I got in the pen and crawled onto the back of a bull, the hair on the back of my neck stood up."

"I bet," I said with a chuckle as I watched the bull finish his round and run through another gate to the back pens.

"It's crazy," Ty explained. "You don't really hear anything or anyone. You're so focused on that bull and staying the hell on."

Smiling, I watched some other men I didn't know move another bull into the chute.

"Do you like being on this side of things?" I asked.

He nodded. "I do. It's like raising race horses, but they're a lot bigger and a lot meaner when they want to be. They're athletes, and they're treated like kings."

"Kings?"

"Yes, ma'am. They're bred to be winners. I've produced more champion bulls than any other bull company."

"Wow. That's impressive."

He tipped his hat and winked. "I know."

Laughing, I turned and nearly tripped on air. Blayze stood there in a long-sleeve, black button-up shirt, jeans, and—Lord above—chaps. I'd watched old footage of him riding in high school and college, but seeing him standing in front of me dressed like a full-fledged cowboy was entirely different. I tried to ignore the throbbing between my legs.

"Wow, you changed."

He smiled. "Can't ride a bull in my hiking gear."

"No," I said with a shake of my head and a nervous laugh. "I guess not."

No wonder women threw themselves at the man.

"Okay," Ty said, "he's a little over three, Blayze, and you're the second rider on his back."

"Fun times." Blayze walked over to the pen where suddenly about six guys had appeared. Ryan and Bradly among them.

Bradly was putting the flank rope around the bull that was used to enhance the natural bucking it would do to try and get the rider off. Turning to look at Blayze, I saw Ryan helping him put his helmet on.

I focused back on Bradly and watched him put the bull rope around the bull's chest, which was what Blayze would hold on to.

Blayze put on his gloves and climbed over the pen. Hunter was the flank man, meaning he would be adjusting the fit of the flank rope. Out in the arena was a younger kid I'd never seen before, who was clearly going to be the gateman. He'd pull the gate open when Blayze gave him a nod.

Blayze rubbed rosin on his glove and then up his rope before drawing the rope across his hand a few times and getting a good grip on it for his ride.

The bull acted up a bit, and Ty put his arm out in front of Blayze to steady him and keep him from hitting the side of the pen. I forced myself to breathe as I watched the whole thing play out. My heart had never hammered so hard in my chest before. It wasn't like I'd never watched Blayze ride a bull. I had the last summer I was in town. But somehow it was different now. Back then he'd seemed so...fearless.

My breath caught in my throat. *"I can be fearless enough for both of us."*

One nod from Blayze and the gate flew open and out went the bull. I covered my mouth with my hand to keep my gasp in.

"Cover him, Blayze!" Hunter yelled as I focused solely on Blayze. The bull changed direction a few times and was giving one hell of a show with his bucking. After a few seconds, a horn went off, and Blayze jumped off the bull with such ease he made it look easy. He landed on his feet, though he stumbled slightly. Knowing what to do, the bull turned and headed out the exit gate to go through the chutes and back out to the holding pen or to the pasture out back.

I turned to Ty and saw him grinning like a fool.

"Blayze has been the only one to ride him the full eight," he said.

Confused, I asked, "I thought you said he was the second rider?"

Ty laughed, and so did Bradly and Hunter.

"I lied. That bull has never kept a single rider on him yet," Ty stated.

"Why did you tell Blayze otherwise?" I asked.

Ty looked at me. "He's like his daddy. Let's shit get in his head too much. If I'd told him no one has been able to ride him for the full eight seconds, the bastard would think about it too hard and get himself bucked off."

"That's risky," I said with a grin.

"You bastard. Ain't no fucking way that bull has only been ridden twice," Blayze said as he climbed over the gate. I couldn't tear my eyes away from him. What was it about Blayze in full-on cowboy mode that made my heart swoon and my head go fuzzy? It reminded me of the younger boy I fell for.

Those big blue eyes shining with excitement. He acted angry, but I could tell he was far from it.

The man climbing up the pen and jumping down was still the boy I fell in love with. The boy I let kiss me. The boy I wanted to be with. When I was younger, it was hard for me to believe that he would ever want a girl like me, and a small part of me still felt the same way. I pressed my fingers to my lips and swore I could still feel that kiss we'd shared. I quickly shook my head when Hunter's voice interrupted my thoughts.

"First one to cover him," Hunter said with a proud smile on his face.

Blayze looked at Bradly. "Not even you?"

He laughed. "No, sir. Only made it four seconds."

With a shake of his head, Blayze focused back on Ty. "He's a good bull, Ty."

Ty grinned. "I know. He's the third-ranked bull in the PBR."

Blayze shook his head. "You got any easier ones?"

Ty laughed. "Like you didn't make that look easy."

"I'd like to not get hurt if I can help it," Blayze replied.

Was that why he wasn't riding professionally anymore? Was he afraid of getting hurt? No way. Blayze afraid? I couldn't see it.

"I see the wheels turning in your head."

Jumping, I turned to see Brock standing there. "When did you get here?" I asked.

He tipped his hat. "Just in time to see him ride. He's good."

I nodded as I glanced back at Blayze. "He's very good."

"Some say he was on his way to being better than me, Ty, and Dirk combined. Now I think Bradly will give the title a challenge. He's still young and has a lot to learn, but it's in his blood and he has Blayze mentoring him."

"He's lucky to have so many amazing bull riders here to train him."

Brock nodded. "That he is."

"What did you mean that you could see the wheels turning in my head?" I asked.

"You were wondering if that was why Blayze doesn't ride anymore. Afraid of getting hurt."

I felt a small puff of laughter slip past my lips. "That's exactly what I was thinking."

Brock drew in a deep breath and slowly let it out. "He has his own reasons, but being afraid isn't one of them."

"I didn't think it would be."

We watched Hunter ride a bull and get thrown two seconds in.

"Better stick to roping!" Blayze yelled out as he helped Bradly get ready to ride.

Brock laughed. "It's a good thing Hunter likes roping more than he likes bull riding."

I looked back to see Hunter let out a few curse words as he climbed out of the arena.

"Watch Bradly and Blayze," Brock said.

I focused back on them. Bradly was adjusting his rope while Blayze was talking to him.

"He's reminding him which way the bull will most likely turn. Reminding him how to move his body with the bull and to expect sudden turns."

Blayze's gaze was intense and Bradly's was focused. When the gateman got the nod from Bradly and the gate flew open, I watched in awe as the nineteen-year-old moved fluidly while the bull did everything in his power to get him off his back.

"That's it, Brad. That's it!" Brock called out.

After the eight seconds were up, Bradly jumped off like it was a kiddie ride. He dusted off his jeans and yelled, "Now that's how you ride!"

Blayze laughed. "Cocky like his daddy."

My nerves were on edge again as I watched Blayze ride two more times. He covered one bull, and was thrown six seconds in on the other. I nearly screamed when I saw him get tossed in the air, the bull almost stepping on his neck.

After the riding was finished, I watched them all gather up the bulls and guide them out into different pastures. Once the animals were out there eating the deep green grass, they looked innocent. Not like the giant beasts they were when they were in the arena.

"You ready to ride?" Blayze asked as he came up next to me. A chill ran down my spine at the sound of his voice—or maybe it was from the warmth of his breath on my neck.

Turning to face him, I made a pouty face. "Bummer, looks like they put up all the bulls."

That brilliant smile of his lit up his face, and my heart fluttered in my chest. "It's a damn good thing I know the owner. Come on."

He took my hand in his, and I tried not to react to how good it felt to have our hands intertwined. Or how he rubbed his thumb over my palm just like he did when we were younger. How many women had he done that to? Did it make their stomachs dance with excitement like it was doing to mine?

"Where are we going?" I asked as I followed Blayze along the fence line.

"Going to say hi to Steel Bullet."

"I'm guessing that's a bull."

"He is, indeed. A world-champion bull. He's retired now and living the good life."

I laughed. "Standing around eating grass?"

Turning to look at me, a devilish smile appeared on his face. "And making babies."

With a roll of my eyes, I said, "I'm pretty sure they don't need him to do that the old-fashioned way."

"Nope, they don't," he said, "But Ty's a good man, and he lets ol' Bullet have a bit of fun every now and then."

He unlocked the gate, and it was then I saw the bull grazing about twenty yards away.

"Don't be afraid of him," Blayze said as we walked toward him. "He was raised on this ranch from the get-go. He's Ty's pride and joy, and he's spoiled. See the pile of sand over there?"

"Yes."

"He loves to play in it. Always has."

I smiled as we drew closer, and Steel Bullet lifted his head and looked at us.

"If he thought we had bread he'd come charging over to get it."

Even though my heart thundered in my chest, there was something in the bull's eyes that said he wasn't afraid. He wasn't angry we were there. He wanted us there.

"When Steel Bullet was competing, Ty said if he wasn't loaded up to leave with the other bulls he'd be pissed and very vocal about it."

"So he enjoyed performing?"

"Loved it. Most of them do."

As we drew closer I slowed my pace, but Blayze walked right up and started petting the bull.

"Some bulls can be moody," he said. "Not all of them like people unless you're feeding them or breeding them. So you always need to be careful around them. But a bull like this is a gentle giant."

Blayze held out his hand, and I took it. With a soft tug, he pulled until I was next to him. "He likes his ears scratched."

It didn't take me long to figure out ol' Steel Bullet was a sucker for a good scratching. He loved my nails and made it clear he wanted me to scratch him instead of Blayze. Before I knew what Blayze was planning, he lifted me up and put me on the back of the bull.

"Blayze!" I whispered, terrified I'd spook Steel Bullet.

With a lighthearted chuckle, he said, "Keep petting him, Georgie."

After a few deeps breaths, I started to use my fingernails to scratch Bullet. He threw his head back, clearly enjoying what I was doing. Then Blayze walked forward a bit and Bullet followed him. I nearly panicked, but when I saw how gentle the bull was being, I relaxed and enjoyed the fact that I was on the back of a world-champion bull. This was a bull that had thrown some of the best riders around—and I was riding him.

"Now you can say you went more than eight on the back of a bull," Blayze said.

"A champion one at that!"

He grinned and gifted me with that dimple. "Are you still scared?"

I shook my head. "No, not like earlier when I was watching you ride."

The words came out of my mouth before I even realized I'd said them. I wasn't about to look at Blayze after I let that little statement slip free.

"Being fearless simply means taking chances on something, Georgie. Trying something new. Not being afraid to jump even though you're not sure of what's going to be on the other side."

My eyes met his.

"Thank you, Blayze. Today has been a lot of fun."

He tipped his hat. "I'm glad. I had fun too."

We walked a bit more while I loved on Bullet, and he continued to graze.

I suddenly realized that we'd been out here for a long time. "What time is it? I'm supposed to help your mom!" I said as I reached for my phone in my back pocket. "Oh my gosh! I'm going to be late now. And I still need to get back to your place and shower."

Blayze reached up and helped me down. "She'll understand if you're a few minutes late."

We quickly made our way back to the barn and said our goodbyes. The moment I got in Blayze's truck, a wave of tiredness washed over me. The more the truck bounced on the country road, the more my eyes grew heavy until there was nothing but darkness.

Chapter Twelve

BLAYZE

I went to say something to Georgie, but when I glanced her way I saw that she was out. She let out a small snore, and I smiled. She must have been exhausted if she could fall asleep within five minutes of sitting down in the truck.

My mind drifted back to early this morning when I had gotten up to get breakfast ready before we'd left for the hike. I'd gone up to her room, figuring she'd need a few wake-up calls if she was anything like my sister Morgan. If I wanted her to get up early I had to start waking her up thirty minutes before we actually needed to get ready.

When I'd heard soft moans coming from Georgie's room, I'd snuck up and put my ear to the door. That was when I'd heard the vibrator and Georgie's mews of pleasure. It had taken every ounce of strength I had not to burst in and ask her to let me finish the job the right way.

Smiling, I tried to picture the moment she'd threw the toy. I'd heard it hit something in the room or bathroom. Then her excuse that it was a book nearly had me laughing my ass off. I deserved a fucking Oscar for keeping a straight face during all of it.

Okay, push all those thoughts away, Blayze.

My phone buzzed and I glanced to see Liz had texted. I nearly groaned as I hit ignore.

Once I parked, I quietly got out of the truck and made my way around to the passenger side. After softly opening the door, I gently shook Georgie on the arm.

"Georgie, we're back at my house."

Her head snapped up and I had to press my mouth closed, so I wouldn't laugh at the drool running down the side of her face.

"Wait, what?" she cried out.

"We're at my place. You fell asleep."

Those sleepy green eyes looked at me, confused. "I fell asleep?"

"Yep," I said with a nod. "Need help?"

She took my hand and slid out of the truck, stumbling a bit until she got her bearings.

"Wow, that hike must have really worn me out," she said with an embarrassed chuckle.

"Or it was the reading all night."

For a moment she looked confused before she remembered her lie. "Right. The book. So good."

"I bet it was," I mused as I stepped away from her.

She tilted her head for a moment before she turned and faced the house. "I better hurry so I'm not too late to meet your mom."

And with that, she went racing off to get as far away from me as she could.

After thirty minutes and nothing from Georgie, I headed to the room she was staying in. As I went to knock, the door flew open. My eyes nearly popped out of my head at the sight before me.

"You look beautiful," I said before I could stop myself.

She glanced down at the overalls she was wearing along with a long-sleeve white T-shirt. When she looked back up at me, her cheeks were a soft pink.

"Thanks. I figured I should be comfortable since we'll be baking."

I smiled when I saw that she'd put her hair up in a ponytail. The look reminded me of the girl I fell for so many years ago.

"We should go," she said, pulling me back to the present.

"Right. After you." I motioned for her to walk first.

As we walked downstairs, I noticed how Georgie's head kept tilting forward. It was clear she was still trying to fight off exhaustion.

"Georgie, if you're tired, I'm sure my mother will understand."

"No! I'm fine."

But it turned out Georgie was more tired than either of us realized. She started off strong with my mother as they made pastry dough together. Then she sat down to roll out a crust as I poured Mom's homemade cherry filling into a pie dish.

"Blayze?" my mother said calmly.

I turned to look at her. "Yeah?"

"What did you do to this girl?" She pointed to Georgie, who had her head down on a pie crust, fast asleep.

"She's exhausted," I said, smiling down at the sleeping beauty who would be horrified to know she was drooling on the crust.

Mom looked at me. "No kidding. Why?"

"Well, she was up nearly all night reading a book. Then we took off for a sunrise hike. Had lunch, walked around Hamilton a bit, then I took her to Ty's to watch how we train the bulls. Oh, I had her ride Steel Bullet as well."

My mother raised a brow.

"In the pasture."

Her body relaxed. Glancing back at Georgie, she slowly shook her head. "Take this girl back to your place and let the poor thing sleep."

"Can I finish the lattice on this cherry pie first?"

Shooting me a dirty look, she pointed to Georgie again. "Get her to a bed."

I shot her a cocky smile. "It would be my pleasure."

"Blayze Shaw!" My mother giggled as she hit me on the arm. "You are terrible."

"I am my father's son."

She grinned. "Amen to that."

After a fruitless attempt to wake up Georgie, I scooped her up and started toward the front door, with Mom ahead of me, she opened the door to my truck.

As I walked, Georgie wrapped her arms around my neck and nuzzled her face into my chest.

"Mmm," she sighed. "Blayze."

Mom turned and gave me a questioning look.

"Don't look at me like that, Mom."

"Like what? Like the girl you were caught making out with behind your daddy's barn years ago is now in your arms saying your name like she's reliving a private moment?"

It was my turn to sound incredulous. "Mom! And you say I'm terrible."

She chuckled. "Trust me, Blayze Shaw. When a woman whispers a man's name like that, well, let's just say her dreams aren't PG."

I felt my cheeks burn. "I don't want to have this conversation with you, Mother."

"Mother?" She gasped as she pressed her hand to her chest. "Oh my. Looks like I struck a nerve."

"Mom, can you please get my truck door?"

Practically skipping by me, Mom opened the passenger side of my truck and watched as I placed Georgie on the seat. I reached up and grabbed the seatbelt and leaned in to buckle her up.

Georgie's eyes opened and I turned my head to say we were heading back to my place. But then she smiled, leaned forward, and kissed me. It was a sleepy, peck-on-the-lips kind of kiss, but it still shot a bolt of lightning through my entire body. I was frozen there for a good ten seconds.

Her head dropped back to the head rest, and she closed her eyes and let out a snore.

I quickly stepped back and shut the door, staring at my truck like it was on fire.

Mom clapped and hopped a little. "I finally, *finally* get to use my mother powers!"

"Your what?" I asked as I shot my mother a confused look.

"My mother powers. Stella has them. She could always tell when someone liked one of her kids—or when they were pregnant—simply by looking at them. Once, she told me she knew I was pregnant with Hunter simply by looking at my gums."

"Your gums?" I asked.

She pointed to her mouth. "Yes! I'm telling you, it's like some weird power I think you get when you're older. For instance, am I surprised that girl just kissed you? No. For one, look at how handsome my boy is." She reached up and cupped my face.

I rolled my eyes.

"And two, that girl fell in love with you a long time ago. I saw it, and so did her momma. Georgie clearly still has feelings for you. The way she looks at you...my oh my."

I looked over at Georgie and then turned back to my mom. "What?"

"Do you not know how to say anything other than questions, Blayze?"

"Georgie's not in love with me, Mom."

She folded her arms over her chest. "She is—she simply won't allow herself to admit it. Kind of how you're doing the same thing."

And with that, my mom turned on her heels and headed back into the house. With a wave of her hand she called back, "Got to run. I have lots of pies to make now that I'm two people down."

The entire drive back to my house, I focused on the road. Or, at least, I tried to. I didn't dare look at Georgie. But when she wouldn't wake up when I tried to get her to walk into the house, I had to pick her up and carry her again. She made another weird sound and whispered my name for the second time and my mother's words replayed over and over in my head.

Then there was the kiss.

I shook my head as I carried Georgie into the room she was staying in. It wasn't a kiss. It was a peck. And she was asleep. It was nothing.

After carefully placing Georgie on the bed, I slipped off her shoes and put them on the floor. I pulled back the covers some and covered her, trying not to wake her up. She smiled and nuzzled her face into the pillow.

Damn. She was the most beautiful woman I'd ever laid eyes on. I lifted my hand and softly ran my finger along her jawline.

"Rest easy, sleeping beauty."

She opened her eyes and looked directly at me before smiling so big my breath caught in my throat. For a moment, I couldn't remember how to breathe.

"Blayze."

Smiling, I lifted her hand and kissed the back of it. "Get some sleep, Georgie."

Her eyes searched my face and it seemed like she was going to say something. Instead, she let her gaze drop to my mouth where I ran my tongue over my dry lips and watched as Georgie's mouth opened ever so slightly before our eyes met once again.

"Do you kiss the same?" she asked.

Frowning, I asked, "What do you mean?"

"Do you still kiss how you did when we were younger?"

A small breath of air escaped my mouth as I softly laughed. "I hope I kiss better now."

She grinned, then closed her eyes and drifted back to sleep. I wasn't sure how long I sat there on the side of her bed and stared at her. Hell, I probably would have stayed there all night had someone not gently cleared their throat from the doorway.

Ryan.

I gave him a nod and carefully got up, quietly making my way out of Georgie's room. After hearing the soft click of her door, I headed to the kitchen. Ryan was leaning against the counter with a beer in his hand and one held out for me.

"You texted for me to get here ASAP," he said. "What's the problem?"

I grabbed my beer and motioned for us to head out onto the covered back porch. If it got too cold, I could simply turn on the heat.

Ryan studied me. "You look really confused."

"I am." I sat down in a chair and pushed my fingers through my hair. "My mom seems to think Georgie…"

He waited for me to finish. Did I really want to tell him she thought Georgie was in love with me?

"She seems to think what?"

"That Georgie has feelings for me."

Ryan leaned back in his chair. "And this surprises you?"

I snapped my head up to look at him. "It doesn't surprise you?"

He laughed. "No. Come on, Blayze. The last time you saw the girl, you were caught just shy of having sex with her behind your dad's barn. You said she was the one."

"The one I wanted to lose my virginity to. I wanted it to happen with someone I cared about. Like you and Mindy."

With a slight tilt of his head, he went on. "Come on. I think we both know Georgie has always meant more to you than that. When she never came back to the ranch, you were devastated."

I sighed. "She's doing an interview about Dad and the ranch. I think things need to stay professional between us."

Ryan pressed his beer to his mouth in a sad attempt to cover a smile before he tipped it back and took a drink.

"You know why I can't open myself up to her, Ryan."

It was his turn to sigh. "Blayze, she isn't Lindsay. She isn't going to play you for a fool and use you like Lindsay did. It's pretty clear to me that you have feelings for Georgie too. I see it anytime you're near her."

I stood and walked over to the door that led outside. I nearly pushed through it to breathe in a lungful of cold air.

"Blayze, you uprooted your entire life for a woman you didn't even care about, so I get having a wall up."

"Because she lied to me, Ryan. You would have done the same thing."

"Probably, and yes, she lied. What in the world would Georgie lie to you about? Dude, you've got to let your guard down with someone. Why not let it be her? See where it goes."

"She lives in Dallas."

Ryan stood. "I'm not saying ask her to marry you. Just see where things go."

Turning, I faced him. He smiled and said, "I see it written all over your face, Blayze. You've never looked at any woman the way you look at Georgiana Crenshaw. For someone who loves to take risks, you're really fighting this. Take the wall down, dude. It's time."

I took a long pull from my beer and stepped outside. Before I shut the door, I looked back at Ryan.

"Lindsay destroyed my trust. Georgie has the power to destroy my heart and soul."

Chapter Thirteen

GEORGIANA

I opened my eyes and sat up in bed. I looked at the side table to see that my phone was plugged in. When had I done that? When had we even gotten back to Blayze's house?

Reaching for the phone, I gasped when I saw it was seven in the morning. One sweep of myself confirmed that I was still in the clothes that I'd worn yesterday to go over to…

"Shit! What happened?" My voice trailed off as I flew out of bed.

I swiped my phone and was about to call Lincoln when I saw I had a text from my father.

Dad: Call me as soon as you get this.

Fear seized my chest and my hands shook as I fumbled to hit the screen to call my father.

"Hey, Georgie. How's Montana treating you?"

I blinked a few times, then rubbed my eyes with my other hand. "Dad, you told me to call you as soon as I could. What's wrong?"

He took in a long, deep breath before he let it out. "I spoke with Ron."

Ron Henderson was the new owner of *Sports Monthly*. I didn't know much about the guy except that he used to play professional football.

"Did you ask about the interview with the Shaws and Blayze?"

"Yes."

"Was it a misunderstanding by the editor?"

He paused for entirely too long. "At first Ron claimed that he didn't know anything about the editor telling you to dig into Blayze's past. After a few minutes, I got it out of him. He did know, and he was the one who wanted the information printed in the article. He wants to shake things up with the magazine. When I first approached him about you doing the interview with Brock, he loved the idea. But then this Doug guy was brought on to help change the image of the magazine, and he's the one who came up with it turning into a tell-all article."

"What?" I nearly shouted as I launched myself into the bathroom. I needed a hot shower and to splash some water on my face ASAP. "I knew you had something to do with me getting that job. Dad, I told you I wanted to get opportunities on my own, not with my father's help."

He sighed. "I know, I'm sorry, sweetheart."

"That doesn't matter right now. Back to Ron. Did you tell him I wouldn't do it?"

"I did. He asked me to talk to you about it. When I told him I wouldn't, he informed me that they'd never hire you again and would never work with me again as well."

I nearly stumbled back. My father had been contributing articles for *Sports Monthly* ever since he retired from bull riding. He'd started off writing guest columns and doing some interviews and had worked himself up to becoming one of their top contributors.

"He said that. Dad, you've been writing for them for years, how could they do that.?"

"Georgiana, I don't even care. I am not going to be involved with the magazine if they're going to turn into a gossip rag. I told him he was a worthless piece of shit. Sweetheart, he was looking for a reason to not work with you. He figured if you wrote an article that leaked information about Blayze, the Shaws would be livid and he would be justified in taking action against you. He planned on pinning it all on you."

Now I was going to be sick. "If he didn't want me to write for the magazine, why not tell me that in the first place? Why not turn down your suggestion of the interview?"

"I think there were a few different reasons. One, he didn't want to make the magazine seem like it wouldn't work with a female journalist. Two, he knew you were close to the family at one point, maybe he thought by using you he'd get the information he wanted. Unfortunately, I'm the one who planted the idea there for him in the first place."

I closed my eyes and sank down to the ground.

"Come home, sweetheart. You've got other work and you still have *Vogue,* and also that fashion magazine in London that adores you. Spend time working on the book you want to write. I told Ron and Kathleen you wouldn't be giving them the story now anyway. Neither one seemed surprised. Ron actually seemed relieved, the bastard."

Trying not to let my thoughts spin out of control, I counted to ten as I squeezed my eyes shut even tighter. I needed to let the sports thing go. I'd lost the passion for it, anyway, if I was being honest with myself. I knew I should leave Montana, but I wasn't ready to yet. I had set out to write an article on the Shaws, and I was determined to do it, even if I did have to pitch it to another magazine. I wasn't ready to leave Blayze. Not yet.

"Georgiana?"

"I'm not leaving. Brock and the rest of the family think I'm here to do an article about the ranch, and that's what I'm going to do."

"The magazine won't print it if it's not what they want."

"That's fine. If they don't print it, they don't print it. I'm not leaving and giving them the satisfaction of running me off."

My father was quiet for a few moments. "I'm proud of you, sweetheart. Write the article how you see fit. I'm sure you can find a magazine that wants it if *Sports Monthly* passes."

Nodding, I said, "I will. I do need to let the family know what's happened. I owe them that much. If Brock says I can still stay and write the article, then I'll finish it and pitch it somewhere else."

"That's my girl. If you need anything, you let me know, okay?"

"I will, Dad. Thank you for everything."

"Tell everyone I said hi. As a matter of fact, your mother wants to come out and visit the ranch soon."

"You should! Especially now that you have the free time."

Dad was on the verge of retiring in a few months, so I was glad he and my mom could finally start traveling like they had always talked about.

He laughed. "We might do that. Talk soon, angel."

"Bye, Dad."

After hitting End, I stripped out of yesterday's clothes and stood under the hot water for what felt like forever. I dried my hair, put a bit of mascara on, and then pulled on some jeans and a sweater. After slipping on my cowboy boots, I made my way to the kitchen only to find it empty. One peek out front and in the garage told me that Blayze was already gone. He had made coffee, though, so bless him for that.

I poured some in a Yeti cup, grabbed my computer and bag and the notebook I had already started making notes in, and headed out to the rental. I wasn't about to let some man dictate how my career would end. Hell to the no. I'd find Brock and tell him everything, then I'd let him decide if he wanted me to continue doing a story or not.

Seven hours later, I barely managed to crawl my way up Blayze's porch and over to one of the rocking chairs before I nearly collapsed into it. To say I was exhausted was an under-statement. I'd spent the entire day following Brock and Blayze around as they'd worked the ranch. I'd truly wanted to see what running a large cattle and grain ranch was like, so I had dove into it with them. They never stopped working. After a good solid five hours of physical work, they'd both retired to their offices and I'd found myself sitting in a stable again. I'd needed the peace and quiet and, honestly, I'd been hoping that Blayze wouldn't find me.

After figuring out what to say to Brock this morning, I'd made my way over to his house. I'd told him everything—including that I was looking for a new magazine to pitch—and he'd told me he wanted me to stay on. We'd both agreed that I needed to tell Blayze everything, and I'd promised I would. I knew he would probably hate me for it, but it wasn't something I could keep a secret anymore.

Kicking off one boot, I groaned. "No wonder all the men around here are in shape." I pulled off my other boot and let it fall onto the porch. The cool air felt good on my swollen feet as I pulled my socks off and stuffed them into my boots.

The sound of Blayze's truck coming up the drive had me sitting up a bit straighter. He parked behind my rental and jumped out like he had the energy of a five-year-old. I'd gone over what I wanted to say to him a million times today. Nothing seemed to sound right. No matter what I told him, I knew he'd have a hard time trusting me because I hadn't told him right at the very beginning.

As Blayze made his way up the porch, he frowned. "You look tired. Are you okay, Georgie?" He looked like he was trying to hide a smile, but he was clearly failing at it.

I shot him a dirty look. "I'm exhausted, Blayze. I think I've done more manual labor today than I have my entire life. And my grandparents owned a horse ranch. Plus, I'm mentally exhausted."

"A horse ranch," he said with a laugh.

"For your information"—I started to rub my foot—"I was responsible for mucking out the stalls. I had to groom my own horse as well and saddle them up anytime we went for a ride. I wasn't raised like a princess."

He winked. "No wonder you were always better at brushing the horses than I was."

Laughing, I replied, "You were obsessed with bulls back then. And girls."

"Nah." He sat down and motioned for me to lift my leg. "Give me your foot."

"You don't have to—"

"Give it to me," he demanded.

Doing as he asked, I lifted it into his lap. The moment he started to massage my foot, I knew I was in big trouble. Blayze's hands on me were dangerous for my lady parts. Add in a massage, and I was sure to give him anything he wanted.

Plus, I really needed to talk to him about the article. I was about to speak when he beat me to it.

"I was obsessed with bulls, but not girls," he said.

"What?" I let out a disbelieving laugh. "You flirted with any woman, young or old. Those big blue eyes and that dimple made all the girls swoon."

"Did they make you swoon?" he asked with a smirk.

My faced heated. "Yes."

"Do they still?" He flashed me a smile so big I instantly looked at his dimple, then up into his eyes.

"I'm not that naïve anymore."

He let out a humorless chuckle. "No, you're not."

"But," I softly said, "when you wink at me, it makes my stomach flutter, so I guess I do sorta still swoon."

That confession seemed to take him completely off guard. He froze, then seemed to realize that he wasn't massaging my foot anymore. He cleared his throat and started moving those skillful hands again.

Moaning, I dropped my head back. "You have no idea how good that feels."

He did something with his thumb to my arch, and I nearly came out of my chair. It hurt but felt so good. Okay, I really had to tell him about the article.

"Are you still the same kind of kisser?" he asked.

Lifting my head, I stared at him. "Excuse me?"

"Last night, after I laid you in your bed, you asked if I kissed the same as I did before."

I was positive my eyes went as wide as saucers, a horrified expression filling my face. "I asked that? I thought I dreamt that."

"You dream about me, huh?" he asked teasingly.

"I was exhausted, Blayze. I'm so sorry."

"For what? The question, or the kiss in my truck?"

I instantly pressed my fingers to my lips, and his eyes tracked my movements.

"We kissed?"

He shook his head. "No, I was putting your seatbelt on and *you* kissed *me*. It was more like a peck. Then you fell back asleep and drool started to come out of the side of your mouth, so I'm not really counting that one."

I pulled my foot away and stood. "It did not!"

Sitting back in the rocker, he laughed. A belly rumbling kind of laugh. "You did. It was all caked on the side of your face when I carried you up to your room."

"You…you…you! Ugh!"

He raised both brows. "Yes?"

I dropped back in my seat again. "I did wake up with drool on my face and pillow. It was gross. I must have been sleeping hard."

"All that reading the night before."

I snapped my head over to look at him. When our eyes met, I wondered if he felt the crackle in the air between us like I did.

Tell him now, Georgie, before he distracts you again!

"Do you want to find out, Georgie?"

I swallowed hard. I knew what he was asking but decided to play dumb.

"Find out what?"

"If I kiss the same."

Blinking rapidly, I looked around.

He lowered his voice a bit. "No dads this time to catch us."

My face instantly warmed.

Blayze stood, and I couldn't tear my eyes off of him. His gaze was heated, and his deep blue eyes looked like deep pools of water in the ocean.

"You want to kiss me," I said.

"Is that a statement or a question, Georgie?"

Shaking my head, I let out a nervous laugh while he stood in front of me and held his hands out for mine. By their own force, my hands lifted to rest in his. He tugged me up and my body crashed against him.

Trying to find my voice, I whispered, "It's a question."

His brows drew down in surprise. "Why wouldn't I want to kiss you?"

I opened my mouth, but my thoughts jumbled around in my head. When I finally found the words to speak, it didn't sound like my voice. I lacked confidence, and I hated that. But there was something about this man. I'd never stopped thinking about him for all these years. Never stopped wondering how different our lives would have been if we'd never gotten caught.

"You have so many beautiful women throwing themselves at you, Blayze. Why would you want to kiss a woman like me?"

His eyes softened, and he put his hand on the side of my face. I leaned into it, loving the way his skin felt on mine. I closed my eyes for a moment before opening them. My breath caught in my throat at the intense look he was giving me.

"Because you're the first woman I ever wanted to kiss. And every time I see you, I can hardly think of anything other than kissing you."

Air slipped out of my lips. My chest warmed, and a rush of sensations filled my entire body. I was hot then cold. I was filled with lust and want, yet so confused how I actually felt about Blayze. Our sexual attraction was over the top, no doubt about that. I had thought maybe it was one-sided, but his words and the way he looked at me said it was mutual. Did I want to go down this road with him? We were two totally different people from two totally different worlds. Not to mention the article, and what Blayze would think of it. If we gave into our feelings, it could change everything. It *would* change everything.

"Maybe you should…"

My words floated away as I stared at his perfect bow shaped mouth. His perfectly soft and plump bottom lip had my heart beating ten times too fast.

"I should what, Georgie?"

My body relaxed, and I realized I was leaning into him. He cupped my face in his hands, looking directly into my eyes. "Tell me," he demanded softly.

"You should kiss me. Yes, you should kiss me right now."

He smiled, and I felt my knees go weak. I reached up and held onto his arms.

"I'm going to kiss you now, Georgie."

"Oh, God," I breathed out. "That's what you said the first time you kissed me."

And then he was there. His mouth pressed to mine. It was soft at first. Then his tongue swept over my lips, and I opened to him. The moment our heat mingled, the kiss deepened. He tasted like mint and honey. The kiss turned passionate, and I wrapped my arms around his neck, reaching up to feel more of the kiss. More of him.

So many nights I laid in bed and thought about those moments behind that barn. The kiss. The feeling of his hand between my legs. Thought about what it would have been like if our fathers hadn't caught us. Thought about what it would have been like to give myself to Blayze.

"Georgie," he gasped as he pulled away long enough for us to catch our breaths. Then he was kissing me again.

I sliced my fingers through his thick dark hair and tugged, causing him to moan and open to me more. I was greedy. I wanted more. God, I wanted so much more.

Blayze lifted me up, and I wrapped my legs around his waist. He moved to the front door and pulled his mouth away long enough to see what numbers he was punching into the key-pad. As soon as the door opened, his mouth was back on mine.

Then I was on the sofa. I lifted his shirt up and over his head. His hand went up my shirt, pushing my bra out of the way to expose my breasts to him. He moaned at the sight and took my nipple into his mouth.

I cried out his name as I arched my body into him. "Blayze! Oh God."

He sucked harder, then gently bit down before he pulled away and blew on my nipple. My body was on fire. The pulse between my legs was like nothing I'd ever experienced before.

"I want you," I said as I fumbled with the buttons on his jeans.

"Fuck, Georgie. Not on the sofa. I'm not making love to you for the first time in my living room."

Before I could answer, the sound of a vehicle pulling up and a horn honking caused us both to freeze. Blayze stared down at me and I looked up at him. I could tell he was as dis-appointed as I was.

"It's Morgan," he said. "She told me she was coming over. Tonight is my grandparents' wedding anniversary. I totally for-got about it."

I closed my eyes and groaned as Blayze quickly got off me and reached for his shirt. I sat up and adjusted my bra.

He stretched his hand down and helped me up. With a smile, he pulled me to him and kissed me once again. He stepped away just in time, leaving me lightheaded as the front door opened and Morgan came bounding in.

"Hey, guys!"

Glancing between the two of us, Morgan stopped and looked at me. Her eyes swept over my disheveled state.

"You look…"

"Tired?" I said with a laugh. "I've been working on the ranch with your father and brother. I think their goal is to kill me."

Morgan laughed. "You poor thing. We've got a lot to do before tonight!"

Looking at her, confused, I asked, "What do you mean?"

Morgan turned and faced Blayze, who had walked over to his small bar and was standing behind it as he made himself a drink. I was positive he was over there trying to hide the bulge in his jeans.

"You didn't tell her that Grams and Granddad invited her tonight?"

"Invited me where?" I asked.

Blayze downed the glass of whiskey, then set it on the bar. "I just got home, Morgan. I've barely had a chance to even talk to Georgie yet."

Spinning around to face me, Morgan looked like a kid in a candy store.

"My grandparents are celebrating their sixtieth wedding anniversary today. I brought a couple of dresses I want to wear, and I was hoping to get your thoughts on them. I thought we could get ready together."

"Morgan, Georgie might be too tired to go."

I shook my head. If it meant spending more time with Blayze, then I was down for it. "I'm not too tired. I love an excuse to get dressed up."

Clapping her hands together, Morgan let out an excited scream. "Great! I'll go get my stuff."

The front door opened and shut and I turned to look at Blayze. We both smiled.

"I'm sorry," he said. "We can pick this up later if you…"

"Yes. I do…want to do that. With you. Later."

He laughed. "Good. Because I want to do that with you too."

My face heated.

"You're sure you're not too tired for the party?" he asked.

"I promise." I bit my lip, suddenly remembering the article. Would he feel more betrayed now that we had kissed? "I need to talk to you about something, though."

He nodded. "Okay. We can talk later."

"Okay, but it's important and..." I looked down at the floor then back up at him. Before I could say anything else, Morgan burst back into the room.

"We're totally the same size, and I have four dresses in here," Morgan announced as she held up a dress bag.

Blayze chuckled. "I thought you said you brought two."

"Two for me, and two for Georgie. I figured she wouldn't have anything formal with her. Come on, Georgie! You're in my room, right?"

"I am. Let me grab my boots off the front porch."

Morgan stopped and looked at me. "Why are they on the front porch?"

"My feet were killing me and the cold air felt good on them."

Morgan chuckled. "Life on a ranch!"

"Leave them. I'll take care of it," Blayze said as he walked past me, his eyes practically piercing mine.

"Thanks," I said softly, wishing his mouth was on my breasts again. He must have been able to read my mind because he raised a single brow, and I had to look away.

"Are you two done giving each other fuck-me eyes?"

"Morgan!" Blayze and I said in unison.

She shrugged. "What? It was *so* obvious when I walked in. The heavy breathing. Blayze making a beeline to the bar. His T-shirt on inside out and your kiss-swollen lips," she said as she pointed at me. "Please. I totally interrupted something. Don't deny it."

"Fine, we won't deny it," Blayze said.

I turned to look at him, my mouth agape.

He shrugged. "What? She clearly knows, so why pretend?"

Morgan smiled. "Oh my God! Are you two sleeping together?"

"No!" I quickly answered.

"Not yet, thanks to you," Blayze said.

My face instantly felt like it was on fire.

Morgan let out a little squeal. "I know what dress you're wearing tonight, Georgiana! Come on! We need to get you showered and not looking like…death."

I jerked my head back as Blayze laughed. When Morgan turned and headed upstairs, I started after her, only to have Blayze pull me back to him and kiss me once more. And yet again, I melted into him.

He drew back slowly. "Don't wear panties tonight."

My eyes went wide. "What?"

With a wink, he headed out the door to the front porch.

"Georgiana!" Morgan yelled. "We have work to do!"

Chapter Fourteen

BLAYZE

"Morgan!" I called out as I looked at the clock for the sixth time. "We're going to be late!"

"One second! Beauty takes time, Blayze!"

Rolling my eyes, I walked over to the bar and poured myself a small drink of bourbon. When I heard Morgan clear her throat, I glanced up and smiled.

"When did you grow up to be such a beautiful young woman?"

She blushed. "You have to say that, you're my brother."

"I don't have to say it, and being your brother doesn't make it any less true. You look beautiful, squirt."

Morgan did a spin. "I know I brought my own dresses, but isn't it beautiful? It belongs to Georgiana. She bought it in Paris, Blayze. Paris! And she's letting me wear it. This is all embroidered lace with a handkerchief hem. The shoes are mine! They match the dress perfectly, don't they?"

I swept my gaze over my sister, taking in her champagne-colored lace dress. It looked stunning on her, and I made a note to make sure I saw it on Georgie at some point.

"Georgie wasn't going to wear it?" I asked.

Morgan smiled. "She wanted me to. She's wearing one of the dresses I brought. It's an off-the-shoulder chiffon dress I bought a few months ago when Mom and I went to New York. Wait until you see her."

"I'm sure she looks…"

I trailed off as Georgie started down the steps. My eyes nearly popped out of my head at the sight before me. The dress was light blue and fit her body perfectly. I loved that she had curves, and I couldn't wait to get my eyes on the rest of her naked body. I wanted to study every inch of her.

Morgan cleared her throat and pretended to hold up a microphone as she said, "And up next, we have Georgiana, who is wearing a Mac Duggal dress in dusty blue. This A-line, off-the-shoulder bodice that's embellished with lace and crystals fits Ms. Georgiana like a glove. It helps that she has a Marilyn Monroe-style rocking body, I might add."

I glanced over at Morgan, who was smiling at Georgie. "Notice how the bottom flares out and is longer in the back. It gives it that perfect elegant touch."

"I do believe fashion is your calling, Morgan," Georgie said. "And if I have a Marilyn Monroe body, then so do you. This dress fits me like a glove."

Morgan laughed. "I love clothes, and I cannot believe we're exactly the same size in everything! My boobs could be a bit bigger, though."

I pretended not to hear my sister talk about her breasts while I looked at Georgie.

"Georgie, you are stunning," I said. "Beautiful. You're gorgeous."

She blushed and tugged a strand of hair behind her ear. The sides of her hair were pulled up in some intricate way, while the rest of it flowed around her shoulders in large curls. She had on a bit more makeup than usual, and the way she had it done showed off her green eyes.

"Wow, you got a *gorgeous* from him," Morgan said. "I only got a *beautiful*."

"You're beyond beautiful, Morgan," I stated as Georgie gave me a soft smile.

I walked up to her and picked up a large curl, twirling it around my finger. "I like your hair down. You always wear it up."

She dug her teeth into her bottom lip. "It's easier to wear it up."

I took in her creamy skin, wanting to reach down and kiss her exposed cleavage. Fuck if I wasn't hard as a rock just from looking at her.

Morgan cleared her throat. "Um, as much as I love seeing my brother dumbfounded by a woman like this, we really need to get going or we'll be late."

Georgie let out a puff of air as she shook her head. "You're too sweet, Morgan. I'm sure Blayze has been left speechless by other women before."

Morgan spoke before I could. "Nope. Not that I've ever seen."

When Georgie's eyes lifted and met mine, I forgot how to breathe.

She bit her lip again. "We should probably go."

I nodded. "Right. We don't want to be late."

After making our way outside, I made my way over to my truck and helped Morgan into the backseat and then Georgie in before heading over to the driver's side.

"Where are we going for dinner?" Georgie asked.

"The country club," Morgan said. "We hardly ever go there. Only for special occasions."

"I didn't know there was a country club in Hamilton," Georgie stated.

I nodded. "My great-grandfather founded it with a bunch of other ranchers. They added a golf course some years later, but my dad and uncles never use it. Granddad does now that he's fully retired."

"So does Grams. She picked up golf a few months back and is already better than Granddad. Pisses him off," Morgan said with a chuckle.

Georgie let out a soft laugh. "I bet. My father loves to golf now. I think he traded his love of bull riding for golfing a while ago."

"Do you golf?" I asked.

Georgie huffed. "No way. If I have any spare time, and I'm at my folk's place, you'll find me riding my horse."

"A woman after my own heart!" Morgan said.

Morgan and Georgie talked the rest of the way into town. When I pulled up to the valet at the country club, they'd already made plans to go riding the next morning. Morgan didn't have classes the rest of the week, and therefore didn't need to be back in Missoula for a bit.

As we walked in, Morgan leaned over and said something to Georgie that made her start to cough.

"I'm just giving you fair warning."

I took Georgie's elbow to slow her down. "What did Morgan say to you?"

Her cheeks turned bright red. "She said your mom was most likely going to think we had sex earlier because my face is glowing."

I shot a look over at my sister, who was now walking ahead of us. She had almost reached the private room my father had reserved.

"Damn you, Morgan!" I whisper-shouted at her as she lifted her hand and wiggled her fingers.

I looked down at Georgie. "Don't pay any attention to her."

She stopped walking and turned to face me. "I have to say this before I explode. You look hot in that suit, Blayze."

I looked down at my black suit, then at Georgie again. "It's not hot at all. I might get a little warm once we get into the room, but I think I'll be okay."

Her mouth fell open before snapping shut. Then she laughed. "I mean you look good. Like I want to drag you into a room and, and…"

I rose a brow. "And what?"

A shy look appeared on her face, but she surprised me by finishing her sentence. "And finish what we started earlier."

"I could see if they have any rooms available."

She let a bubble of nervous laughter slip free. "What? Sneak away from the party to have sex?"

I shook my head. "If I get you naked in a bed, I plan on being there all night."

A voice cleared next to us, and we both jumped.

Morgan was standing there with a wide grin on her face.

"I knew it!

She turned on her heels and started back toward the entrance of the room.

I took Georgie's arm, and we followed. "It's going to cost me a fortune to keep her mouth shut."

"We can split it."

We both looked at each other and laughed. No one had ever been able to make me laugh like Georgie could.

The moment we walked into the room, all eyes were on us. The first person I saw was Ryan, staring at Morgan like he'd never seen a woman before. Poor bastard had it bad for my sister. And she looked at him in the same way.

As we walked farther into the room, Georgie asked in a low voice, "Are Morgan and Ryan a thing?"

"Aw, you noticed that, too, huh?"

"How can I not? His jaw about hit the floor when she walked in, and she's one to talk about fuck-me eyes."

I chuckled. "They're not a thing."

"Well, someone should tell them they could heat up a room with that spark between them."

Georgie took two glasses of champagne off a waiter's tray and handed me one. "All she talked about was Ryan while we were getting ready. Of course, it was more like, 'Ryan thinks he knows it all.' Or, 'Ryan told me I couldn't barrel ride, so I had to prove him wrong. Ryan thinks I'm still a little girl.'"

"Really?" I asked as I watched Morgan walk up to Ryan. They exchanged a few words and Morgan walked off, Ryan following her every move.

"Guess it'll be left up to fate," I said.

I turned back to Georgie, hit with the sudden urge to ask her to stay in Hamilton. Was it fate that brought her back to me? Would it really be so cruel and take her from me again?

"What's wrong?" Georgie asked.

I shook my head and forced a smile. "Nothing. I was just thinking that you're right."

She lifted the glass to her lips and said, "I almost always am."

"Blayze, sweetheart!"

We both turned to see my grandmother walking toward us.

"Hey, Grams," I said as I gave her a kiss on the cheek. "Happy anniversary."

She beamed up at me. "Thank you, sweet boy." Then she turned to Georgie. "My goodness. I remember you as a little girl with pigtails running after the boys demanding that they let you play cowboy—and now look at you. You look like a movie star!"

Georgie smiled and leaned in to kiss my grandmother. "Happy anniversary, Stella. You look beautiful."

"Thank you, dear. The two of you together look stunning. What cute babies you'd make."

"Grams," I warned.

On her face was a mockingly innocent expression. "What? I'm only saying that when the two of you walked in here, everyone's heads turned. Then the whispers started."

"Whispers?" Georgie asked.

Grams gave me a heartfelt look. "This young man has been throwing out compliments to women his whole life, it seems. You know I practically raised him when his father was on the circuit."

Georgie nodded. "I did know that."

"Well, the boy could toss out compliments and flirt like it was second nature. But I can honestly say, I've never seen him smile at a woman the way he smiles at you."

"Oh," Georgie said as she looked down at her drink and blushed.

I sighed. "Grams, please."

"What? I'm simply stating a fact. You've had women throw themselves at you nearly your entire adult life, but I've never seen your eyes as full of happiness as they were when you walked in with Georgiana."

"Okay, Mom. Don't embarrass the boy."

I nearly hugged my father for stepping in and putting a stop to Grams' speech.

"Psh, I'm only speaking the truth. Oh, look, Linda and Louie are here!"

And just like that, Grams was off.

"Thanks, Dad," I said as I reached for his hand to shake it. He pulled me in for a quick hug and a slap on the back. Then he turned to Georgie.

"Georgiana, you're stunning this evening. Not as beautiful as my wife, but a close second."

"What about Morgan?" I asked.

"Okay, you're a close third behind my beautiful wife and daughter."

"Nice save," I said.

He nodded and held his hand out to Georgie. "Do me the honor?"

"I'd love to," she replied as she handed me her drink. "Do you mind?"

"Not at all."

I watched my father whisk Georgie onto the dance floor.

Frank Sinatra's "The Way You Look Tonight" started, and I couldn't have torn my eyes off of Georgie if I tried.

"She has certainly grown up to be a beautiful woman."

I nodded as I turned to my mother and kissed her on the cheek. "Mom, you look beautiful."

She beamed. "And you look as handsome as ever. You seem to be happy about Georgiana being here now."

With a half shrug, I replied, "I never minded her being here. I minded her writing about me."

"Well, you don't have to worry about that anymore."

I gave her a questioning look. Before I could ask what she meant, she put her hand on my arm.

"I know how fiercely you've guarded your heart, but the

way you look at her reminds me of the way your father looks at me."

I pulled my head back some. "Mom, I'm not in love with Georgie. There's a physical attraction there, sure, but I haven't seen her in years, and she's only been here a few weeks."

My mother's mouth pressed into a tight line. Then she patted my arm before placing her hand on the side of my face. "I want you to be happy, Blayze. You deserve someone who will make you so unbelievably happy—like your father has for me."

Even though my mother wasn't my biological mom, she never once treated me any differently than Morgan and Hunter. In fact, she was probably more protective of me than of my siblings. And I loved her so much for that. She was the only mother I had ever known and the one woman whom I knew would never let me down.

I leaned over and kissed her cheek. "I love you, Mom. And someday it will happen when it's supposed to happen."

She nodded. "That day may be sooner than you think, Blayze Shaw. If you'd let down that wall you've built. Remember, I now have the mother power."

Before I had a chance to respond, my father and Georgie appeared.

"There's my beautiful wife," Dad said as he leaned down and kissed Mom.

My mother gave Georgie a huge grin. "Georgiana, you are stunning in that dress. And the one you let Morgan wear—my goodness, it's breathtaking. She said you got it in Paris?"

Georgie nodded in excitement. This was clearly her element. Fashion. Why was she writing for a sports magazine when this topic made her entire face light up?

"I did. During fashion week. I was covering the designer for *Vogue*."

"Well, at least you can focus on that now," Mom said with a laugh.

Georgie drew in a long breath and then exhaled. "Yes."

What did that mean?

"Over the last few months, I've discovered my heart is really more in fashion."

Dad and Mom both nodded. Okay, then why were we doing this interview if Georgie wasn't interested in doing sports writing?

"Does your dad do any writing for *Sports Monthly* anymore?" I asked.

Georgie paused. "My father left the magazine recently. There have been some changes that neither of us are on board with."

"What kind of changes?" I asked.

She looked directly into my eyes. "The kind I'm not comfortable with."

I felt myself growing angry. Was someone at the magazine making Georgie do something she didn't want to do?

"Well, good for you, standing up for what you believe in, Georgiana," Mom said. "It's a hard area to break into, especially for women. You showed them you can do it, and you should be proud of that and proud that you stood up for what you thought was right."

Georgie reached for my mother's hand. She looked as if she wanted to say so much more. And there was a pained expression on her face.

"Enough of this talk," Dad said. "How beautiful is all of this for Mom and Dad?"

Mom quickly added, "We had so much fun planning this party. Stella was against it at first. She didn't want to make a fuss, but after a little bit of pressure, we were able to talk both of them into it."

Dad smiled as he looked over at Grams and Grandpa dancing. "They both deserve a party to celebrate their love."

"That they do," I agreed.

The song changed, and Dad looked at Mom. "Shall we?"

Placing her hand in my father's, she beamed up at him. "We shall."

Georgie and I watched them make their way to the dance floor where Dad swept my mother into his arms.

"I want that," Georgie said softly. "For a man to look at me like that, with such love and admiration."

My mother's words came back to me. *The way you look at her reminds me of the way your father looks at me.*

I glanced down at Georgie while she stared at my folks dancing.

"Would you like to dance?" I asked, placing the two glasses I still held on a small table.

"I'd love to dance."

I took her hand in mine, laced our fingers together, and walked out onto the dance floor.

Drawing her against my body, I couldn't help but notice how well we fit together. We moved in unison as we danced to a slower song. I pressed my hand tightly against her lower back, and she wrapped her arms around my neck. Our eyes met, and it took everything I had not to kiss her.

When she smiled up at me, something in my chest felt like it cracked open. I wasn't about to try and figure out what in the hell was happening. I wasn't going to think about how my heart felt like it was beating three times harder in my chest. Or how I wanted to ask her to go back to my house and spend the rest of the night in bed. The need to explore her body and learn what she liked nearly had me losing my mind, and I was unable to think clearly.

"Where did you just go?" she asked as she studied my face.

I shook my head. "Nowhere."

Her eyes filled with something that looked like sadness, and I hated seeing that. I wanted to be honest with Georgie. Hell, she deserved honesty. But I also didn't want to ruin tonight.

"I'm not asking you for more than this, Blayze."

"This?" I asked.

"Being with you while I'm here in Montana. I know we both have separate lives, and I know you want a ranch wife and kids."

My heart ached at the idea that Georgie didn't want a family. Or maybe it was that she didn't want it with me.

"You don't want kids?"

Her eyes brightened. "I do," she said with a soft laugh. "I'd like at least two. I hated growing up without any siblings."

"It's not all it's cracked up to be," I said, winking.

She shook her head. "Liar. I see you with Morgan and Hunter. Even with Bradly the other day. You loved helping him with his riding. It was written all over your face."

"You got me there. I do enjoy it. I'm older than Morgan by six years, and I'm thirteen years older than the youngest cousin. I know they look up to me and follow my example, so I try to be as strong as the examples I had growing up."

Her eyes searched my face. "Your dad and your uncles?"

"Yes. If I could be like anyone, I'd want to be like my father. Hell, I'd take being at least ten percent of him."

"You are like Brock. In more ways than you think, Blayze. Watching the two of you together has been fascinating. You move the same. Think in the same way. Do you know how many times you both acted in unison without even speaking while you worked side by side today? And your father is clearly so proud of you."

I let out a humorless laugh. "I'm not sure about that. I think he wanted me to follow in his footsteps."

She gave me a confused look. "You have."

"No," I said with a shake of my head as I looked over the people dancing until I found the man I was talking about. "Bull riding. When I gave it up in college, everyone said it was because I was too afraid. That wasn't it at all."

"Then why did you give up bull riding? And don't tell me it was because you wanted to run the ranch."

I looked back down at her. "That was part of the reason. I'll tell you the other one later. I don't want to ruin tonight."

Her brows drew together, and for a moment she looked like she was going to ask me another question. Instead, she dropped her head down to my chest. When the song was over, I took her hand and led us through the crowd.

"The family will all be sitting together," I said.

"Oh, I don't have to sit with the family."

Stopping, I put my hand up to her face. "Yes, you do, Georgie. And you're sitting next to me."

Her tongue came up and swept over her lips as her cheeks turned a beautiful pink.

Dinner seemed to drag on for what felt like hours. There were a lot of stories, laughter, and a few tears. I handed Georgie a napkin when she started to cry during my grandfather's toast to Grams. Truth be told, I teared up myself.

I glanced at my watch and Morgan leaned over. "Just go already. My God, if you look at your watch one more time, Mom is going to notice."

"I can't leave you here, and you know it."

She rolled her eyes. "Yes, you can. Stand up, take the girl's hand, and walk out of here. Jesus, I can practically feel the sexual tension dripping off of you."

I turned and looked at my younger sister. "For fuck's sake, Morgan."

She took a sip of her drink. "I call it like I see it, big bro. How about I ask Mom something, pull her into a deep conversation, and you and Georgiana slip away."

"How will you get back home?"

Glancing down the table, she answered, "I'll ask Ryan or Mindy to drive me."

I looked over to see Ryan talking to Dirk. Mindy was in a deep conversation with Merit, Dirk's wife.

I surveyed the rest of the table. It was clear everyone was in conversation, and if we left, they'd most likely think I was asking Georgie to dance again.

"I owe you," I said to Morgan as I reached under the table and took Georgie's hand. After a small tug, she looked up at me.

"Grab your purse, we're leaving."

Her eyes went wide, and she looked past me at Morgan. Her cheeks flushed, and Morgan chuckled.

"God, you two are so cute. Go!"

We both stood and Georgie reached for her purse as she nodded like I had asked her a question. We headed to the dance floor then weaved in and out of the people. Everyone in Hamilton seemed to be at this anniversary party, and someone was going to see us leave, but in that moment I could not have cared less. Let people talk.

Once we were clear of the room, I pulled Georgie closer to me and we started down the hall toward the lobby of the hotel that was attached to the country club.

"Isn't this cozy."

The sound caused me to freeze, and Georgie stumbled to a sudden stop.

I looked behind me and saw Lindsay standing there.

Fuck.

Without saying a word, I started to walk again. Georgie glanced over her shoulder.

"Not even a hello for your ex—"

I spun around. "Not a fucking word, or you'll hear from my lawyer."

Lindsay flashed an evil smile. "Oh, I forgot about that little piece of paper." She looked at Georgie. "Georgiana Crenshaw. The one who got away."

"I'm sorry?" Georgie asked as she stared at Lindsay with a confused expression.

"You don't know?" Lindsay laughed. "Oh, this is rich, Blayze. The girl who broke your heart and pushed you into the arms of another has no idea you've been pining over her since you were in high school."

Georgie turned and looked at me. "What is she talking about?"

"Nothing. Let's get out of here."

Placing my hand on Georgie's elbow, I turned her around and guided her out the door.

Georgie remained silent, thank God, as I handed the valet my ticket. When my truck pulled up, I looked down at her. "Please don't ask me what Lindsay meant, Georgie. Not tonight."

She gave me a soft smile. "I won't. When you're ready, we'll talk about it."

I cupped her face in my hands and kissed her. "The only thing I want to think about tonight is you and how I'm going to explore every inch of your body."

Her eyes sparkled with desire. "I like the sound of that."

Chapter Fifteen

GEORGIANA

The drive back to Blayze's house seemed to take forever. I wasn't sure why I was so nervous. Okay, that was a lie. I was nervous because this was Blayze. I'd dreamed of him making love to me for way too long. He was my first crush. The first boy who'd ever kissed me. The first boy to ever touch me intimately, and the first boy who'd broken my heart in two. He had the power to do it again, but I wasn't a shy little girl anymore. I was experienced, and I knew exactly what I was doing.

But the moment we slept together, everything would change. There was no way I was even going to write an article now. Not even the original story idea. Something inside me had shifted tonight. The more I was around the Shaw family, the more I realized I didn't want to use them in that way.

The sound of the truck turning off pulled me from my thoughts. I turned and looked at Blayze, who was staring at me with eyes so dark with lust and desire my insides trembled.

"Are you sure?" he asked me.

"I've never been so sure of anything in my life."

He smiled and his dimple appeared, making my stomach tumble.

Blayze got out of the truck and jogged around to my side. He opened the door and reached for my hand, helping me slip out.

After lacing his fingers in mine, we headed into his house and straight to his bedroom. My heart hammered in my chest when I heard the sound of the door shutting behind us.

My eyes scanned the massive king-size bed, and a strange thought hit me. What would it be like to wake up every morning in his arms? In this room, in this bed. What would it be like to be his?

I closed my eyes and pushed away those crazy thoughts. This was for right now, and that was okay. Blayze walked up behind me and pressed his mouth to my neck, kissing me so softly that desire bloomed in every single one of my nerve endings. I was acutely aware of how my body reacted to him.

"You're so beautiful, Georgie," he whispered as he ran his tongue over my skin, then followed the path with light kisses. His teeth grazed my earlobe before he gently bit down on it, causing me to lean back into him and moan.

He pushed his hips into me, allowing me to feel how much he wanted me.

When his hands lifted up to my breasts and squeezed softly, I dropped my head back against his chest. "Blayze," I whispered in a needy voice. "Please."

He started to slowly unzip my dress while I focused on keeping myself upright. I'd never had a man go so slowly, as if he wanted to commit every moment to memory. I did as well. Once I told him I was no longer doing the interview, I'd have to leave the ranch. Tonight might be our only night.

I squeezed my eyes shut. I didn't want to think about that right now. I wanted to be in the moment.

When his fingers came up to my bare shoulders, I jumped. He chuckled and slowly pushed the dress down my arms, allowing it to pool at my feet.

"Christ," he growled. "You're not wearing anything under it."

"You told me not to."

"Fuck, if I'd known you were naked under that dress all night, I would have hauled you up to a room in the country club."

I laughed. "Good thing I didn't tell you."

"Turn around, Georgie."

Doing as he asked, I watched him lick his lip and take in my naked body. He closed his eyes and moaned, and I felt a rush of wetness between my legs.

"You're perfect. So fucking beautiful."

I felt my cheeks burn under his intense gaze.

He took a few steps back and started to undress. All I could do was stand there and watch him. I focused on his hands as he removed one item after another until he stood before me gloriously naked. His body was beyond built. Broad shoulders and a strong chest led into a trim waistline and a six-pack. My eyes locked on his dick. His large shaft jumped against his perfectly fit lower stomach, and I had to concentrate on not drooling. Moving my eyes lower, I was mesmerized by his thick, strong thighs. No wonder he could ride a bull so well.

My gaze lifted to his. "I've never seen a more beautiful body in my entire life."

"I could say the same thing. You're perfect."

I blushed.

"Lie down on the bed, Georgie."

I did as he asked, moving myself up until I was on one of the large down pillows. My breathing doubled as I watched Blayze crawl onto the bed, his mouth and hands exploring my legs while he licked and kissed his way up slowly. He spread my legs apart and placed a kiss on my inner thigh. I let out a groan of pleasure, even as I squirmed and fought not to cover myself. I'd never had a man look at me the way Blayze was. As if this was the first time he'd ever seen a woman naked. I felt like a goddamn queen.

"I could look at you for days and not get enough of you."

I blinked as I watched him. He let out a low growl and looked up. Our eyes met and heat bloomed deep in my stomach.

"I want to taste you."

Swallowing hard, I opened my mouth to speak, but only a small puff of air came out.

"May I?" he asked.

"I've...no one has...I've never had that done before, Blayze."

A wicked smile spread over his face as he kept his eyes fixed on me and leaned down. Never once breaking our connection, he licked through my lips and I gasped, feeling a rush of exotic pleasure.

"Oh God," I panted.

"Did you like that?"

All I could do was nod.

"Then you'll really like what I'm going to do next."

My neck ached as I watched him cover my clit with his mouth, laying his tongue flat over it. He moved his lips in the most wicked of ways, and I'd never felt such pleasure before. He flicked that key bundle of nerves, then licked and sucked.

"Oh my…oh my God!" I cried out.

"Keep watching me, Georgie. I want to see your face when you come on my tongue."

Oh. My. God.

"Blayze," I said on a rush of air.

He started to lick, bite, and suck as my head swam with a feeling I had never experienced before in my life. The things his mouth were doing had me dropping my head back and grasping at his comforter.

"Watch me," he demanded.

Lifting up, I rested on my elbows and watched him feast on me. He was going to ruin me forever.

Then he slipped his fingers inside of me, and I felt my orgasm about to let loose.

"Blayze! Oh God. Yes! Yes! What are you doing to me!" I cried out.

"That's it, baby," he said, pumping his finger in and out before covering my clit with his mouth once again.

Then it happened. The most intense, mindblowing orgasm I'd ever experienced raced through my body. I thought I was going to black out as stars burst behind my closed eyes, and I screamed out his name. I'd never screamed out a man's name before.

He wasn't stopping. He kept licking with his mouth and pumping with his fingers until I found myself trying to get away from him. It was pleasure and torture all in one. God, I'd never experienced anything like it in my life.

"It's too much!" I cried out.

And then he was over me, his body against mine. When I opened my eyes, I was staring into the most stunning blue eyes I'd ever seen. His dark blue eyes pierced my green. I could get lost in that gaze.

"I have a condom on," he whispered before he pressed his mouth to mine.

When? How had he put one on so quickly without me even knowing?

I wrapped my arms around his neck, struck by how tender his kisses were. That and the taste of myself on his tongue nearly had me coming again. Impossible. You couldn't come just from a kiss.

He kissed me like he adored me. When he drew back, he said my name and I knew no man would ever say it with so much passion again. "Georgiana."

God, it was the most erotic thing I'd ever heard. How could my own name turn me on?

Wrapping my legs around him, I tugged him forward. "I want you, Blayze."

He kissed my neck and whispered in my ear, "I *need* to be inside you, but I don't want it to end too soon."

I placed my hand on the side of his face and smiled. "We have all night."

And with that, he pushed inside me and I gasped, flexing my inner walls.

"Fucking hell, Georgie. You're like a goddamn vise."

I giggled. "Kegel exercises."

"Don't do that again, or I'll come before we even start."

Reaching up, I captured his mouth with mine as I attempted to relax and adjust to the fit of him inside of me. It had hurt slightly when he first pushed inside, but the burning sensation quickly faded.

Blayze slowly pulled out then pushed back in.

"You're so wet."

"It's you, Blayze. You make me this way. God, I've wanted you for so long."

He buried his face in my neck. "So have I, Georgie. Fuck, I've dreamed of making love to you."

The confession nearly brought tears to my eyes, and Lindsay's words from earlier flooded my brain.

"The girl who broke your heart and pushed you into the arms of another..."

I felt a tear slip free, and Blayze saw it. He leaned down and kissed it away. "Are you okay?"

"Yes," I managed to get out. "Don't stop, Blayze. Don't stop."

His movements were slow and beautiful as he worshiped my entire body with his. I moved my hands slowly down his back, squeezing his ass when he pushed inside me again.

"More," I demanded. I needed to feel him. I wanted to remember how he felt inside of me for days. "Blayze, I need more...please."

He lifted slightly and brought one of my legs up, opening me wider to him. Then he moved faster. Harder.

I could feel my orgasm building. God, it felt so good. I'd never had sex like this before, and I knew I never would again. Not with any other man.

"Blayze!" I cried out in frustration, my orgasm just out of reach.

He reached down and played with my clit and that was all it took. I exploded around him. My name fell from his lips as he moved faster and harder. His lovemaking quickly turning to fucking. I loved it. I loved all of it.

"I'm coming!" he called out right before he shuddered and came.

When he finally stopped moving, he dropped down over me, keeping most of his weight on his elbows. Our breathing was quick and hard. Sweat glistened off of both of us as we looked into each other's eyes.

"That was…" he started to say before he swallowed and dragged in a long breath of air.

"Amazing."

He nodded. "Magical. I've never experienced lovemaking like that before, Georgie."

My eyes burned as I tried to hold back the tears. I softly ran my finger down the side of his face. "Neither have I."

"I don't want to move, but I need to get this condom off." Blayze rolled off of me. "Don't move. Let me clean up."

All I could do was nod. There was no way I could form words as I laid in the bed, completely relaxed after two mind-blowing orgasms and the best sex of my entire life.

I pressed my hand to my mouth as I smiled and tried to keep from squealing like a little girl. Had it all been a dream? It felt too perfect to be reality. When I brushed my fingers against my kiss-swollen lips, and felt the soft abrasions on my skin from Blayze's day-old beard, I sighed.

The sound of the water turning off caused me to turn. I watched Blayze walk out of the bathroom naked, completely comfortable in his own skin. He crawled onto the bed and pulled me against his body, holding onto me like he was afraid I would run.

"I need you to know that I don't do this often, Georgie. I know I've always had a reputation as a flirt, but I don't make it a habit to sleep around. I learned a lesson a long time ago that taught me to guard myself—and that included sex."

Turning in his arms, I lay on my side and faced him. "What kind of lesson?"

He closed his eyes and exhaled before he met my gaze. "The day at the barn, when we were caught and you were so upset?"

I nodded. "I was embarrassed more than anything, Blayze. I never regretted it, and I'm sorry I said that."

His eyes drifted down to my mouth and then back up. "I was hurt by your words and young and stupid. You already know I went to that party and slept with Lindsay."

I nodded.

"I'm so sorry I hurt you like that. As an adult, there were so many times I wanted to reach out to you and tell you what a complete asshole I was. When you left without saying goodbye and never returned any of my calls or texts, I let anger dictate my feelings for you."

"We were both young. I do know that if we hadn't been caught, I would have easily given myself to you, Blayze. I wanted you to be my first, even though I said those hurtful words to you."

He ran his finger down my cheek. "I wish I could go back in time and have you be my first."

I laughed under my breath. "My first time wasn't how I pictured it would be either."

"Was he not gentle?" Blayze asked as he tucked a piece of hair behind my ear. I reached up and took out the hair tie that had been holding part of my hair up. Blayze ran his fingers through my curls, then kissed the tip of my nose.

"He was inexperienced like me. We fumbled a lot, and it wasn't anything I was going to go home and write in my journal about. It was prom night, my junior year. His name was Scott, and I liked him. Didn't love him, and he didn't love me. We never promised each other anything. I trusted him, and he trusted me. It hurt like a son of a gun, and he came way too soon. I think he might have pumped three times and then bam. He was done. He was sweet about it, though, and made sure I at least had an orgasm. He used his hand, and I had to show him what felt good."

"I hate him."

Laughing, I asked, "Why?"

"I hate every man who's ever touched you or made love to you."

I shook my head. "There haven't been that many. Three to be exact. And what we just did felt like making love. The other times felt like sex. I wasn't in love with any of them. We dated, it felt like something we should do, and that was that. I didn't date Mitch or Pete for long. I never felt connection with them. I cared for them, but…"

My voice trailed off. When I looked at him, he had a pained expression on his face.

"That night with Lindsay, the moment it was over, I knew I had made the biggest mistake of my life."

Propping my head up on my hand, I asked, "Why?"

He cleared his throat and rolled over onto his back to stare up at the ceiling.

"I started riding bulls more after that summer. My father said something was fueling me to push myself to ride more and more. To be better. I'm not sure if he was right or not. I remember being really angry with myself. With you, my dad, my mom. But when I climbed up on the back of a bull, I was lost to it all. It was just me and the bull, and I had something to prove to myself more than anything. I already knew my dad was proud of me. But I wanted to see how good I was."

"Did the anger wear off? Is that why you stopped riding?"

Blayze shook his head. "No. During college, when I could come home and help on the ranch, I found myself longing to be here more and more. I love this place, and it had always been my plan to run it alongside my dad and uncles. Bull riding became second in my life, and the ranch moved to number one. I decided to stop riding and focus on finishing up school so I could get back to the ranch."

"So you quit bull riding to ranch? That's the only reason?"

His eyes met mine. "I still did some riding every now and then. It was kind of hard to get rid of the itch to ride. I did some benefit rides, and a few times I did some local stuff. There was a lot of pressure for me to get back on the circuit, and I'll admit I was thinking about it. Then it all changed one night."

"What happened?"

"I was at a party and Lindsay was there. She'd been dating this bull rider named Lane West."

"Lane West?"

He nodded. "Yeah, he was on the Unleash the Beast Tour for a bit, but got bumped back down to the Velocity Tour. Anyway, he and Lindsay came up with this grand plan to get me off the tour."

I lifted my head. "What?"

"Lane had no idea I was walking away from the PBR. He considered me a threat. Anyway, I was at this party, pretty fucked up, and drinking my sorrows away."

"Why were you upset?"

Turning his head to look at me, he exhaled. "I saw you in Dallas at a benefit my father was attending. You were with your parents and some guy. He had his arm around you, and at one point he leaned down and kissed you."

I tried to hide my shock. "Pete. That was Pete."

"Well, seeing you all grown up and fucking beautiful on the arm of another guy set me off. I left the dinner and flew home. Hit up a party that next night and Lindsay was there. She came on to me, told me she and Lane had broken up, and we hooked up. Or at least she told me we had because I didn't remember anything the next morning. It was meaningless. I told her all I wanted was sex, and she said that was all she wanted too."

My heart started to hammer in my chest. I had a feeling I knew where his story was going.

"I woke up the next morning in a bed with her next to me. I honestly didn't even remember anything that had happened. I got up, got dressed, and left. Three months later, she was at my door telling me she was pregnant. My entire world turned upside down. Ironically, that day I had decided I was going on the Unleash the Beast Tour. I was going to give it one year before I came back to the ranch. And then here was this woman I honestly didn't like very much telling me she was pregnant and positive that it was my kid. I talked to my parents, and we talked to Lindsay and her parents about getting a paternity test while she was pregnant. But there were some risks involved in that. She swore up and down I had been the only guy she'd slept with during that time period. Something always felt off, though. Especially since I'd blacked out that night."

"What happened next?" I asked.

"Her parents were devastated and ready to disown her. She begged me to marry her right away so that she could save her relationship with them. So, I agreed. Her mother pretty much took over the wedding plans, which was fine by me. My mom, I think, was in a state of shock and knew I didn't love Lindsay— or even like her. My father was devastated, because he didn't want me to end up in a relationship like he'd had with my bio-logical mother. It was all fucked up. The disappointment in my dad's eyes every time he looked at me nearly killed me. A week before the wedding, I got a phone call from someone I used to ride with on the circuit in college. He asked to meet up with me and said it was important. I drove to Billings where he was rid-ing that weekend. We met up, and he dropped a bomb on me."

I held my breath and waited.

"Lane had gotten drunk the weekend before, right after he won an event. He told this friend of mine that he'd managed to make sure I wasn't going to be on the pro circuit. This mutual friend had informed him that I wasn't planning on doing the tour—I had never told him that I'd actually decided to do it for that year. He told me Lane started laughing his ass off. Then said something about how I was about to be played like the fool I was. I dug around, started asking some people close to Lind-say, and ended up connecting with this girl named Wanda. She was a buckle bunny and followed the Unleash the Beast Tour around. She said that Lindsay and Lane asked her to join them one night. It wasn't something she was into, but she had the hots for Lane so she agreed. That night, Lindsay confessed to her that she and Lane had come up with a plan to get me off the upcoming tour so that Lane didn't have to compete against me."

I felt my heart start to pound. "You've got to be kidding me!"

He shook his head. "No, I wish I was. They came up with this plan, and then I just so happened to open the door for them at that party. They saw I was drunk, Lane pretended to leave, and Lindsay slipped something into my beer. Wanda said that Lindsay told her I passed out the moment I hit the bed. She got me undressed, got herself undressed, and then crawled into the bed and waited for me to wake up. She was always planning on lying and telling me that she was pregnant. She knew her parents would be furious and that she could talk me into marrying her because I wouldn't want to disappoint my mother and father. Once we got married, she was planning on faking a miscarriage, then divorcing me and trying to get money from my father to keep quiet about it all."

I gasped and sat up, pulling the cover up to shield my naked upper half. "Holy shit, she lied about it all? But why would your dad pay her to keep quiet?"

I saw the hurt still on his face. It was all I could do to keep from leaving and going to find that skank!

"I have no idea, but their grand plan almost worked. If it hadn't been for that old friend of mine and Wanda, I would have married her."

Reaching for his hand, I wished I could take all of his pain away. I also couldn't help but feel guilty.

"I wish you'd talked to me that night at the benefit," I said. "Pete and I were already broken up. We actually broke up on the way to the party, and he was being a gentleman by still accompanying me."

He slowly shook his head. "You've got to be kidding me."

I frowned and squeezed his hand. "Ugh, I hate Lindsay. I hate her."

Chapter Sixteen

BLAYZE

I could see the anger on Georgie's face and the wheels turning in her head. I would hazard a guess that she was thinking about beating Lindsay's ass.

"Is that why you left her at the altar?" she asked.

I froze. "What?"

Her face went pale as she realized what she'd said.

"How did you know that?"

Georgie sighed. "Wendy, Mindy's sister told me. That night at The Blue Moose, Mindy let it slip that Lindsay was the woman you were arguing with. But that was all she told me."

I stared at her. "Why didn't you tell me you knew?"

She shrugged. "I didn't want you to think I was snooping around in your business. I figured if you wanted to share that part of your life with me, you would."

I believed she was telling me the truth. "Very little people were at the wedding, and it was on the ranch, so it was easy to keep prying eyes out. We only had family and close friends there. I dug a bit more, and it was pretty easy to find out that

Lindsay wasn't pregnant at all. I asked about going to the doctor together, and she gave me one stupid excuse after another. Then I confronted Lane the morning of the wedding. Took a private plane to Tacoma where he was riding that weekend. Told him I knew the truth, and he broke like a cheap piece of furniture. Confessed to the whole fucking plan to get me off the tour and to get money from my family. I threatened him and told him not to tell Lindsay that I knew the truth yet. I wanted to handle her myself. Called my dad from the plane, had him bring his lawyer in, and we drew up a non-disclosure for both Lindsay and Lane to sign."

"Why?"

"I knew I wasn't going to have a future in the PBR because it wasn't really in my heart to follow that path, and I was fine with it. In a way, it was a blessing in disguise. But I knew my brother and Bradly wanted it, and I didn't want stupid family gossip to follow them out on the circuit. My father and uncles worked too fucking hard to build the Shaw brand. I wasn't going to let my mistake ruin that reputation. So I stood there and watched Lindsay walk down the aisle. When she turned to face me, I leaned down and told her Lane confessed everything. Told her to meet me in my father's office, and then I walked away."

"And she met you in there, I'm guessing?"

I nodded. "She did. She admitted that she wasn't pregnant, and that they came up with the plan to get me off the circuit and to try and get money from the family. Since she hadn't actually done anything yet, we couldn't charge her with anything. She signed the non-disclosure, and I told her if I ever saw her anywhere near me or my family again, she'd regret it."

Georgie slowly shook her head. "All so you wouldn't join the tour?"

I nodded. "And money. It was really about the money."

"Blayze, I'm so sorry. What a bitch."

Glancing back up at the ceiling, I said, "After that, I had a really hard time trusting anyone."

"I'm so sorry."

"Why are you sorry?" I asked as I looked over at her.

"You wouldn't have left Dallas if you didn't see me that night."

I laughed and sat up, facing her. "If I had acted like an adult and had come up and spoken with you instead of running off like a wounded pup, then it wouldn't have happened."

"Was that why you were so against me being here?"

I placed my hand on the side of her face. "I was scared to death to see you again, Georgie. No matter how much time has passed, the thought of you here, in my house with me, it just…"

My voice trailed off.

She smiled. "I know; I felt the same. I've thought about you so many times. I even told my parents at one point that I kept comparing all the men I dated to you."

I tugged the comforter down, exposing her breasts to the chilled air. Her nipples instantly got hard. "What do we do now, Georgie? I don't want this to end."

She dug her teeth into her lower lip. "I don't want it to end either, but I live in Dallas, Blayze."

"But you can do your job from anywhere. I would never ask you to give up your work."

Georgie looked away, and I could see the conflict on her face.

"What's wrong?" I put my finger on her chin and drew her gaze back to mine.

"I'm not writing the article anymore."

I frowned. "Because we slept together?"

"No, that's not it at all. The magazine recently sold, and they want to go in a direction I'm not willing to."

"Wow," I said, drawing back some. "Does this mean you're leaving early?"

Her gaze lifted and met mine. "I mean, I do already have my calendar cleared for the next few weeks."

Smiling, I pulled her up onto her knees. "I don't want you to leave, Georgie."

"I don't want to."

I moved until my back was against the headboard. "Then stay."

"Okay," she whispered softly.

"Climb on top of me."

She blushed, and it was the sweetest yet sexiest thing I'd ever seen. "Blayze, there's more. I need to tell you—"

I pulled her into my lap, and we both moaned when her warm pussy hit my already-hard dick.

"Take me inside you, Georgie. Ride me and make yourself come."

Those eyes of hers grew big and round and I loved that I could make her blush like that.

"But…"

"Now, Georgie. Fuck me."

Her mouth fell open slightly as her eyes grew darker. She liked it when I talked dirty to her. I was going to have to remember that.

She lifted, but before I guided myself into her, I pushed two fingers inside and groaned when I felt how wet she was.

With my hands on her hips, I guided her down until she'd taken me completely. "Are you okay?"

She nodded. "A bit sore. I haven't had sex in a while before all of this."

"Do you want to stop?"

"No!" she quickly said.

I slid my hand around her neck and pulled her mouth to mine. With her hands on my chest, she started to move.

"Blayze," she whispered softly. "I need to tell you what the magazine wanted from me. What they wanted me to write."

I pressed my mouth to hers. "Later. The only thing you need to do right now is come."

It didn't take her long to find the spot that gave her the most pleasure. She pushed up and moved, and the way her tits were bouncing forced me to have to bite down on the inside of my cheek so I wouldn't come.

"Touch yourself, Georgie."

She brought her hands up to her breasts, cupping them before she found each nipple and started to play with them. Christ, I was about to come.

"I'm so close, Blayze."

"Yes. Take it, Georgie. Fall apart on my cock."

She rode me faster, then dropped her head back down and took my mouth in hers. The kiss was raw and passionate. Then I felt her squeeze around me, and I knew she was about to come.

"Blayze!" she cried out as she ripped her mouth away. Her eyes met mine, and I watched her fall apart. Not a moment later, I was calling out her name, coming so hard I nearly passed the fuck out.

Georgie dropped her head to my chest and dragged in air.

I knew I needed to figure out a way to keep her in my life, and I only had a few weeks left to do it.

When we could both finally breathe without sounding like we'd ran a marathon, she lifted up and looked at me with a stunned expression.

"Blayze, we didn't use a condom."

My hands, which I had been moving over her body in gentle strokes, froze. "Are you on birth control?"

She bit down on her lower lip and nodded.

I let out the breath I didn't even realize I was holding. "I'm so sorry, Georgie. I got so caught up in everything—I'm so sorry. I'm clean, I swear to you."

When she gave me that innocent smile, I felt my dick twitch inside of her.

"I've never had sex without a condom before. You felt... you felt so good inside of me bare."

It had felt even better than the first time, and in my clouded haze, I'd figured it was just the position. But it was because there hadn't been a barrier between us.

"It felt more than good, Georgie."

She kissed me softly, and I held her—still inside of her—and moved until I was sitting on the edge of the bed.

"Let's go take a shower."

Georgie let out a giggle as I stood and carried her into the bathroom. I kept hold of her while I turned on the shower. Once it was warm, I stepped inside and stood under the stream of water. Georgie pushed her fingers through my wet hair and pressed her mouth to mine in a kiss that left my knees weak.

Pushing her against the shower wall, I moved in and out of her until I was hard again. Then I made love to her, vowing to do whatever I needed to do to keep her from leaving me again.

◆ ◆ ◆

The morning light shone through my bedroom window, and I rolled over. When I reached my hand out, the bed was empty. I opened my eyes and saw Georgie standing there, dressed in one of my T-shirts and holding two cups of coffee.

"I made us some breakfast, if you're hungry."

Sitting up, I scrubbed my hands down my face before looking up at her and smiling. "Breakfast sounds amazing."

She handed me the coffee, and I brought it up to my nose to smell the wonderful aroma. "That smells good."

"I made pancakes, bacon, and scrambled eggs."

My stomach growled and Georgie chuckled. "Let me slip on some sweats, and I'll meet you in the kitchen."

She winked and my heart stumbled in my chest. Memories of last night came crashing back to me. I felt a small pang of panic, knowing that I wanted to keep her in Montana, but also knowing that I kept my heart guarded for a reason. But this was Georgie. And what we had shared last night and this morning was unlike anything I had ever shared with a woman.

Heading out of the bedroom, Georgie tossed over her shoulder, "Don't take too long."

Five minutes later, I was standing in the kitchen while Georgie handed me a plate. I piled the food on and sat at the bar. Georgie sat down next to me, and we ate in a comfortable silence.

"Are you busy today?" I asked as I finished off the last of my eggs.

She laughed. "I have a totally open schedule now."

"Good."

She looked down at her plate. "I've been tossing around the idea of writing a romance novel, so I may look into doing that. I'm not sure."

I raised a brow. "A romance novel, huh? Do you need to do any research for it?"

A wide smile spread across her face. "Such as?"

"Romance means sex, so if you need any help researching interesting sexual positions, I'm down to try them out if you are."

She let out a burst of laughter, and I couldn't help but join in.

"If I think of any, I'll be sure to let you know."

I stood and made my way over to her. With my hands on her hips, I lifted her up and put her on the counter. She yelped, and I quickly figured out why. My sweet girl was sans panties.

"No panties?"

She bit down on her lip and shook her head.

"I think one of your scenes should be your hero giving your heroine a mindblowing orgasm on the kitchen counter."

Georgie swallowed hard. "How would he do that?"

I saw the wicked gleam in her eye, but also heard the vulnerability in her voice.

Spreading her legs open, I grinned as I placed a kiss on the inside of her thigh. "First, I'll kiss up your leg like this."

I pressed another kiss to her skin, then another as I worked my way up her leg.

"And then?" she asked in a breathy voice.

"I'll see how wet you are with my fingers."

She wrapped her fingers around the edge of the counter as she hissed out a breath.

"Does that feel good?" I asked, curling my finger into her and then slowly pumping.

"Yes."

"Do you want more?"

She nodded.

"Tell me."

Her cheeks turned bright red. "Blayze."

"Tell me what you want, sweetheart."

Georgie's chest rose and fell. She closed her eyes and drew in a deep breath before she snapped them open again and looked down, watching me finger her.

"I want your mouth on me."

I smiled. "On you where?"

"Oh God, Blayze, I can't say it."

As I started to withdraw my fingers, she grabbed my hand.

"I want your mouth on my pussy."

Growling, I gave her what she wanted.

"Jesus," she cried out, her hands instantly pushing into my hair and pulling my face closer.

She moved against my mouth, taking control, and it made my dick so fucking hard it nearly hurt.

"Yes. Blayze. Oh God, yes. I'm going to come! Oh my God!"

Her moans of pleasure were nearly my undoing. I stood, pushed my sweats down, and moved her closer to the edge of the counter, pushing into her fast and hard. When she gasped, I paused.

"No! Don't stop."

"I need you, Georgie."

She nodded. I moved in and out a few times, but the angle was wrong. As I pulled out, she protested with a soft groan. I picked her up and carried her over to the table in the breakfast nook. Turning her, I bent her over the table and kicked her legs apart. I needed to be inside of her. I needed to feel her around me.

"Have you ever been fucked from behind?" I asked, my mouth against her ear as my body weight pushed her onto the table.

She shook her head. "No."

I felt myself smile. Another fucking first.

"Hold on to the table, Georgie."

After she did as I asked, I positioned myself and pushed in again. I grabbed her hips and moved fast and hard.

"Blayze!"

"Am I hurting you?" I asked, slowing. I might have been losing my goddamn mind, but the last thing I would ever do was hurt her.

"No! I want more! Please, I need more."

And more is what I gave her. Pounding into her, the sound of my body hitting hers echoed through the kitchen, and it wasn't long before I felt her clench around me.

"Fuck, Georgie! I'm going to come."

"Yes! Yes!"

As I exploded inside her, she called out my name. It felt like my orgasm went on forever. When it finally slowed, I looked down at Georgie. Her light brown hair was sprawled out on the table, her T-shirt was pulled up, and her bare ass was looking up at me.

What the fuck had I done? I took her like a fucking savage.

She was panting, her pussy still spasming around my dick. With a quick look around, I grabbed a nearby hand towel, pulled out of her, and wiped myself off. I bent down and did the same to her.

"I'm sorry, Georgie," I whispered as I softly cleaned my cum off her. She pushed off the table and turned to face me.

"What are you sorry for?"

I tossed the towel into the laundry room and rubbed at the back of my neck. "I just fucked you over my damn kitchen table. I…it…"

"Was amazing," she said with a smile as she made her way over to me. She lifted her hand to touch the side of my face. "It felt good. I loved that we were able to lose it like that with one another. It made it so much hotter, and I liked that position."

I raised a brow. "Did you?"

Her cheeks turned pink. "I mean, I like when we make love, but that was raw and full of passion."

I nodded. "It was."

Glancing down at the floor, I cleared my throat before looking back at her. "I've never had a woman here in my house. That was new for me." I chuckled.

She stepped closer to me. "Well, it was a fabulous way to start the day."

Laughing, I pulled her to me and kissed her. "Let's get dressed. I've got something fun planned for today."

She raised a single brow. "What is it?"

"You'll see. But dress comfortably."

"Okay, that could mean anything. You won't tell me?"

"Fine," I said with a smile. "We're going to the fall festival."

Her face lit up. "For real? Will there be a corn maze?"

"Yes, a haunted one."

She clapped in excitement.

"Tons of festival food, sack races, hay rides, and a pumpkin patch."

"How much time do I have?" she asked as she spun on her heels and started to head to her room to change.

"One hour! We're meeting everyone at my folks' place."

The shower turned on and I fought the urge to go join her. After holding off for a solid two minutes, I raced into the bathroom. Needless to say, no one was pleased we were late.

Chapter Seventeen

GEORGIANA

I watched Blayze take the hand of his younger cousin, Avery Grace, and guide her out to the makeshift dance floor that was in the middle of Main Street. We had finished dancing, and it was probably a good thing the slow song had changed to a fast one, because I was nearly ready to drag Blayze to a hidden spot and have my way with him.

The fall festival had been a blast so far, and I was so glad I had decided to stay in Montana. Just this day alone had been worth it, never mind all the amazing moments I'd spent with Blayze the last few weeks.

We had raced Ryan and Morgan in the sack race and lost, which Morgan made sure to remind Blayze about every moment she saw him. I'd eaten more food than I should have, and I was counting down until we did the corn maze later that night. The fall festivals in Texas were nothing like this. Yet another reason for me to come back to Montana. I had gotten an email on the way to Lincoln and Brock's house with an offer I couldn't refuse. *Vogue* had lined up an interview with one of the

UK's up-and-coming designers, and they wanted me to handle it. I'd agreed. But it meant I now had to leave Hamilton in less than a week. I'd really wanted to stay through Halloween. I'd told Blayze about it and he had seemed happy, but I could tell from the look in his eyes, he hadn't wanted me to leave.

The sound of Avery Grace's laughter caused me to focus back on her and Blayze. I couldn't help but smile at the sight of them. Blayze loved all of his cousins as if they were his brothers and sisters. I had watched him give them advice over the last few weeks, help them through difficult situations, and even tease them now and then. My chest ached at the thought of leaving, and I still needed to tell Blayze the rest of the reason I wasn't writing the article for *Sports Monthly*. Every time I tried to, something came up or I got distracted. Or, I was too scared of what he would say.

"I've seen that look before," a female voice said from behind me. I smiled and turned in my chair to see Lincoln standing next to me watching her son and niece. "What look is that?" I asked.

She turned to me, silently giving me a questioning look that asked if I really wanted to play dumb.

"That look of longing on your face directed at my son."

My cheeks burned, and I fought the urge to press my hands to them to cool them off. It was a chilly fall day, and I'd wished more than once I'd brought a heavy jacket. Especially as the sun went down.

Lincoln continued on as she looked back out toward Blayze. "The first time I realized I was in love with Brock…"

"Oh, I'm not in love with Blayze!" I blurted.

She raised a brow, and when I pressed my lips tightly together, she went on.

"I didn't want to admit to anyone that I had feelings for him—let alone myself. He was so grumpy, and we'd initially gotten off on the wrong foot."

"You and Brock did?" I asked.

She laughed as if remembering the moment. "Yes. He was a real jerk to me the first time we met. But there was something about him that struck me, and I had to know more about him. Maybe it was his eyes, or the broody way he had about him."

Glancing back out at the street dance, I nodded. "They do have some beautiful blue eyes in the Shaw family, don't they?"

Lincoln nodded. "That they do. Anyway, I was so scared. Not only was I new to Hamilton, but I was finding myself attracted to a man who I wasn't sure felt the same way about me. A man who kept everything locked up inside. Breaking down walls with Brock Shaw was very hard. I'm going to guess Blayze is a chip off the old block."

I chuckled. "I'd say so."

She looked back toward the dancing, and I was surprised by her change in subject. "Blayze told me you're leaving and heading to London. Morgan is green with envy."

"I wish she could come with me."

"I'm sure she does as well. How long will you be over there?"

"Not long, a few days, or maybe a week. Just long enough to make sure everything is set up for the interview. The designer wants her own photographer to do the photos, so I need to meet with them the day before the photoshoot. Then I'll do the interview the next day."

"Do you always have to be at the photoshoot?"

Shaking my head, I replied, "No. But *Vogue* wanted me there to watch since the designer isn't a model and has never done a shoot before. She's pretty new to all of this, and has shot up in fame rather quickly. She's young, too, my age, so I think the magazine wants to make sure she's comfortable with everything. This is her first big interview since her designs have gained popularity."

"How did they? Gain popularity, I mean."

"The Princess of Wales has worn three of her dresses in the last few months. She's exploded since then. Everyone wants to wear her designs."

"Ahh," Lincoln said knowingly. "It only takes one person to blow up a career."

"Or take it down."

I could feel Lincoln's eyes on me. I wasn't sure why I'd made the comment. Something in the back of my head was giving off warning signs that I couldn't ignore. *Sports Monthly* had let the whole Shaw interview go too easily when my father had told them I wasn't writing the piece. Something felt wrong. I'd had my father's lawyer check my contract with them, and I was legally able to cut ties and walk away from the assignment since I hadn't been paid yet. But since they'd been pushing for the interview so hard, it seemed strange they'd let it go so quickly.

"What about Blayze?" Lincoln asked.

Turning my body to face her, I asked, "I'm sorry?"

Lincoln sat down in the chair next to me. "It doesn't take a rocket scientist to figure out the two of you are together."

"We're not–"

She put up her hand. "Something changed at Stella and Ty Senior's anniversary party. But I'll be the first to admit that I saw it in Blayze way before that. The moment you came to town, I saw a difference in my son. When he didn't think anyone was watching, he'd watch you. He fussed about you being here at first, but anyone with eyes could see he wasn't very heartbroken about you staying at the house with him."

I blinked rapidly and opened my mouth at least five times to say something, but nothing came out.

"A blind man could see that the two of you are attracted to each other. Everyone sees it, but you both need to let your guards down and be adults. Talk about the future and what you both want." She paused. "Brock told me about your conversation regarding the magazine. Blayze hasn't mentioned to him that *Sports Monthly* knows about what happened with Lindsay."

A twist of guilt hit me in the chest. "I haven't told Blayze yet. I keep trying to and something always changes the subject, or we get distracted, or..."

My voice trailed off.

Lincoln smiled gently. "A word of advice: The longer you keep something in, the harder it is to tell the person. Tell him. You did nothing wrong, Georgiana. If anything, you stood up to the magazine and protected the family. Which Brock and I are grateful for."

She looked back out at the dancing. "It makes my heart happy to see my son happy—and he clearly is when he's with you. Even when the two of you were younger, I used to tell your mother, 'Callie, those two are going to end up falling in love.'"

I let out a small puff of laughter.

"And don't think for a moment I believed that tale about you two getting twisted around in the maze and leaving Lily and her friends wondering where you went."

My face heated.

"I was young and in love once, too, you know."

I shook my head, about to say that I wasn't in love, but I found I didn't want to deny it. Was I in love with Blayze? I thought I was when I was younger. My eyes drifted back to see him swing Avery Grace around, causing her to let out a whoop of excitement.

"This might come across as harsh," Lincoln stated as I looked back at her. "But I don't want to see my son hurt."

I opened my mouth to tell her I would never hurt Blayze. At least, never on purpose. The time I'd spent with him had been the most amazing moments of my life. The sex was out of this world, but the endless hours we'd spent lying in his bed and talking was something I would always hold dear to my heart. We'd talked about everything except what I actually needed to talk to him about. I'd been putting off telling Blayze what the magazine had really wanted me to write about for far to long. So I could respect Lincoln's worry, and I wasn't about to argue and say that me leaving Hamilton couldn't possibly hurt Blayze. I knew it could. And it had been clear to me he wasn't thrilled about me leaving for London.

"I would never hurt him, Lincoln. I mean I…" I let my words trail off as I almost said I loved him. "I don't want to pressure him or force him into something he isn't ready for or doesn't want."

She reached for my hand and gave it a squeeze. "How do you know what he wants if you haven't asked him?"

Standing, she reached down and kissed me on the cheek, then turned and walked away. I looked at Blayze and then back at Lincoln. She was right. Blayze and I needed to talk. About everything. And I wasn't going to put it off another day. I had an evening to plan.

I stood and looked around. When I spied Mindy, I started to make my way over to her. I was so focused on getting to her, I bumped into someone in the crowd.

"I'm so sorry," I said before I saw who it was.

Lindsay.

She glowered at me before forcing herself to smile. "Don't you think it's a little strange to be fucking the son of the man you're writing an article about?"

My entire body froze. How in the hell did Lindsay know about that? "I'm sorry?"

I hadn't told anyone other than the Shaw family about why I was originally in Hamilton. Had someone else said something? Every time Brock or anyone in the family introduced me, it was always as an old family friend's daughter.

Lindsay gave an evil laugh. "Please, you don't think I know why you're here? When it comes to Blayze, I know everything."

I narrowed my eyes at her. "What is that supposed to mean?"

She let her eyes move up and down my body. "I don't get what he sees in you. I never have, to be honest. You're kind of plain and a little too curvy, if you know what I mean."

I balled my fists, ready to teach this woman a lesson. Before I could reply, she went on.

"You know what makes me giddy?"

"I don't have time for this," I said as I went to push past her.

"I fucked him first." I stilled. Her words sent a pulse of anger through my entire body. "It was me he came to when you rejected him."

"I never—"

I clamped my mouth shut.

"I feel bad for you. You don't see that Blayze isn't the type of man to settle down. He likes women. He loves to flirt with them, and God knows how many he's slept with. You're the new filly in town, and he simply wants…" She leaned in and licked her lips as she looked down my body. "A taste. Once he gets it, you're no longer interesting to him. I know."

I took a step toward her, which caused her to take a few steps back. I looked her up and down and then smiled. "Don't feel too sorry for me, Lindsay. The sex is amazing, and he can taste as often as he likes."

Her eyes grew dark, and for a moment I couldn't help but wonder if Lindsay actually wanted Blayze.

When she finally pulled her anger in, she let out a low chuckle. "Enjoy it while you can, Ms. Crenshaw. It's about to all be over."

Turning on her heels, she walked away, making sure to swing her hips.

"What did she say to you?" Morgan asked as she took my elbow and turned me to face her. Her eyes went wide. "Are you okay? You look like you're about to be sick."

I slowly shook my head. A feeling of utter panic filled my chest, and I felt like I couldn't breathe. I swallowed the lump in my throat. "She knows I was here for the article. She knew I was working for *Sports Monthly*."

Morgan looked confused.

"Morgan, I never told anyone! I don't think anyone in your family would have said something to her. But she still knew about the article."

Morgan shook her head. "Georgiana, I don't understand why you're so upset. Who cares if she knew?"

I looked over her shoulder in an attempt to find Blayze. I needed to speak to him. Now it all made sense. How Doug had known about Blayze being engaged. Lindsay had told him. And why they didn't care that I wasn't doing the article anymore. Lindsay was going to give them an interview herself.

"I need to talk to Blayze. Your dad! I need to talk to them!"

I pushed past Morgan as she called out my name.

"Georgiana!"

The sound of my father's voice caused me to spin around.

"Dad, what are you doing here?" I asked as I made my way over to him. I stopped short when I saw the look he had on his face. It was sad or angry. I couldn't tell.

He looked past my shoulder at Morgan, then down at me. "We were coming to surprise you and Brock." He looked disappointed as he looked into my eyes. "You told me you didn't give Doug anything."

I shook my head in confusion. "I didn't. I didn't give anyone anything. I even deleted what I'd started to write from my laptop."

"Did anyone at any time have access to your laptop, Georgiana?"

The anger in his voice scared me. "No! Dad, what's going on?"

He looked around. "Ron sent me a little something I didn't see until we landed. I've been trying to call you. We need to find Brock. Now."

My head was spinning. "Dad, I think Doug has been in contact with Lindsay."

He grabbed me by the elbow and started to walk toward Brock, who was standing with Lincoln, Ty, and Tanner.

"What's happening?" Morgan asked from beside me.

"I'm not sure," I said.

"Whatever it is, I don't think it's good," she said.

All I could do was walk alongside my father. When he spotted Brock, he called out his name. Brock turned, and so did Ty, Tanner, and Lincoln. They all smiled at the sight of my father. Then Brock's smile disappeared.

"Holy shit! Jeff, what are you doing here?" Ty said, pulling my father in for a hug and a slap on the back.

"I'm afraid I'm not here for a friendly visit. I came to warn you," he said as he turned to Brock.

A feeling of dread settled over me and I pressed my hand to my stomach.

Brock glanced from me to my father, a look of worry on his face. "What do you mean?"

Dad turned to me. "Did you tell them?"

"Yes! Of course. But I haven't told Blayze everything yet."

Brock gave me a look of disappointment.

"Haven't told me what?" Blayze asked as he walked up.

Something was about to happen, and my father hadn't even given me a heads up. I answered Blayze as I twisted my fingers together.

"That Doug, the editor from *Sports Monthly,* wanted me to find out about your broken engagement and to dig up dirt on the family."

Ty and Tanner looked confused.

Blayze, also looking confused, turned to me. "You said Wendy was the one who told you about the wedding."

"She did!" I quickly said. "But Doug initially told me you had been engaged."

His eyes went cold.

"So you knew before I told you, and never said anything?"

"I thought it was a rumor, and I wasn't even going to write about you since they wanted it to be more of a gossip piece."

Blayze shook his head. "You came here to dig up dirt on me?"

"NO!" I shouted. "The editor told me all of this after I was already here. I wasn't going to do it."

"So that night I told you everything."

"I told you, I wasn't writing the article. I informed them that next day I wasn't going to be turning anything over. That I wanted nothing to do with writing anything about you or your family."

Hunter walked up to the group. "I think we have a problem." He held up a magazine, and I nearly dropped to my knees when I read the title.

"The Real Story of Why Blayze Shaw Left PBR."

"What in the fuck?" Blayze said as I stared down at a picture of him in a tux standing at the altar with Lindsay.

"Where did that picture come from?" I asked, looking up at my father.

"My guess, Lindsay gave it to them when she gave them her interview."

"What?" Blayze and Hunter said at the same time.

My eyes found Blayze, and I desperately wanted to reach for him as he stared down at the magazine.

"How did Lindsay even know the magazine was doing an interview on the family, and how did Blayze get pulled into this?" Hunter asked.

Blayze's eyes jerked up and met mine. I shook my head. "I didn't say anything to her or anyone. I swear to you, Blayze."

"But you knew about the engagement and the wedding. Why not tell me your editor told you and made it seem like Wendy told you?"

"Wendy did tell me the story about you leaving Lindsay at the altar. That was it. I didn't know anything other than that you were possibly engaged before."

His brows pinched together. "The call you took in my truck that first day? You knew since then they wanted a piece on me, and you lied to me about not writing about me."

"No!" I quickly said. "I mean, yes, that was when he told me they wanted to go in a different direction. But that's a moot point, I never had any intention on writing it that way."

I kept staring at Blayze, trying to get him to believe me. "I was told when I landed in Atlanta, after leaving Paris, that I was going to Montana to do a *where are they know* story on Brock and his brothers. And Dirk Littlewood. Once I got to Montana, this editor I'd never met before said he wanted me to interview you as well. I called my father as soon as I found out the magazine wanted to go in another direction."

Blayze frowned. "But you never told me. You never told any of us. Why? Why not tell us they were changing the angle? You kept pretending you were going to do the article."

"After I decided not to write the article at all, I told Brock. I was going to write it as it was origanlly supposed to be, until I found out they wanted to go in a different direction. I swear to you," I pleaded. "I would never hurt you or your family."

"Okay, everyone stop coming at Georgiana from all angles," my father said. "She told me what was happening. She said she contacted the magazine and was pulling herself off the assignment. She also promised to tell Blayze they were digging for information on him."

I spun to face Blayze. "I was going to tell you. I tried to tell you a few different times. The first time was when…" My cheeks flamed. "Things kept happening. I was going to tell you tonight. I swear to you, Blayze. I told Brock and your mom."

The look of hurt on his face had my breath catching in my throat.

"You know how I am about my privacy. You didn't think this was something I needed to know right away?"

"Blayze, I tried multiple times to tell you."

"Didn't try hard enough," Blayze spat out.

Lincoln glared at him. "Blayze, that's enough."

Blayze reached down and grabbed the magazine, crumpling it in his hand as he shook it in my face. "Who gave them this information then?"

"I don't know! Earlier, Lindsay said–"

"I saw the two of you talking. Did you work with her–"

My father stepped between me and Blayze.

"Son, you need to stop and think before you say something you'll regret."

"I trusted you," Blayze said, still staring at me. "I trusted you, and you lied to me."

I shook my head as my heart broke into a million pieces.

"I know I should have told you right away, and I regret I didn't try harder."

He scoffed.

"Blayze," Lincoln said calmly as she walked up to her son. She put a hand on his shoulder. "I think we should take this back to the ranch to talk it out. People are starting to stare."

Blayze stepped around my father. "The time for talking is long past."

"Blayze," I said on a sob. "Please, I'm so sorry—"

Pointing at me, Blayze cut me off. "Leave me alone. You're the last person I want to talk to right now."

I took a few steps back. "Wh-what?"

"Blayze, that's enough," Brock said.

"Let's all calm down here," Ty added as he walked around to Blayze's other side.

235

Blayze gave me a look so full of disappointment that I gasped. Tears started to fall down my cheeks as I shook my head.

"I let you in," Blayze said, "and you ended up destroying me all over again."

"Blayze!" I choked out, reaching for him. He jerked his arm away, making me stumble. I could see my father start after him.

"No! Don't!" I put my hands on my father's chest. Turning, I looked Blayze in the eyes. "Can you honestly stand there after the time we've spent together and believe I would purposely hurt you?"

For a brief moment, I saw the anger slip away before something else appeared.

A wall.

Pushing his fingers through his hair, Blayze looked back at me. "We don't have anything else to say. You've got an hour to go back to my house and get your things out and get out. Have fun in London."

Then he turned and walked away. Not a moment later, I collapsed into my father's arms and started to sob in earnest.

"Brock, you know she didn't have anything to do with his," my father said.

I could hear Brock let out a long exhale. "I know she didn't."

"It was Lindsay!" Morgan said. "I walked up and heard Lindsay saying something to Georgiana, and she was clearly upset."

My entire body felt numb, and my legs were giving out.

"I need to get her to the hotel," my father said. "Morgan, will you please go get her things?"

"Yes. Of course. Of course."

As we left the festival, I called Blayze and sent him text after text. He ignored it all. Before my father brought me to his hotel, we went to Brock's house. Everyone was there. I shared what Lindsay had said to me. I knew why Blayze was so angry with me, but I also knew part of his anger was toward the article. That didn't excuse why I hadn't told him yet. A small part of me had worried if I told him, he would react exactly like he was.

Once we got to the hotel in Hamilton, I fell onto the bed and cried myself to sleep.

I didn't remember the drive to Missoula. Or the drive from the airport in Dallas to our family's ranch. I didn't even remember how I got up to my old childhood bedroom. The only thing I remembered was sitting on the window seat in my parents' dining room, crying until the tears would no longer come.

Chapter Eighteen

BLAYZE

The doorbell rang, followed by loud knocking. "Go the fuck away!" I called out.

More knocking.

I got up and made my way into the kitchen, grabbing another beer before I found myself back on the sofa in my living room.

The sound of the front door opening caused me to turn and see who in the hell would dare ignore my demands to be left alone.

Ryan and Hunter stood there. Both of them had looks of pity on their faces. I couldn't help but laugh.

"Maybe we shouldn't have let him wallow away like this for a week," Hunter said as he stared at me with disapproving eyes.

"A word of advice, little brother," I said. "Don't ever fucking give your heart to a woman. They're trouble."

Hunter walked in, picked up an empty beer bottle, and then set it back down.

"I get why you're pissed, I really do. Georgiana should have told you when she told Mom and Dad. But don't you think your anger is geared more toward the fact that Lindsay gave the magazine that information?"

Looking up at my younger brother, I frowned. "And who told her about the article? Georgie was the only one who knew about it besides us."

Ryan huffed. "Do you honestly think Georgiana told Lindsay she was there to write an article about your family, and they came up with this plan to out you? Blayze, think about it."

Drawing in a deep breath, I dropped back onto the sofa. "Well, she clearly found out somehow. If not Georgiana, then who?"

Ryan walked up to me and glanced down at the coffee table. "Jesus Christ, have you even showered or eaten real food in the past week, Blayze?"

"I'm sure I have. Morgan brought me something to eat a while ago, and Mindy was here last night being all motherly. I finally yelled at her, and she left."

Ryan shook his head. "Dude, I've never seen you like this. If you'd stop drinking your sorrows away and actually talk to Georgiana, you could fix all of this mess."

I snapped my head up to meet Ryan's gaze. The room spun, and I had to reach out to steady myself.

"I fucking trusted her, and she kept this from me."

"She didn't," Hunter said as he sat down on the sofa next to me. "Georgiana said she told you the magazine wanted to her to write something she wasn't comfortable writing. Then she told you she wasn't writing the article at all. Stop and think a goddamn second why that is! She didn't want to hurt you. And she was probably afraid to tell you because you'd react exactly like you are right now."

I stared at my brother, the room felt like it was spinning. I was so done talking about Georgie.

"You want a beer, little bro?" I grabbed him by the neck, pulled him to me, and then kissed him on the top of his head.

"This isn't getting anywhere." Hunter pushed me away. "He's too drunk."

Ryan stood. "We need to sober his ass up."

"I don't want to be sober. So if you both could leave..."

Ryan and Hunter exchanged a knowing glance.

"You know what to do," Ryan said.

Hunter nodded. "I'm on it."

I watched Hunter walk toward my kitchen. "Whoa, dude, can you walk in a straight line? Shit. You're making me dizzy."

My brother ignored me.

Ryan reached for my arm. "Come on, Blayze, it's time to sober you up."

"No!" I said, batting his hands away from me and nearly falling off the sofa. "I don't want to sober up. I don't want to feel or remember anything."

Ryan let out a frustrated breath. "That's exactly why we need to sober your ass up. Come on, let's go."

The last thing I remembered before I passed out was being pushed into my shower, fully clothed, and the water hitting me. The next time I woke up, soft light was spilling in through my bedroom window.

I snapped my eyes shut and let out a groan as I scrubbed my hand down my face. It took me another minute to slowly sit up. My head was pounding like someone had a drum in there.

"And he lives."

Cracking open one eye, I saw Rose standing in the doorway of my bedroom.

"What are you doing here?" I asked, my mouth dry as cotton.

"Let's see, Ryan called me and said you've been locked away in your house for a week, not answering calls or texts, and drinking yourself to death. He and Hunter came by last night, threw you in the shower, and poured coffee down your throat until you passed out. I got in this morning and told them I'd stay with you to make sure you didn't die from alcohol poisoning."

I rolled my eyes. "I'm fine. I told my mother I was fine when she called me non-stop for three days in a row."

Rose walked over to the bed and sat down on the edge of it. "What do you expect, Blayze? You stormed away from the fall festival and didn't talk to anyone. Your parents tried to talk to you, as well as Hunter, Georgiana, and her father. You wouldn't talk to anyone. Georgina called like twenty-five times. She's left you at least five voice messages, and I swear like sixty texts. You're pushing everyone away."

I shot Rose a dirty look." You were looking through my phone?"

"Don't worry, I didn't answer them. But you need to call Georgiana back."

"I don't want to talk to her, Rose. I don't want to talk to anyone."

Tossing the covers off me, I headed to my bathroom.

"Blayze, I don't understand you. She made a mistake. Why are you blowing this up so much? So she didn't tell you right away about what they wanted her to write about. Who gives a shit. She didn't write the story. She didn't work with Lindsay and go behind your back. She was afraid the moment you found out you would push her away...and look what we have."

Trying to ignore the ache in my chest, I grabbed my toothbrush. "I really don't need a lecture."

Rose leaned against the doorjamb and folded her arms over her chest. "You really won't give her a second chance?"

I shook my head. "I said some pretty hurtful things to her and…"

My voice faded away.

Sighing, Rose dropped her arms. "Talk to her, Blayze. The only way you're going to be able to move on, with or without Georgiana in your life, is to talk to her."

Deep down, I knew it was true. The moment Georgiana had started to cry and plead with me at the festival, I'd known the truth. Hell, the last week I kept going over every moment with her. The night we made love for the first time she had told me she had something important to tell me, and I put her off. Every time she wanted to talk, I would do something to distract her. Had I done it because I was worried about what she had wanted to say?

Fuck. Fuck. Fuck. I screwed up so fucking badly. But I'd been blindsided again, and fuck if that didn't make me so angry.

I started to brush my teeth.

"She's in London."

I ignored the way that made my stomach feel queasy.

"She left to go there earlier than planned, and is going to stay for a bit longer than she intended."

"Good for her."

Clearing her throat, Rose asked, "What about Lindsay? Have you done anything with that piece of shit, or have you been too drunk to deal with her level of crazy?"

Ignoring her, I walked over to the dresser and pulled out a pair of sweatpants and a long-sleeve shirt. Rose let out a frustrated sigh. "I'll be down in the kitchen. I've got Ryan's hangover cure waiting for you."

I couldn't help but smile at her. "Thanks."

After Rose shut the door, I sat down on the edge of the bed. I had been so worried about letting Georgie in and her hurting me. The only person who was to blame was me. I let my anger and hurt about Georgie not telling me the truth about the story right away cause me to be blind. To not see the amount of times she mentioned needing to talk to me. I was in a bubble of pure happiness and bliss, and I was also terrified of losing her again.

"You're fucked up in the head, Shaw," I said before I quickly got dressed and headed down to the kitchen.

Rose was sitting at the island. I glanced over at the other side of the kitchen, remembering back to the morning when I had Georgie up there. Then I looked at the table, and I shook the memory away.

"I have a theory," Rose said.

Pouring myself a cup of coffee, I replied, "I'm breathless with anticipation to hear it."

She scoffed. "You were scared."

I turned on my heels. "I'm sorry?"

The way Rose looked deep into my eyes made me feel like I was under a microscope. I had the urge to look away, but there was no way she was going to win. The girl was so much like her mother Kaylee.

"You fell in love with her. Hell, you might have always been in love with her."

"You're letting your romance novels spill into real life."

"You were scared that you were falling in love with Georgiana. You didn't want her to leave because you weren't sure she would come back to Montana, so when this happened you jumped on the chance to blame her, to push her away."

Jesus, it was like the woman had been in my mind only moments ago. I took a sip of the foul-tasting hangover drink, which Rose had left on the counter for me then chased it down with a sip of coffee. When I didn't answer, she glared at me.

"Why do men do that? Why are you so afraid to tell a woman how you feel?"

"Women do the same thing."

She crossed her arms over her chest again. "Tell me, oh great one, where you've witnessed this, because I'm dying to hear it."

I wanted to say something about Morgan and Ryan, but I had no right to talk about them to Rose. And I had no fucking clue about Rose and her love life.

Her expression softened. "Blayze, call her back."

"I'm suing Lindsay."

Rose's eyes went wide. "Change of subject, but I'm glad. She shouldn't be able to get away with what she did."

"I'm also suing the magazine. If we win anything, it will go to the community center."

She smiled. "I hope they both get everything that's coming to them."

I nodded. "So do I." Pulling in a deep breath, I exhaled. "Maybe it's for the best things didn't work out with me and Georgie. She has a whole different life in Dallas. Can you honestly see her living on a ranch and being a cattle rancher's wife?"

Rose nodded. "Yes! I *can* see that, because anyone with eyes saw the way she looked at you, Blayze. She loves you, and you're too freaking scared to see it for yourself or admit that you love her too. Look at my mother! Your mother. They love this ranch, Blayze. And so do Timberlynn and Merit."

"They're different. And my mom wanted this life. She moved to Montana first. She wasn't traveling to fashion shows and jet-setting all over the world. She was here. With me and Dad and then with all of us."

Rose blinked a few times, then slowly shook her head. "So a woman can't have a career and be a wife and a mother? I do believe your own mother had a career and still does. Or is it that Georgie would be traveling the world and seeing new things? You were the one who decided to walk away from the PBR, Blayze. You decided *this* was your life. Do you begrudge Georgiana for following her dream when that's the very thing you did?"

"I'm going for a run. Thanks for stopping by, but as you can see, I'm alive."

"Blayze."

Her pleading voice forced me to stop and face her.

The stiffness in her body relaxed as she said, "If you love her and let her go like this, you'll regret it for the rest of your life."

I stood there for a few moments while her words settled in. I knew I would regret it more if I gave my heart to Georgie and she destroyed it.

Clearing my throat, I said, "If you see my dad, tell him I'll be in my office after I go for a run."

A look of sadness swept over Rose's face as she softly replied, "I'll tell him."

◆ ◆ ◆

One month later

There was a light tap at my office door, and I looked up and smiled. "Hey, Mom."

I went to stand, but she held up her hand. "No, don't stand. I finished up a ride earlier and thought I would come in and say hi. Are you sure you don't want to move your office up to your grandparents' place? Ty Senior said his office is waiting for you."

With a shake of my head, I replied, "Nah, I like being down here. It's easy for the guys to find me if something is wrong. Plus, I enjoy the smell of the hay and the sweat of the horses."

She laughed lightly. "You are your father's son."

"How was your ride?" I asked as I leaned back in my chair.

"Good. Gingersnap isn't like Elly; she likes these cold days. She was itching to run, so we had a bit of fun."

"Best to let her get it out of her system before we get a good snowfall."

"Christmas is in two weeks."

"I bet Aunt Kaylee and Rose have already put up trees."

With a beautiful smile, my mother nodded. "Rose mentioned stopping by your place with Avery. They want to decorate your tree."

"What about Morgan?" I asked.

A look of disappointment crossed my mother's face. "You would know what's happening in your sister's life if you ever came to Sunday dinner, stopped by the house, or simply answered a text message."

"It's been busy on the ranch, Mom, you know that."

"Really?" she said with a quirk of her brow. "You dad seems to find time to eat and to catch up on what's happening in his family's world. And the rest of the family meets once a week at your grandparents' house for our weekly dinner. You've been absent for over a month, Blayze."

"I've been..."

My voice trailed off. I had been about to repeat my earlier comment about being busy.

"You've been riding. Ty told me. Said you volunteered to be the headline ride in the charity rodeo."

"Are you upset by that?"

"That my son is crawling onto the back of a bull? No, it's in your blood and something I came to terms with when I married your father. Am I upset because you're doing it simply because you think it will chase away your feelings for Georgiana? Yes."

I sighed and pushed my fingers through my hair. "I'm not doing it because of that."

She folded her arms over her chest.

"What?" I asked with a bitter laugh. "As much as you want to believe you have some weird mom power, it was never like that."

Mom frowned. "You won't even give the girl a chance to talk to you, Blayze."

"I've heard all of this from Morgan, Ryan, Mindy, Hunter, and Dad—hell, even Rose. The list goes on. I get it, everyone's Team Georgiana."

She slowly shook her head. "We're always Team Blayze. But it was clear to all of us how you felt about her, and the fact that you pushed her away so easily—"

"Should tell everyone I'm over her. It was just a fling, that's all."

Mom lifted her chin. "Well, that's good, then. You've moved on. I'll be sure to let Morgan know."

"Why do you need to let Morgan know?"

A frown appeared on her face as she moved back toward the door to my office. "She's in England. Georgiana invited her to stay for a week. She's staying with a friend of Georgiana's on the coast. Morgan thought you weren't returning her texts or calls because she went to see Georgiana, but I'll assure her it was simply because you didn't know she was there."

I swallowed the lump in my throat. "I'm sorry, Mom. I kind of remember Morgan telling me she was going."

Mom put her hand on her hip, then pointed at me. "You would have known had you come to dinner last weekend. Please come tomorrow. For me?"

The guilt of avoiding my family hit me even harder as my mother gave me a pleading look. I smiled. "I'll be there, I promise."

She headed out of my office, then popped her head back in. "If you want to know if it's a rumor, I'm sure Morgan can tell you."

"If what's a rumor?"

"Oh, that's right, you weren't at dinner last week, so you didn't hear."

I exhaled in frustration. "Heard what, Mom?"

She had an innocent look on her face. "Apparently, Georgiana was asked to stay in England by the brother of the fashion designer she went there to interview. I think it's his beach home that she and Morgan are staying in. I believe Morgan said he's a lord or a viscount or something along those lines. Friends with Prince William or Harry. One of the two."

"A lord?" I asked.

She shrugged. "You know the British, they have all those titles over there. Be sure to text your sister back, please, so she knows you're not upset with her."

I nodded. "I will."

And just like that, my mother was gone. After arguing with myself for about ten minutes, I finally pulled up Google on my laptop and typed in Georgie's name along with *Vogue*. The article Georgie was writing on the fashion designer hadn't been published yet, but there was a photo of her at some event with the fashion designer on her left, Lady Mary Douglas. And on the other side was a tall, good-looking bastard with blond hair, dressed in a suit. I read the first few lines.

"Lord David Douglas and Lady Mary Douglas hosted a charity party for the Wales Orphanage fund. Guest of Lord David Douglas was American journalist, Georgiana Crenshaw."

I studied Georgie's face. She was looking up at the guy and smiling while he stared down at her, clearly enthralled. I reread the one line that stood out. "Guest of Lord David Douglas."

I closed my laptop and stared down at it. She didn't look upset or sad. She looked happy. The guest of Lord David—why wasn't she the fashion designer's guest?

And what rumor was my mother talking about?

"A fucking lord," I mumbled, nearly knocking my chair over as I got to my feet.

Chapter Nineteen

GEORGIANA

I stood on the cliff and watched the water below roll in, wave after wave. It was freezing out, but it was the only thing that numbed my body and made me forget how badly my heart ached. I hadn't realized that inviting Morgan to visit would remind me so much of Blayze. I had given up trying to call or text him. It was clear he wanted nothing to do with me. He wasn't interested in knowing the truth.

Closing my eyes, I drew in a long breath of salt air. The air here was different than that of Montana. It was salty and damp, compared to fresh and dry.

"How did I know I would find you here, Georgiana?"

Smiling at the familiar British accent, I glanced over my shoulder to see David walking up.

"It's peaceful."

"And freezing. Why don't you come back in? Morgan and Mary are worried about you being out here for so long."

Turning, I wrapped my shawl tightly around my shoulders. "I guess I can't stay hidden away here by the sea forever, holing up in an old castle on the beautiful coastline of England."

He laughed. "When you say it like that, it sounds glorious."

"Thank you for letting me stay here. And thank you for letting me invite Morgan. She adores your sister Mary, and I think she's totally in love with your daughter, Mia."

David chuckled. "Mary has found a fellow fashion lover in Morgan, and it's refreshing to have someone here who isn't looking to take advantage of her new success. They both get so lost in talking about designs. It's been good for Mary."

I nodded. "I know this newfound fame is hard on Mary. I hope the article isn't stressing her out more. Being featured in *Vogue* is going to put her even more on everyone's radar."

He shook his head. "This is her dream, Georgiana. I think she's a bit overwhelmed, but she's following a dream, and I'm proud of her for it."

"Morgan told me that Mary asked her to come work for her."

He nodded. "She did, and Morgan was honored but turned her down."

"She's very much a family person, and I don't think even a dream job could pull her away from Montana."

David looked up at the cloudy sky. "Mia adores your Morgan."

"Morgan and I both adore her as well."

We continued to walk toward the large stone house that looked like a small castle. Turrets and towers rose above the trees, giving the house a romantic, fairytale-like appeal. David and Mary's family had owned the home for generations. David was now living there, raising his four-year-old daughter alone after his wife passed away during a tragic ski accident.

"What about you, Georgiana. Will you stay in England?"

I let out what sounded like a laugh, but was more of a sigh. "I have to admit, I've fallen in love with it here, but I can't hide on the other side of the world forever."

"Has he called you yet?"

I had shared with Mary and David what happened with Blayze after getting to know them both and growing so close this past month. Mary must have seen the heartache on my face because she'd instantly drawn me into her circle and had made me feel like an old friend from that very first day on the photoshoot. Of course, I had grown protective of her during that time as well. At twenty-four years old, she was shooting to stardom in the fashion world, and it was clear she wasn't fully prepared for the success. David was a wonderful older brother, though, and was making sure no one hurt his baby sister. And David understood me in a way Mary didn't. He, too, was hiding, but I knew that his loss was so much bigger than mine.

I closed my eyes to keep the unshed tears at bay, then opened them. "I don't think he wants to speak to me."

"From what Morgan says, her brother loves you."

I laughed. "No, I think that's what Morgan hoped for." I glanced up at David. "He wouldn't even let me explain."

My voice trailed off. I'd told him all of this before.

I felt a few tears fall free, and I quickly wiped them from my face.

"Love is such a crazy emotion, isn't it?" David said.

I let out a low, humorless laugh under my breath.

"Everyone tells me I need to move on, to find a mother for Mia. I can't even think of that right now. My heart still feels as if someone ripped it from my chest. There are some days I wonder how I'm even still alive because of the void I feel in my heart. The only reason I keep going is for Mia."

I stopped walking and took his hand. "I'm so sorry, David. Mia is a part of Louise that will always be with you."

He smiled down at me. "You're right, I know that. It doesn't make the pain any less."

All I could do was nod. David took a step closer, and his eyes fell to my mouth as he brought his hand to the side of my face. He brushed a tear away with his thumb. I knew what he was thinking because it had crossed my mind before as well. We could get lost in one another, if only for a little time. Forget all about how broken we were as we fell into each other. But at what cost? If we slept together, we'd both feel guilty.

He leaned down, and for a moment I nearly lifted to bridge the kiss. But then I stepped back. "I'm sorry, David. I can't."

He closed his eyes, and I saw the hurt on his face. It had nothing to do with my rejection. He longed for his wife. He longed for the closeness.

"We could pretend we were with them," I said, "but when it was over, we'd both know the truth."

He cleared his throat and looked out over the countryside, letting out a long breath of air. "Yes, we would. I'm sorry, Georgiana."

I took both of his hands in mine and gave them a squeeze. "I think maybe it's time we both leave the sanctuary of this place and figure out a way to move on."

David looked back at me and gave me a weary smile. "I think you're right, love."

Turning, we both started for the house, neither of us saying word.

◆ ◆ ◆

"Hey, you busy?"

Glancing up from my laptop, I smiled at Morgan as she walked into the massive library in David's house. Floor-to-ceiling bookshelves covered most of the walls except for one, which was covered by a huge stone fireplace and flanked by two massive windows. Dark blue velvet drapes hung on either side of the windows and pooled onto the floor. It was one of the most stunning libraries I'd ever been in. And it had been the perfect place to start writing my first book.

I hit save on my document and shut the laptop as I returned her smile. "I'm not busy at all."

Morgan made her way in and sat in the chair next to me. She kicked off her slippers, pulled her legs up, and rested her chin on her knees. "I heard from Blayze finally. He didn't even know I was here."

My heart skipped a beat at the mention of his name. I tried to keep my emotions in check as I replied, "How could he not know you were here?"

She gave me a half shrug. "He's been avoiding everyone and hasn't been to any family dinners since you left."

It broke my heart that Blayze was missing the weekly Shaw family dinners.

"Why isn't he going?"

Her eyes lifted to meet mine. "I think he knows he fucked up and doesn't want to face anyone."

I drew my brows in. "Fucked up how?"

"By doing what he did to you. Now he's let it go on for so long that his pride is what's keeping him from contacting you."

I frowned. "Men and their pride."

She rolled her eyes. "Tell me about it. Why can't they admit when they've messed up? I don't understand it. It was so clear to everyone how much Blayze liked you. Why would he be willing to let you go simply because he's too much of a coward to let you in?"

Leaning back in my chair, I let out a puff of air. "It wasn't all his fault. I should have told him everything the moment I found out."

Morgan nodded. "Fair enough. But that still doesn't give him the right to act like nothing happened between you. I've never seen my brother as happy as he was when you were there. There was a light in his eyes, and he smiled all the time."

"Maybe I'm just that good in bed."

She crinkled her nose before we both laughed.

"Did you love my brother?"

I swallowed hard and fought the sting in the back of my eyes as I glanced out of the large windows. It was raining and gloomy outside. After getting my emotions under control, I looked back at Morgan.

"I still do love him. I think I fell in love with him a long time ago. I just never realized it until I saw him again. And a part of me knows I'll always love him."

I shrugged, feeling my chin tremble.

Morgan dropped her legs and moved to the edge of her chair. "Then what are you doing here in England?"

Confused, I drew my head back. "What do you mean?"

"Why are you hiding away here in this stunningly beautiful—yet depressing as hell—old house? Why aren't you back in Montana fighting for him?"

"Blayze made it clear he doesn't want me, Morgan."

"God!" She dropped back in the chair and stared at the ceiling. "Why does love make people so freaking clueless?"

"I'm sorry?" I asked as I watched her jump up and move closer to the table I was sitting at.

She put her hands on the desk and leaned forward. "He's bull riding again."

My heart dropped. "What?"

"Hunter told me he's been riding at Ty's almost every day."

"But it's winter."

"Ty has an indoor arena. But that's not all. Blayze signed up to be the headline rider at a charity rodeo, and even though my mother won't admit it, she's terrified. Hunter said my dad keeps assuring her that Blayze will be okay, but she thinks he's riding because it's the only time he doesn't think about you."

My eyes went wide. "Wait, but there are no rodeos in December."

"It's a charity thing that's being held at the Hamilton community center. The arena is indoors, so events can be held there all year. It's like a PBR event center."

I stood and walked over to the window, wrapping my arms around my body to ward off the sudden chill.

"Georgiana, he asked about you."

I spun around. "Blayze did?"

Nodding, she smiled. "He didn't text me, he called. He asked how you were doing. He also asked about David."

"David?" I asked in confusion. "How did he know about him?"

She shrugged, but I saw the hint of mischief in her eyes.

"What did you say?"

Morgan didn't even appear to be sheepish. "I might have said something to the family at dinner before I left about David asking you to an event, and about how rumors were flying around England that the two of you are together."

My mouth fell open. "That's not true."

Shrugging once again, she added, "And Mom might have mentioned David to Blayze."

"What did she say?"

Morgan smirked.

"What did you tell everyone about him?

With a wicked grin now on her face, she replied, "I said David was Mary's hot brother, and that he invited you to stay here to mend your broken heart."

I was positive my eyes were as round as saucers. "You did not say that!"

"I sure as shit did. If you two aren't going to do something about your feelings for one another, then I am."

I waited for her to go on. When she didn't, I let out a frustrated sigh and tossed my hands up in the air. "What did he say to that?"

"Which part? About the hot single guy or your broken heart?"

"Both, Morgan!"

"He didn't say anything about David. He ignored it, but he asked me if you were okay. I told him if he wanted to know how you were, it was up to him to ask you."

I chewed on my lower lip. "When did he call you?"

She smiled. "About an hour ago."

My eyes jerked to where my phone was sitting on the table.

"Remember that pride thing?" Morgan said as she walked over to me. Placing her hands on my arms, she gave me a squeeze. "Go back to Montana, Georgiana. Show him he's worth it, because for some stupid reason he doesn't think he is."

A tear rolled down my face. "And if he doesn't feel the same?"

She reached up and wiped it away. "I know my brother, Georgiana. He's madly in love with you and doesn't know how to say it or apologize for being a complete and utter dickhead.

He should be the one running here to England and falling on his knees, but honestly, I'm tired of waiting for him to wake up. It's time you grabbed the bull by the horns."

I felt a laugh-sob slip free, and Morgan pulled me into her arms. I held onto her tightly until we both broke apart.

Morgan cupped my face in her hands. "Christmas is in two weeks. Come back to Montana with me."

Sniffling, I nodded and whispered, "Okay. I'll go back with you."

Letting out a scream of delight, Morgan jumped up and down, making me laugh.

"Come on," she said as she pulled me to my phone. "Let's see if there are any seats left on my flight home!"

Chapter Twenty

BLAYZE

I watched a cowboy climb onto the back of a bull. We were at the charity rodeo in the indoor area at the Kaci Shaw Community center. It always felt special to ride here, even though I had no memories of my biological mother.

Bradly was also riding tonight and had left to go grab his lucky charm or some other bullshit. I was itching to climb onto a bull. To feel that power under me and to just be lost, even it was only for eight seconds. After my phone call with Morgan two days ago, where I had to listen to her glowing description of Lord David, my mind had been in overdrive. I wrestled with the question of did I stay here and wait, or did I fly to England to tell Georgie how I felt? Obviously, I was still on this side of the pond because I had obligations.

Ty and Dirk were standing off to the side as they looked at the bulls being loaded into the chutes for the riders. The stands were full of people and noise, but when I glanced at the crowd, it felt like everything was so far away. Like I was in a fog watching it all happen, but I wasn't a part of any of it.

The last two nights I'd hardly slept, and when I did finally fall asleep, my dreams were about Georgie. Some good, some not. I woke up around one this morning with sweat pouring off me after I dreamed she was getting married to Lord whatever his name was.

"Fuck," I mumbled as I attempted to get my head straight. I needed to have a clear head before I climbed up onto my bull.

"Blayze?" a voice called out, pulling me from the spinning thoughts in my head.

The voice belonged to Uncle Ty, who had come up on my left. I saw Blake Hardy, the sheriff, standing there next to Ty.

"Blake, you guarding the place tonight?" I asked.

Laughing, he reached out and shook my hand. "Nah, here to watch. I also had some news that I thought you might like to hear regarding Lindsay and Lane."

"If it's good news, hit me with it."

"Lindsay was served with her law suit for violating your NDA. And Lane has been charged with tax evasion. Seems he hasn't been paying Uncle Sam."

My mouth fell open. "No shit?" I asked.

"No shit."

Ty smiled. "Karma is a bitch."

"Amen to that," Blake said. "You probably won't see a dime out of her from the lawsuit."

I waved that off. "I just wanted her held accountable. It was never about the money."

Blake nodded. "Well, I wanted to let you know. Have a good ride and stay on!" He hit the side of my arm. "You're not a young buck anymore."

Ty and I both laughed. "Thanks, Blake. For everything."

He tipped his hat. "No problem at all."

Looking at Ty, I slowly shook my head. "Tax fraud?"

He laughed. "Are you surprised? I hope they throw the damn book at her."

I pushed my hand through my hair. "So do I."

"You okay?" Ty asked as he slapped my back. "You seemed a little off earlier."

"Yeah, I'm fine."

He raised a brow and gave me a knowing look. "You still want to ride?"

I didn't even have to think twice. "Yeah, I'm still going to ride."

"Your head needs to be in the right place, Blayze. Is it?"

I forced a smile. "It will be. I'll be fine, Uncle Ty. I promise."

"Bradly's up in a few. That's also why we were looking for you."

"I need to take care of one thing, and then I'll be there."

Ty gave me a weary nod, then turned and headed up the steps to the bucking chutes. I pulled out my cell phone and hit Georgie's number. It went straight to voicemail.

I covered my ear so I could hear when the beep sounded to leave a message. The announcer was giving stats on the next rider.

"Hey, Georgie. It's me, Blayze. Um, listen, I know I don't deserve to even hear back from you, and I don't want to do this over the phone. Can you call me back, Georgie? Please. I should have said it the moment I saw you open that hotel door, but I'm saying it now because if I were you I'd probably never talk to me again. I love you, Georgiana. I love you, and if you don't feel the same way…"

My voice trailed off. I didn't want to think about how I'd feel if she no longer wanted to be in my life. Hitting End, I closed my eyes and counted to ten before I ran up the steps.

The bucking chutes were always crazy. Stock contractors, friends, parents, and other bull riders either stood around and waited for their turn, or were helping the next rider up.

I looked to see Bradly getting his helmet on. Ty met my gaze and jerked his head for me to get my ass over there.

"Get in there and move the bull. He's wedged against the gate, and we can't get the flank strap on the bastard."

Doing as my uncle said, I used a piece of wood to get the bull away from the gate. Once Bradly climbed on, I held onto the back of his vest as he adjusted the rope and the strap. The bull was getting impatient and was starting to get feisty in the chute.

"Fuck!" Bradly yelled out as the bull pushed against the gate. Moving to get him off it, I yanked on Bradly's vest.

He didn't say a word, which told me he was fine.

Letting go, Bradly hit his hand, adjusted in the seat, and gave the nod. The chute gate flew open, and Bradly and Spitting Fire took off.

"Cover him, Bradly!" I yelled while Ty and Dirk shouted out too. I watched with pride as my younger cousin rode the shit out of the bull. Eight seconds seemed like a lifetime, and when the buzzer went off, I turned to Uncle Dirk who looked proud as hell.

"That's my boy! That's my kid!" he yelled.

Ty and I both laughed as Bradly came running back into the chute to get away from Spitting Fire. He climbed up, and Uncle Dirk pulled him into a hug and slapped his back.

"Damn good ride, Bradly. Damn good!" Dirk said. I was sure Aunt Merit was in the stands sending up a prayer of thanks.

The way Bradly looked at Dirk made my chest squeeze. He loved his daddy, and there was nothing better than getting that approval from your father. Especially when your father was one of the best bull riders in history. Though not as good as my dad—or so Dad would say.

I felt a hand squeeze my shoulder, and I turned to see the man I had just been thinking about.

"You good to go, Blayze?"

I nodded. "Yes, sir."

"And you want to ride?"

Again, I replied, "Yes, sir."

Dad looked as if he was in deep thought for a few moments before he said, "All right. I'll be one of your flank men."

I grinned like a little boy who'd been let loose in a candy store. "Don't get too used to it. I'm only doing it for charity."

He tossed his head back and laughed. "I've heard that before."

We turned around, and I froze. Coming up the steps as fast as she could was Georgie.

"Georgie?" I asked in surprise.

A look of relief washed over her face, and she ran toward me. Given the determined way she was moving, I braced myself right before she launched herself into my arms and wrapped her legs around me. A few people around us whistled, and someone called out to get a room.

"Georgie, what are you—"

Before I could finish, she pressed her mouth against mine and dug her hands into my hair, knocking my cowboy hat off. She held me tightly, and I deepened the kiss. Then she suddenly pulled back, her green eyes meeting my blue.

"I love you, too, Blayze."

For a moment, I was stunned into silence. The only thing that came out was a puff of laughter. "What are you doing here?"

"Morgan said you were riding today. I'm not here to tell you not to ride, but I'd be lying if I said I didn't care about what happened to you. But I won't ask you not to ride. I just…I needed to tell you that I love you. I listened to your message as we were walking in. I had spotty service driving out here."

"Georgie, I've got so much to say, and I need to apologize."

She shook her head and kissed me again. "Don't. We can talk later."

"Blayze!" Ty called out.

I smiled at her. "I need to ride, baby. Wait here, okay? Stay right here. Do. Not. Leave. Again."

Georgie nodded. I knew it wasn't the first time she was up on the bucking chutes since her father also rode bulls once upon a time, nor was it the first time she'd ever watched me ride a bull from this vantage point. I simply needed her close by.

After getting my helmet and vest on, I stood in front of my chute. As much as I wanted to talk to Georgie, I needed to focus. My mind needed to be on the ride. A few deep breaths, and a good hard stare at the bull in the chute, and I fell into line. It was like I had never stopped riding. I climbed onto the bull with my father in the front, Ty in the back. Dad adjusted the flank strap as I got my rope in place and hit it a few times to get it right. I adjusted my seat and saw Hunter out of the corner of my eye, ready to open the chute gate.

Dad grabbed my vest and leaned in. "Cover this bull, son."

He stepped away as I raised my hand and gave the nod. The gate opened and Tank took off. Everything else around me faded away while Tank did his damn best to get me off his back. But I wasn't going to have it.

He spun, jumped, kicked, and spun in the other direction, giving me the fight I needed. I heard the buzzer, got my hand out, and did my best to clear the bull as I leapt off of him.

The moment my feet hit the ground, I looked for Tank. He was going after a bull fighter, so I rushed back to the chute, jumped up on the pen, and felt my father grab my ass to yank me up.

His strong arms folded around me as he hugged me.

"Jesus Christ, where did you learn to ride like that?" he asked, pushing me back and grinning. I could see the pride all over his face.

"I learned from the best of the best."

"Bullshit," Uncle Ty said from the side. "You learned from three of the best."

That was something I couldn't argue with. Hunter and Bradly both came up and gave me a hug.

"Fucking way to cover it, dude!" Hunter said, a proud grin spreading across his face. Bradly repeated almost the same sentiment.

Then I saw her. Standing in the background with a look of relief on her face as she watched me interact with my cousins.

"Excuse me, boys. I have a girl to kiss."

She met me halfway and once again threw herself into my body. I wrapped my arms around her tightly and held her close.

"I love you, Georgiana Crenshaw, and I don't ever want to walk away from you again."

She drew back, tears streaming down her beautiful face. "I think two times is enough."

I slowly shook my head. "I'm so sorry, baby."

She pressed her fingers to my lips. "Listen."

They announced my score. I was the last rider up, and I had the highest score.

Her eyes gleamed with pride, and a wide smile broke out on her face. "You won."

Pulling her back into my arms, I said, "I sure as hell did, and not because I rode a bull named Tank."

Chapter Twenty-One

GEORGIANA

After the bull riding event was over at the charity rodeo, the fun started. Or, at least, that was what Morgan said as she dragged me over to the concession stand for what she stated was a rodeo must-have. Corndogs and funnel cake. The only difference with this rodeo was that everything was inside a large, open barn. Rodeos weren't a normal event for the dead of winter, and for a last-minute charity fundraiser, the town had done an amazing job. Of course, it helped that there was an indoor arena that Brock, Ty, Tanner, and Dirk had all gone in on with some other folks a number of years ago.

Blayze had wanted us to leave right away, but when his father and mother told him it would be rude, he'd been forced to make the rounds with Brock, Ty, and Dirk. Bradly had joined them as well, so it wasn't hard for me to slip away from all the "shop talk."

"Jesus, Blayze acted like I was stealing you forever when I suggested going and getting food," Morgan said. "Does he even care that we've been on the longest flight of my life?"

I chuckled. I had to admit, I was exhausted, and the last thing I was looking forward to was a corndog.

"What did you say to him? What did he say to you?" Morgan asked, right as Rose spotted us and called out our names.

"Georgiana! Morgan!"

"Rose!" I hugged her as hard as she hugged me. "How was school?"

She rolled her eyes. "Good. I'm so glad it's winter break. I need it."

"Amen to that!" Morgan handed me a beer I hadn't asked for.

"Oh, I didn't want—"

Rose took the beer from me and winked.

Morgan turned and handed me my corndog and funnel cake. She eyed Rose drinking the beer and hissed, "If your mom and dad see you, Rose Marie, you're going to be in so much trouble."

"Then we'll make sure they don't see. Besides, I'll be twenty-one soon."

Morgan rolled her eyes and handed Rose a corndog. Rose shook her head. "I want the funnel cake."

"Too bad, I don't want the corndog so…"

We made our way through the crowd and to a large table where a slew of Shaw and Littlewood family members were gathered. Even Stella and Ty Senior were among them.

The moment Stella spotted me, she smiled big and bright.

"Oh, my darling girl! You've come back."

Moving my arms out to the side so she wouldn't hit the corndog or funnel cake, I attempted to hug her. Blayze appeared at my side and took a bite of the corndog.

"You can have it," I said as he waggled his brows and divested me of the disgusting dog.

"Gladly!"

I nearly gagged when he took a bite.

"Don't tell me you don't like corndogs, Georgie," Morgan said with a laugh.

"She's never liked them," Blayze stated as Ryan appeared.

"Do you remember the first time she ever ate one?" Ryan said. "She threw up all over Mindy."

I pressed my hand to my mouth. "Oh my gosh, I forgot about that."

"I don't think Mindy has," Ryan mumbled.

Laughing, I looked over to see Morgan watching Ryan. Her eyes were filled with…was that longing? She seemed to snap herself out of it and looked away. At that exact moment, Ryan stole a glance at her. He let his gaze roam over her, even though she was wearing jeans, boots, and a winter coat.

I faced Blayze. "What was the reason for the charity event?"

He finished off the nasty corndog and wiped his mouth on his sleeve. "A local boy who's big into the rodeo was diagnosed with cancer. His parents don't have the money to take him to this specialty hospital in Billings, so the town got together to fundraise."

Rose Marie walked up and rubbed her hands together. "Is it me or is it freezing in this barn?"

"It's just you," Morgan stated with a mouth full of funnel cake. Ryan laughed and pulled a piece off and popped it into his mouth. I wasn't sure if he saw the dirty look Morgan tossed his way or not.

"Well, I'm freezing. My nipples could cut glass!"

"Rose!" Morgan exclaimed on a bark of laughter.

Kaylee shot her daughter an odd look that was both proud and disappointed.

Rose rolled her eyes. "You're just mad you didn't think of it first, Mom."

"Touché," Kaylee replied.

Warm breath hit my neck. "Dance with me?"

I couldn't put the funnel cake down fast enough as Blayze took my hand and led me to the makeshift dance floor.

With my body pressed against his, I finally felt at peace. I hadn't felt that way in nearly two months. A Drake Milligan song played—"She"—and Blayze held me tighter.

We danced without saying a word, even though we had so much to talk about. For right now though, I simply wanted to be held by him. He spun me around, then brought me flush against him again. I looked up into his eyes.

"Do you miss riding?"

He frowned as he thought about it for a second. "No. I don't miss it."

"Morgan said you've been riding more lately."

Lifting his hand, he tucked a piece of my hair behind my ear. "You look tired, Georgie."

"Not gonna lie, I'm exhausted. The last-minute flight back with Morgan was filled with long layovers in Atlanta, and then a bumpy flight to Montana. Then driving here from Missoula was a real fun adventure. I have never gripped that little handle on the door so hard in my life. Morgan drove like a mad woman to get to the rodeo in time for me to see you ride. And did I mention it's snowing outside?"

Blayze laughed. "Gotta love that sister of mine. Thank you for inviting her to England. Mom said she had a wonderful time."

"I hope she did. She met a lot of people in the fashion industry."

He tilted his head when I let out a yawn. "That's it, we're leaving."

"No! I'll be fine."

Placing his hand on my lower back, he started for the large table. "I'm going to take Georgie back to my place," he told everyone. "She's about to fall asleep."

Rose Marie laughed. "Ryan just took Morgan home. She literally fell asleep while they were slow dancing."

I chuckled. "We've had a long couple of days."

"Who's going to drive her car back to the ranch?" Blayze asked.

Dad walked up to us and leaned down to give me a kiss on the cheek. "I'll drive it back. Ryan said he'll swing by and drop Georgiana's bag off on your front porch."

Blayze shook his father's hand. "Thanks so much, Dad."

Glancing down at me, he asked, "You ready to go?"

I nodded, then proceeded to say goodbye to those at the table. Stella and Ty Senior had left a while ago with Tanner, Timberlynn, Ty, and Kaylee.

The moment I climbed into the truck, I dropped my head onto the headrest, and that was the last thing I remembered until I felt Blayze lift me out of the truck.

"I can...I can walk," I mumbled, nestling my head against his warm body.

He chuckled and headed up the steps and into the house. I had nearly dozed off again by the time he put me down on his bed. I attempted to help him take off my coat and boots—they were the same clothes I'd been in since Morgan and I left London.

I sat on the edge of his bed, but nearly dropped down to the pillow as Blayze grabbed a T-shirt and handed it to me. I put it on and then crawled under the covers.

"We should talk," I softly said before I breathed in a deep breath. The pillow smelled like Blayze. Smiling, I felt him pull the covers over me.

"Get some sleep. We can talk tomorrow."

All I remembered was a soft kiss on my forehead before I drifted off into a dreamless slumber.

◆ ◆ ◆

Warm breath tickled my neck, and I stretched and opened my eyes. It only took me a moment to realize I was in Blayze's bedroom. I didn't even need to look at my surroundings; the way he placed kisses on my neck and along my jawline told me exactly where I was. Blayze leaned over me, those deep blue eyes sparkling with delight.

"Good morning."

I sat up as I replied, "Good morning. My goodness, did I even move in my sleep? I feel like I blacked out."

He chuckled and put a tray in front of me. My eyes widened as I saw coffee, orange juice, two pieces of toast with butter and cinnamon sprinkled on them, and a bowl of cereal.

"How did you know I liked cinnamon on my toast?"

Blayze winked and my stomach fluttered. "You stayed with me remember? I watched and paid attention."

I wanted to sigh at the sweet gesture. I smiled as I looked down at the tray. "Is that Cap'n Crunch?"

A sheepish smile appeared on his handsome face. "It is. I bought some after you left. I remembered it was your favorite when we were little. I don't have any eggs or anything, so this is it as far as breakfast goes."

With a shake of my head, I picked up the orange juice. "No, this is perfect. Thank you."

He moved a bit on the bed until he faced me. "I want to apologize for the way I treated you that day at the street fair."

I opened my mouth to tell him he didn't need to say he was sorry, but he held up his hand.

"Please, let me say this. Just eat your breakfast while I talk."

Nodding, I set the orange juice down and started in on the cereal.

"The day our fathers caught us, we were young and maybe we weren't ready to take that step, but I knew I wanted to take it with you. Even at sixteen, I knew my heart would always belong to you. So when you said that it had all been a mistake and that I wasn't the type of guy you wanted to give yourself to, it hurt more than I think I realized at the time."

"Blayze, I was…"

My voice faded as he raised a brow.

"I ran off and did the one thing I've regretted to this day," he said. "After that, I decided I was going to be the guy you thought I was. So I kept flirting, and I never dated anyone seriously—although, I think that had more to do with you than I wanted to admit. I didn't sleep with a ton of women, but I had my fair share. Then Lindsay pulled that little stunt on me, and I once again blamed you because seeing you was the reason I'd gotten drunk that night. When I saw you with that guy in Dallas, it brought up all those damn feelings again from when I was sixteen. I didn't know how to work through it. So I found myself in a pickle with the one woman I never wanted to be in a pickle with."

I couldn't help but give him a sad smile. "I never meant to hurt you."

He nodded. "I know that now, but back then I was still hurt. You were scared, embarrassed, and well, my pride was broken.

It was broken again in Dallas. Then again with Lindsay. Don't get me wrong, I was glad I dodged that bullet. But it shook my faith in women, and I swore I wouldn't settle down until I was good and ready and had found a woman I could trust."

Blayze drew in a deep breath and exhaled. "When I found out about you knowing what the magazine wanted and you hadn't told me, I used that as an excuse to push you away. I was still hurt that you hadn't been upfront and honest with me, don't get me wrong, but after I settled down, I got to thinking about all the times you kept saying you wanted to talk to me and how I pushed it off. I don't know, maybe deep down inside I was scared of what you were going to say. So it was easier for me to put it off. I blamed you, Georgie, when I played a big part in the reason you hadn't told me."

All I could do was stare at him, not sure what to even say.

"My wall came up, and once again it was fortified by my goddamn pride. I couldn't sleep for days after that. I drank nearly every night until I passed out. I was so pissed at myself for treating you that way and letting you go—telling you to go. Then one week turned into two. Then a month. Then you stayed in London, and I tried to tell myself it was for the best. That maybe we weren't meant to be together."

Tears burned at the back of my eyes, and I shook my head. Blayze smiled and reached for my hand.

"I know that's not true, Georgie. Because I honestly don't think I could live this life without you in it. I've been so fucking miserable without you here. I miss seeing your smile, hearing your laugh. Those green eyes of yours that I could get lost in for hours have been in my dreams ever since you left. I love you, and I can say without a doubt that I've never loved anyone else but you."

I felt a sob slip free as I went to move, but then realized the tray was in the way. Blayze chuckled, picked it up, and set it on the floor.

"I love you too," I said, "and I would never in a million years do anything to hurt you or break your trust. I know I should have told you about the article from the very beginning, and I regret that more than anything. I could have been more forceful about telling you, but I think a part of me wanted to pretend everything was okay. I think we both were feeling that way. And I'm so sorry Lindsay hurt you again. So terribly sorry."

Blayze pulled me onto his lap and held me close. And for the first time in nearly two months, I felt like I was home.

Chapter Twenty-Two

BLAYZE

I held Georgie in my arms as she melted into me. God, it felt so good to hold her. She was where she belonged. I truly believed it in my heart and soul.

"Georgie, I know I have no right to ask you this, and that you have a career you love, but I would really love it if you stayed here in Hamilton. With me."

She drew back and smiled. "I was really hoping you would say that because I'm no longer doing freelance writing."

I could feel my brows pull down in confusion. "What do you mean? You're not writing for *Vogue* anymore?"

"No," she said with a shake of her head. "When I was in London, I got to see this whole other side of the fashion industry. I love to write, but I think I found what I really love writing."

"The romance novel?" I asked in shocked surprise.

"Yes," she giggled. "The romance novel. And watching Morgan in action with Mia in England, and seeing how she has an eye for fashion gave me another thought. I've already asked my mom and dad for their advice about it, and I even talked to your dad at the rodeo to get his opinion as well."

I remembered seeing Georgie and my father speaking together, their heads bent close in what looked like a serious conversation.

"You've really got my curiosity piqued."

She climbed off me, turning to face me. I could see the excitement on her face. "That day we walked around Hamilton, I saw a building that was available for rent. The idea kind of sparked then, but I pushed it away. It resurfaced again in England."

Reaching for her hands that she was rubbing together nervously, I laughed and said, "Georgie, tell me."

She inhaled a deep breath and then exhaled it all in a swoosh. "I want to open a boutique store in Hamilton that carries affordable designer clothing. I think Morgan would make an amazing partner, and she could design a line of clothing exclusive to the store. I mean, if she wants to. I think if given the chance, she could really make a name for herself as a designer. I also took business classes in college, and I know Morgan has as well. With both of our parents help, I really think this could be an amazing opportunity for everyone."

I stared at her, letting her words sink in. My heart did a weird dip as I realized what she'd said.

She nervously chewed on her lip. "You don't like the idea? Do you think it wouldn't work?"

Clearing my throat, I finally found my voice. "I think it's an amazing idea, I'm just…the fact that you want to bring Morgan in on this is…this would be her dream, Georgie."

She beamed back at me. "She told me how much she loves Hamilton and her family and the ranch. She adores her horses, but I know she wants a career in fashion. I would love to have more of a home base and still be able to do something I'm passionate about—which is fashion. After I talked to my father about it, he offered to buy the building if we officially decided to go through with the plan. I thought maybe Morgan might like to live above the store and have a design studio there as well. Your dad agreed and said he thought she'd be over the moon about the plan. Do you think she will? I mean, you're so close with her, and I'm hoping I didn't read the situation wrong."

I pulled Georgie onto my lap and pressed my mouth to hers. She giggled and wrapped her arms around my neck as I pushed her back onto the bed.

"I think she's going to love it, Georgie. And if it means I get to wake up and go to sleep every night next to you, I'm all for it. I'm here to support you in whatever way you need."

She traced my jawline with her finger. "That means the world to me. Thank you, Blayze."

"I'm the one who should be thanking you. I love you, Georgie."

Her eyes filling with tears, Georgie softly said, "I love you more."

Smiling, I rubbed my nose against hers. "Impossible."

I moved my hand down the side of her body and under her T-shirt.

"I want to make love to you."

She arched her body into mine. "Yes, please, Blayze."

I moved quickly, pulling off her panties and T-shirt. Then I ripped my own shirt off and pushed off my sweatpants.

"God, I want to be inside you so fucking bad."

Her cheeks blushed as she spread herself open. I crawled over her. "I'm sorry, baby. I can't do foreplay right now," I said.

She wrapped her legs around me, pulling my body down to hers. "I don't need it. I need you inside me, Blayze. Now."

I pushed my fingers into her and found her soaking fucking wet. My mouth instantly watered. Being inside her would have to wait a bit longer. I rolled us over, and she gasped.

"Climb up here and sit on my face. I want to taste you."

Her eyes darkened with desire.

"Hold onto the bedframe, Georgie, and make yourself come on my tongue."

She moaned as she moved up my body. Spreading her legs, she positioned herself over my head. I reached up and licked her, causing her to gasp.

"I need to hear you scream my name, baby."

Georgie moved her body, rubbing her pussy against my mouth. I nearly came undone at the taste of her. The feel of her.

"Oh God," she whimpered as she held onto the bedframe and slid herself up and down my mouth. I reached up to grab her ass, pulling her onto my face.

"Blayze. Jesus…I'm so close."

I moved my hand and pressed my finger against her ass with the slightest amount of pressure, and she jerked. When I did it again, while sucking on her clit at the same time, she exploded. I felt like a greedy bastard who hadn't eaten in days. I slipped my tongue between her lips so I could feast on her cum.

"Oh God. Oh God. Oh God, Blayze!"

The sound of my name ripping from her mouth had me hard as fuck. I pushed her up and down my body. She seemed to still be lost to her orgasm as I moved her onto her back. Lifting her leg, I positioned myself and pushed inside.

"Blayze!" she cried out, and I swore I felt her coming again as I moved into her hard and fast.

"Yes! God, yes, harder!"

"That's it, baby, tell me what you want."

Her head thrashed back and forth as she gripped the bed-frame and wrapped her legs around me.

"Fuck," I gasped, feeling my balls pull in. I was about to come.

"I'm coming! Blayze!"

I exploded into Georgie with an orgasm so fucking strong, I thought for sure I would pass out.

When we both came back to Earth, I was hovering over her body, vaguely aware I'd managed to keep most of my weight on my elbows. My breathing was fast and hard, and so was Georgie's. She ran her fingertips up and down my back softly as she opened her eyes and met my gaze.

"That…was naughty."

I smirked. "Do you like naughty?"

She nodded. "Very much so."

◆ ◆ ◆

Christmas Eve was finally here, my absolute favorite time of year. And having Georgie by my side at Grams and Grandpa's house made it even more special. Years ago, when everyone started having kids, the family took a vote and decided that we would do Christmas Eve lunch together as a family, while Christmas Day would be spent at our respective homes. I loved seeing my grandparents and cousins, don't get me wrong, but being able to open gifts on Christmas morning and hanging out at home was a tradition we kids quickly got on board with. Mom and Dad kept it light, and every year one of us got to pick what we would all have for Christmas dinner. When it was his turn, Hunter always asked for a roast. Morgan wanted hamburgers on the grill. Many a Christmas, my father would be outside grilling in a snowstorm, and he never once complained about it. I always picked potato soup. It was one of my favorite meals that my mother made.

The large table in the formal dining room was set with all the trimmings. The plates, glasses, silverware, napkins, and even the napkin rings were Christmas themed. It was always Morgan's and Rose Marie's job to make the flower arrangement for the centerpiece, and to say it had improved over the years was an understatement.

Us kids always sat in the living room where Grams had set up two long tables. Even though most of us were grown, we still sat out there to this day. This year, though, Georgie was to my left and Morgan was to my right.

The meal was traditional. Christmas ham and turkey with homemade cranberry sauce, mashed potatoes, green beans, stuffing, rolls, and every kind of dessert you could think of. Cherry, apple, and pumpkin pie. Brownies, about six different types of cookies, fudge, peppermint bark…it was endless. That was because every year Mom, Aunt Kaylee, Aunt Timberlynn, Aunt Merit, and Grams all had a baking day. They spent the entire day baking different treats to put in containers for family and friends. The leftovers were put out on Christmas Eve. It was Ryan's favorite time of year because he was always invited over for Christmas Eve lunch, and Grams would pack up all the leftover desserts for him to take home.

"Ryan, must you talk with your mouth full?" Morgan spat out.

Ryan looked across the table at Morgan and frowned. "I wasn't even talking."

"You were. Bradly asked you a question, and you answered with a big ol' bite of mashed potatoes in your mouth."

Looking confused, Ryan turned to look at Bradly who shrugged. "All I said was 'yep.'"

"With your mouth full."

"Then stop staring at me while I eat, ya creeper."

Morgan set her fork down and glared at Ryan. "I wasn't staring at you."

Rose coughed and covered her mouth with her napkin. Morgan snapped her head over and shot Rose a dirty look. "What?"

"Nothing," Rose quickly said as she reached for her glass of water and took a sip, most likely to hide the smirk on her face.

Letting out a huff, Morgan picked up her fork and got back to her meal. I looked at Ryan and nearly lost it laughing when he smiled and winked at Rose.

Georgie leaned in and whispered, "Is there something going on there between them? The way they look at each other..."

I shook my head. "Not that I know of. But it's pretty clear they like each other."

"You're okay with that? Your best friend having a thing for your baby sister?"

Nodding, I wiped the corners of my mouth. "I know him. Trust him with my life. I'd fully support it—if they both ever got their heads out of their asses."

Georgie giggled.

After we all helped clean up, it was time to open gifts. To say Georgie was overwhelmed by the noise and the chaos would be an understatement.

"I can't keep up with any conversation!" she said over the chatter in the room. "How can anyone think in this?"

Grinning, I took her hand and kissed the back of it. "You should have seen it when everyone was little. One year they tried to get us all to take turns opening gifts, so that each family could see who the gift came from. By the time we got to Avery Grace, the other kids had lost their patience. I swear to you, wrapping paper went everywhere! Toys flew across the room as we dove back under the tree for more. Tanner used to play Santa and hand the kids their gifts, but he actually had to dive out of the way when Nathan came running at him full speed to grab another present. To this day, no one knows how the tree didn't fall down. That kid face planted right into it."

Georgie let out a laugh. "I can only imagine. What will it be like when the kids start having kids?"

A warm sensation moved through my body as I looked into her eyes. "I don't know, but I can't wait to find out."

Red spread across her cheeks, and she looked out over the room. Everyone was finished exchanging and opening gifts, and Morgan made her way over to us. She flopped down on the sofa next to my chair and sighed.

"I'm exhausted."

"Too exhausted for my gift?" Georgie asked.

Morgan sat up and smiled. "You already got me that beautiful silk blouse and scarf."

"This is another gift."

Morgan winked. "Because I'm your favorite. I get it."

I rolled my eyes as Georgie chuckled. "Grab your jacket, and we'll meet you out by Blayze's truck."

My sister jumped up so fast I nearly broke my neck watching her move.

"Give me five minutes!"

I stood and reached for Georgie's hand to help her up.

"I have a feeling she's excited," Georgie mused.

Watching my sister hurdle over Josh and Nathan, who were sitting on the floor playing with Gram's new chocolate lab, I nodded. "Just a little."

Chapter Twenty-Three

GEORGIANA

"Morgan? Are you going to say anything?" I asked as she stood in front of the building on Main Street that would hopefully house our boutique.

Tears streamed down her face while she simply stood there, staring at the sign in the window that said something new was coming soon.

Blayze put his arm around his sister. "Hey, not to rush you and this experience, but the snow is coming down harder, and I can't feel the tip of my nose anymore."

Morgan spun to face me. "A boutique? You want to open a boutique and have me be your partner?"

I nodded. "Not only my partner, but I want you to design a line of clothing that will be exclusive to the store."

She let out another round of sobs and more tears as she turned and looked back at the building. Blayze leaned back and raised his brows, silently asking me if his sister was okay.

"If you need time to think about it, I completely under-stand," I said. "I know you still have a semester of school left and—"

"Yes!" Morgan screamed out, causing the people walking by to all turn and look at her.

"She's excited about a new clothing store coming soon," Blayze stated.

"Oh my God, yes! Georgiana, this is my dream. I never imagined it would come true so soon. I don't know what to say. I mean, I'm broke, and I'm not sure how I'm supposed to help pay for this."

I laughed. "You will more than make up for that with your clothing line. Besides, your father and mine are helping us both reach this dream by backing us financially until we can start bringing in income."

Morgan wiped her tears away before she launched herself into me. I nearly fell backward, but was able to keep myself standing as she sobbed into my jacket.

When she started to mumble something, I took her by the arms and held her out a bit. "Sweetie, I can't understand a word you're saying."

"I don't know how to thank you!" Turning to Blayze, she blurted out, "You have to thank her for me with some amazing sex or, or, like a trip somewhere!"

The look on her brother's face was priceless. As for the people walking by—let's just say they picked up their pace as they tried to avoid us.

"You couldn't have just suggested taking her on an amazing trip?" Blayze questioned.

Morgan waved him off with her hand. "Really, Georgiana, thank you so much for this opportunity. I love you!"

"Oh Lord, here come the waterworks," Blayze mumbled. He was right. I started to cry, which made Morgan start to cry again. Then we both hugged one another and cried some more.

Blayze rolled his eyes. "Okay, let's take this back to the truck where there's heat and your tears won't freeze on your face."

By the time we dropped Morgan off at her grandparents' house and had made it back to Blayze's, I was emotionally and physically exhausted.

"How about a foot massage?" Blayze asked as he took my hand and led me over to the sofa.

"If you do that for me right now, I'll do anything you ask."

He raised a brow. "Anything?"

I dug my teeth into my lip. "Anything."

Blayze picked my foot up and began to move his fingers in a way that nearly had me melting into the sofa.

"That feels so good."

I closed my eyes and relaxed. We remained in a comfortable silence until Blayze put my foot down and grabbed the other one.

"There's something I want to show you tomorrow morning," he said. "Are you up for an early morning adventure to watch the sunrise?"

My eyes snapped open. "I am not hiking in this freezing cold weather, Blayze Shaw. I love you, and I love sunrises, but I have to put my foot down on this one. I'd rather get on a bull."

His eyes lit up with excitement.

"Okay, I wouldn't, but I really, really don't want to go hiking in the cold."

Blayze chuckled. "Would it help if I said Duke and Elly are going with us?"

That caused me to sit up some. "Riding?"

"If you're up for it."

Smiling, I answered, "I'm always up for riding."

He pushed harder on the ball of my foot, and I gasped. "Lord, you're good with your hands."

"So I've been told. And my mouth."

An instant ache formed between my legs, and I squirmed. Blayze lifted his brows. "Problem?"

"Not at all."

He slowly slid his tongue along his upper, and then his lower lip, and my heart picked up its rhythm.

"That is not fair, Blayze Shaw. Besides, I want to do something different. I want to pleasure you with my mouth next time."

He dropped my foot instantly. "When?"

Laughing, I leaned closer to him, and in the sexiest voice I could manage, I purred, "How about now?"

Blayze shot up off the sofa and started to unbuckle his pants. I watched in delight as he shed his clothes faster than lightning.

"I need a shower first," he said as he reached down and pulled me up. Pressing his lips to mine, he smiled against them. "Have I told you today that I love you?"

I drew back slightly and our eyes met. "You have. This morning when you woke up. After breakfast. On the way over to Stella and Ty Senior's house, in the kitchen when you whispered it in my ear, and I think you said it twice on the drive over here."

He tsked. "That's not nearly enough."

"Let's go take a shower."

Those blue eyes of his turned dark and his dimple appeared, causing my heart to feel like it dropped a bit in my chest.

Once we were in his room, I stripped out of my clothes and stepped into the hot shower. Blayze washed my body first before I took over and washed him. Pushing him onto the small bench in his shower, I dropped down and took him in my mouth. I'd never given a man a blow job before, so I had no idea what to do, but Blayze seemed to be enjoying it.

"Jesus, Georgie. Fuck yes. Oh God."

Smiling, I used my hand to stroke him at the same time. I heard a friend of mine once say she would lightly graze her teeth over the edge of a guy's dick because it was sensitive there. I tried it and Blayze grabbed a fistful of my hair and moaned in pleasure. It felt so good to have this kind of power over him. To know it was me who made him moan and buck his hips.

"Christ above, that feels good. Faster, Georgie, fuck, I'm so close."

I moved my hand and my mouth faster. Sucking harder as I got to the tip. Blayze grabbed onto the edge of the seat and gasped for air. "I'm going to come. If you don't want to…"

His words fell away as I sucked harder, taking him in deeper.

"Georgie!" he cried as warm jets of his cum hit the back of my throat. Not gonna lie, I almost gagged, but hearing his moans of pleasure pushed me past it, and I took in all of him. Every single drop he spilled into my mouth. When he slumped back, I slowly let his dick fall from my lips.

"Was that good?"

He let out a strangled laugh. "That was fucking amazing. Hell, I've never come so hard."

While his eyes were closed, I rinsed out my mouth and gave a little shudder. Cum tasted horrible. Did men really mean it when they gave you oral sex and said it tasted like honey? I highly doubted it. One day I'd work up the nerve to ask Blayze.

I stood and let the hot water run over my face and body. "I've never done that before."

When I looked down at him, I saw that he was watching me. My newsflash had caused him to jerk his brows up in surprise. "Are you serious?"

"Yep, you were my first."

He stood. "And I'll be your last."

His words hit me in the chest, but in the most amazing way. I wrapped my arms around him and kissed him. "You are most certainly the last."

◆ ◆ ◆

"Georgie. Georgie, wake up."

I rolled onto my back, aware that the warmth of Blayze's body was no longer pressed against mine.

"No! It's too early. Go back to bed, Blayze."

He kissed each corner of my mouth. "Merry first Christmas."

I looked up to see the most handsome man I'd ever laid eyes on smiling down at me.

"Merry first Christmas."

I yawned and let out a long, pained noise as I stretched my entire body out.

"What time is it?" I asked.

"It's six."

Sitting up, I exhaled. "That's right, the sun doesn't rise until eight-something."

"Eight eighteen, to be exact. Come on, we need to get going."

I tossed the covers off me. Blayze was standing there with his robe at the ready, and I shuffled my way into the bathroom.

"I talked to my dad," I said as I put toothpaste on my brush. "He said my Ford Bronco will be leaving Texas on January fourth," I said. "My parents plan on flying up the next day. I think I'll fly back with them, clean out my place, and pack and ship anything else I might need. I doubt there's much. I traveled so much I didn't really pick up a lot of stuff along the way."

When I turned to look at him, he was starting at me. "What?"

Sometimes I feel like I need to slap myself to believe you're really here to stay."

"Don't do that! I rather like that handsome face of yours."

Blayze laughed. "Get ready, we've got somewhere to be."

After getting ready, I dressed in a pair of thermals I had bought the other day, as well as a pair of jeans. My long-sleeve shirt, along with my down jacket, should keep me warm.

"I'm glad Morgan talked me into buying these winter riding gloves," I said a while later when I jumped out of Blayze's truck, sipping on the to-go coffee I'd made before we left. I also had on a scarf and a comfy cotton hat.

"It's a chilly morning for sure," Blayze stated as we walked into the barn to find Hank standing there with Duke and Elly saddled up and ready to go.

"Hank! Merry Christmas!" I said, walking up and giving him a hug. "You didn't have to come down here and do this for us on Christmas morning!"

He blushed slightly. "I overheard Blayze making his plans, and I offered. I'm leaving and heading to the house soon. My wife is probably still in bed."

I peeked over at Blayze. "Lucky me, I have a boyfriend who likes to go on early morning adventures."

Winking at me, Blayze held onto Elly so I could mount her. "Best boyfriend ever."

"That you are," I said as I settled into the saddle.

"She likes the cold weather, so she might be a bit frisky," Hank warned.

Giving Elly a pat and scratch on the neck, I said, "A girl after my own heart."

"I owe you, Hank," Blayze said as he hopped up onto Duke.

With a wave of his hand, Hank called out, "Enjoy the ride and the sunrise."

"We will!" I called back.

Elly followed Duke as we headed down a nearby trail. It was dawn, so the horses could see. I marveled at the beauty of my surroundings. A light dusting of snow covered the ground and the limbs of the trees. It was a beautiful sight, especially knowing it was Christmas Day.

"I don't think I'll ever get used to how beautiful it is here," I said.

The trail opened up to a wider one, which I was pretty sure was an access road that twisted up the side of the foothills.

"It's the most beautiful place on Earth, if you ask me."

I smiled as I looked over at Blayze. He wore a black cowboy hat that made his blue eyes pop. "Aren't your ears freezing?" I asked.

"Nah. When you grow up in Montana, you learn real quick what temperatures you need a winter hat for, and when you can get away with wearing a cowboy hat."

I rolled my eyes as I smiled.

The road was a nice incline, and even with the fresh snow, the horses didn't have a problem going up it at all. It was a winding road, though, and a few times I tried not to look at the ledge. As we neared the top, Blayze started to look nervous.

"What's wrong?" I asked.

"Nothing at all. Just making sure there aren't any icy patches the horses might step on."

As we crested the last little hill, I sucked in a breath at the sight before me. The top of the foothill was an open clearing. The sun was getting closer to rising, and the whole valley below was filled with light. I slipped off Elly and looked at Blayze. "Where are we?"

He gave me the biggest, brightest smile I'd ever seen on him. Full-on dimple and all.

"My favorite place on the ranch."

"The horses?" I asked.

"They'll be fine." Blayze reached for my hand. "Come on, I want to show you something."

I stared down at the picturesque view. "Is that the whole ranch?"

"It's a good portion of it. Behind that small hill is where Ty and Kaylee live. And off to the north is where Tanner and Timberlynn live."

Looking down, I saw cattle in the pastures. It looked as if someone had taken a shaker and sprinkled them all out. To the right was another large pasture where horses dressed in blankets pushed through the snow to find what grass might be left. I saw a truck driving in the distance and pointed. "Who's that?"

"That's Rancher and Solo," Blayze responded. "They're going to throw out feed for the horses, and then Decker and Clay will get the cattle. Don't worry, we pay them double time on Christmas Day. But a cattle ranch can't stop running even on a holiday."

I wrapped my arms around my body as I let my eyes sweep across the landscape. "Look at how the light is reflecting the clouds off those small lakes. And the snow-covered mountains. It's…it's so beautiful."

"Look," Blayze said as he pointed.

Turning, my mouth dropped open. The sun was cresting over the mountains in the distance and the sky was turning orange and yellow. The hues blended together, making the scene look like something right out of a painting.

I pressed my hand to my mouth as I stood there in awe. The sunrise we had seen on our first hike was stunning, but there was something so special about this one. I wasn't sure if it was because it was rising over the ranch that I would soon be calling home, or if it was because Blayze and I had finally found our paths coming together.

"Look how the fields are cast in a soft, warm glow," I whispered. "And the sky. It's turning the most beautiful shade of pinkish-orange I've ever seen. I wish I had a camera."

When I turned to look at Blayze, he wasn't looking at the sunrise. He was watching me.

"You're missing it, Blayze!"

He shook his head. "No, this is exactly what I've been waiting for. I've waited a long time for this moment."

Smiling, I looked back at the sky. "It's breathtaking."

"It is," he agreed.

Rays of sunlight seemed to burst from behind the mountains, and I stared at it in awe.

"Oh, Blayze. Look at how…"

My voice trailed off when I turned to see Blayze down on one knee, holding an open ring box in his hand. I covered my mouth with both hands and dropped down onto my knees, feeling a rush of sobs break free.

Tears formed in Blayze's eyes, and he had to clear his throat to speak.

"Georgiana Elizabeth Crenshaw, I would like to spend the rest of my life watching sunrises and sunsets with you. And maybe I'm asking way too soon, but I've waited long enough to make you my partner in this life. Will you marry me?"

With my entire body shaking and tears streaming down my face, I launched myself into Blayze. He caught me as I wrapped my arms around him and cried. He held onto me tightly and told me he loved me. I couldn't stop crying.

I pulled back and our eyes locked. I cupped his face with my shaking hands and said the words that naturally came.

"I love you so much! Yes! Yes, I'll marry you!"

Blayze blinked to hold back his own tears and he pulled me back into him. I let out a rather loud yell of happiness while he laughed, or maybe cried. I wasn't entirely sure. All I knew was I had never been so happy in my life.

After what felt like forever, Blayze stood, bringing me up with him. He smiled, placed his finger on my chin, and lifted my eyes to meet his.

"May I put the ring on now?"

I gasped. "Oh my gosh! Yes!"

Looking down at the open box, I felt another onslaught of tears come on. A stunning oval-shaped diamond that sat in what looked like a white gold or platinum band glimmered up at me. The colors of the sky seemed to reflect in the diamond as I looked at Blayze.

"This is beautiful."

"It was my mother's. I mean, my biological mom, Kaci. My dad gave it to me the other night when I told him I was going to ask you to marry me. He'd been holding onto it for me for when the time came."

I wiped a tear off my cheek and slowly shook my head. "Oh, Blayze."

He took the ring out, and I quickly removed my glove. We both looked down at my hand, then at the glove, and laughed at the same time.

"Will the glove fit back on over the ring?" he asked.

"I think so!"

He slipped it on, then brought my hand up to his mouth and kissed the back of it. "I swear to you, Georgie, I'll do whatever it takes to make you happy every single day for the rest of our lives."

My stomach dipped and turned as I stared down at the ring on my finger.

"It's a perfect fit," I whispered, glancing up at him.

Winking, he replied, "I always thought so."

Epilogue

MORGAN

SOPHOMORE YEAR OF COLLEGE - TWO YEARS FROM PRESENT DAY

"This Halloween party sucks. We should have stayed at our dorm and studied like I suggested," Krista said as she glanced around the room.

We were at one of the frat houses for what everyone said was the most epic Halloween party on campus. So far we'd been hit on by nearly every male in the room. I watched more guys take girls up those stairs than I cared to count.

"We need to find Heather, and then we can leave."

Krista rolled her eyes. "She's probably in some room with her dress up to her waist and some guy in her—"

"Krista!" I squealed.

She gave me a befuddled look. "What? You know I'm right."

I laughed, then stood on my toes in an attempt to look over everyone.

"Would you like to dance?" a voice said from behind me. Turning to look over my shoulder, I couldn't help but smile at the guy's costume.

"A skeleton ringmaster. I love it."

He smiled back.

"Whoever did your face makeup should be given some kind of award," Krista stated.

"Thank you," he said, his voice sounding a bit muffled. "Dance?"

He held his hand out to me, and I looked over at Krista. "For fuck's sake, go dance," she said. "At least one of us needs to have some fun. I'll go find the whore."

"Krista!" I said with a pleading look.

"Fine." She rolled her eyes. "I'll go find the tramp."

I let out an exasperated sigh as my best friend turned on her heels and headed up the steps in search of the third person in our trio of friends.

Turning back to the stranger, I placed my hand in his. We weaved our way through the crowd of people on the makeshift dance floor. The frat house was in a historical home right off campus, and it looked like we were in the old ballroom.

The skeleton drew me to him, and I cleared my throat and took a step back. It was a little bit too close for my comfort.

"Sorry," he said with a wicked gleam in his eyes. "What's your name?"

"Morgan," I answered. "You?"

"Rich."

"Nice to meet you, Rich," I said as we moved to the slow song that was playing. His hand drifted a little more down my back, but I wasn't sure if I was imagining it or not.

"Are you in the frat?" I asked.

"No, my best friend is, though."

I nodded.

"Are you in a sorority?"

"God, no!" I blurted out. "Not that there's anything wrong with them. That's just not my scene."

It was his turn to nod.

"You look familiar to me," he said. "I wonder if we're in any classes together."

Looking up at him with a bit of a flirtatious grin, I replied, "I couldn't tell you since I can't see what you look like."

"Tell me you don't like the mystery of it."

"It is pretty neat," I said, laughing somewhat nervously. He was for sure moving his hand down.

"Can I kiss you, Morgan?"

Okay, that was a first. Guys didn't usually ask—they just dove in.

"Um…"

"Do you have a boyfriend?"

I shook my head as a memory of Ryan holding me while we danced resurfaced in my mind.

"Then what harm is one little kiss?"

I licked my bottom lip and noticed how he reacted to it. Pressing my mouth into a tight line, I looked around. The place was packed with people. What would the harm be? If I thought about it, I freaking deserved a kiss for staying at this stupid party for as long as I had. If a guy pinched my ass one more time, I was going to scream.

"I guess one kiss would be harmless."

He smiled, and I couldn't help but notice his perfectly straight teeth. I suddenly wanted to know what Rich looked like.

I reached up onto my toes, and he leaned down. The kiss was soft at first. Nice. He licked my bottom lip, and I opened to him. When his tongue touched mine, I could taste beer and peppermint. Gum, maybe?

He moaned and deepened the kiss. At least one of us was getting something from it because I felt nothing. He was a good kisser, but still…nothing.

When he grabbed my ass with both hands and pulled me against his body, I gasped at the feel of his hard erection. I put my hands on his chest and pushed as hard as I could.

"Stop!"

A few people turned and looked at us, and he stepped back and ran his hand through his hair. "I'm sorry."

Wiping my mouth, I exhaled. "Listen, I'm not interested in anything."

"You kissed me, though."

Frowning, I said, "That doesn't mean I want to go any further with you."

Taking a step closer, he leaned down. "Are you sure, Morgan? Because I really, really want to f—"

"Found her!" Krista said as she pushed between me and Rich. My eyes were wide with horror because I was pretty sure he'd been about to say that he wanted to fuck me.

"Great, let's go," I said as I grabbed Krista and Heather's hands and practically ran from the party.

"What was that about?" Krista asked when we got outside.

I dragged in a few deep breaths. "Christ," I said. "I hate men. The guy asked me to kiss him. I thought it would be harmless, but I swear he wanted to take me right there on the dance floor."

Krista rolled her eyes. "Men are pigs, especially when they've been drinking."

I looked at Heather. "Where were you?"

She blushed and looked away.

Krista scoffed. "About to have a threesome with two guys."

My mouth fell open. "What?"

Heather laughed. "Just because some of us are saving ourselves doesn't mean the rest of us can't play and have fun."

"You're either going to end up pregnant, or with some STD," Krista said as we hooked arms and started to walk down the street toward my car.

"There's something called a condom, Krista. You should try one," Heather said. "You need a good pounding to jolt you out of your virtue."

A strange feeling crept up my neck as I glanced over my shoulder and back at the party. My eyes scanned the outside and porch, but thankfully, I didn't see the skeleton ringmaster guy.

Facing forward again, I shook off the feeling and counted down the days until I got to go home and see my family.

And Ryan.

Ringmaster

I watched her walk away with her two friends. My mouth still tasted of her. It wasn't enough. I wanted more. The sting of her rejection burned, but I needed to remind myself that she wasn't like her whore of a friend, Heather. Morgan was a good girl.

And good girls were always worth the wait.

Look for *Cherished Enough*, book 2
in the Love in Montana series on June 6, 2023.

ABOUT THE AUTHOR

Kelly Elliott is a *New York Times* and *USA Today* bestselling contemporary romance author. Since finishing her bestelling Wanted series, Kelly has continued to spread her wings while remaining true to her roots with stories of hot men, strong women, and beautiful surroundings. Her bestselling works included *Wanted, Broken, Without You,* and *Lost Love.* Elliott has been passionate about writing since she was fifteen. After years of filling journals with stories, she finally followed her dream and published her first novel, Wanted, in November 2012.

Elliott lives in Central Texas with her husband, daughter, and two pups. When she's not writing, she enjoys reading and spending time with her family. She is down to earth and very in touch with her readers, both on social media and at signings. To learn more about Kelly and her books, you can find her through her website, www.kellyelliottauthor.com.